Rings That Bind

Rings That Bind

A novel by

M. Leo Doucet

Published by The WryPen

a division of Slamyrbach Studios

This is a work of fiction inspired by real experiences. Names, characters, places, and events have been reimagined for the story. While certain elements are drawn from the author's life, the narrative is a work of the imagination.

ISBN 979-8-9957976-1-6

First Edition

2026

For my loving wife, who has patiently supported and tolerated me for more than 30 years.

And for my children, who have taught me more than I taught them.

Five hundred and eighty-nine pieces of eight

Pay them up

Or seal your fate

Five hundred and eighty-nine pieces of eight

Pay them up

Before it's too late

— from "Five Hundred Eighty Nine"

Table of Contents

CHAPTER ONE

The Debt of the Sea

The sea had been watching them for days.

Not with malice — not yet — but with the patient attention of a thing that remembers every hull that ever scarred its surface. It breathed beneath the Providence in long, rolling swells that lifted the ship and set her down again with a mother's indifference, each rise and fall a reminder of who truly held dominion here. The sky bruised slowly, purples bleeding into black along the western horizon, and the wind shifted quarter by quarter until it carried the smell of something old and metallic, like blood on a whetstone.

Then the patience ended.

The storm descended — a black wall of sky and salt that swallowed the horizon whole. Rain lashed the deck of the Providence, hammering her timbers as if testing their resolve. Lightning clawed the heavens, striking jagged scars across the night. The air stank of tar and ozone, the taste of iron on every drop. Waves no longer breathed — they reared, snarling, white-capped and furious, slamming the hull broadside as though the ocean had made a fist and was using it.

The Providence groaned. Timbers spoke in the language of stress — deep, percussive cracks that traveled through the keel and up through the soles of men's boots. The bowsprit dipped beneath a wall of green water and came up streaming, the figurehead blinded by foam. Rigging sang in frequencies that set the teeth on edge. Somewhere above, a block broke free and swung in a lethal arc, trailing rope like a severed vein.

It found a man.

The block caught a young rigger across the chest — a sound like a mallet striking a side of beef — and the force of it lifted him clean off his feet and over the gunwale. For a heartbeat he was there: arms wide, mouth open, eyes white with a surprise too sudden for fear.

Then the sea took him. His hand broke the surface once — pale, grasping at rain — and Elias Tidewell lunged for it, half his body over the rail, one boot hooked under a cleat, his massive arm reaching into the black water as though he could haul a man back from the deep by will alone. Their fingers touched. Slipped. The wave closed over the place where the rigger had been, and the sea offered nothing — no cry, no ripple, no evidence.

Elias pulled himself back aboard. He stood at the rail for three breaths, water streaming from his arm. Then he turned and went back to the foresail without a word. His hands found the line.

At the wheel stood Captain Wry Slamyrbach.

He had seen it. All of it. The block, the body, the hand in the water, Elias reaching and failing. His jaw clenched once. His knuckles whitened on the spokes. But his hands did not leave the wheel, because a captain who lets go of the wheel to save one man drowns thirty.

Broad-shouldered, hat pulled low, his fur mantle dark with rain and sea, weathered hands locked on the spokes as though he and the wheel were fused from the same oak. His coat snapped like a torn banner in the gale. He didn't flinch when the sea reared against him; he leaned into it, as though daring the ocean to prove itself greater. He had stood at this wheel through typhoons in the Eastern Passage and through squalls off the Banks that would have sent lesser ships to the bottom. The sea knew him. He knew the sea. And between them ran a thread of mutual respect that was indistinguishable from war.

But the wheel fought him tonight. Each wave that hit broadside sent a shudder through the rudder and up through the spokes, and his back — a souvenir from the Orient — seized with a pain that shot from his knees to his spine. He shifted his weight, set his teeth, and held. No one saw. No one ever saw. That was the point.

But tonight, Elias saw. From the foresail, the Bosun's eyes found the Captain's stance — the slight lean to the left, the way his right hand gripped the wheel — and filed it away without expression. He had been sailing with this man for twenty years. He knew that body's ledger as well as he knew the ship's.

The Captain's eyes betrayed nothing. Piercing blue, the kind that read men before they'd finished speaking, they swept the deck in a single measured pass. He saw everything: the lines that strained too tight, the man whose grip was slipping, the angle of the foresail that would tear if not trimmed in the next thirty seconds. He saw fear. He cataloged it the way a surgeon catalogs wounds — by severity, by urgency, by what could wait and what could not.

To the crew, his silhouette against the storm was half comfort, half curse. Below the quarterdeck, men shouted over the wind. Lines strained, sails cracked like thunder, boots slid across the soaked planks. Water poured through the scuppers in sheets, and every few seconds a wave broke over the gunwale and sent men staggering, clutching at anything bolted down. The sea was inside the ship now, ankle-deep in places, sloshing between barrels and gun carriages, turning the deck into a tilting, treacherous sheet of salt and oak.

And in the chaos rose a voice — sharp, bitter, unmistakable.

"Storms and debts!" Rafe Cutler bellowed, his words carrying even through the thunder. "That's what we've got! A captain chasing ghosts while we break our backs for a promise of coin we've yet to see!"

Several men glanced up from their labor, their eyes catching Rafe's fire. He was no common grumbler. Tall, lean, moustached, his jaw square as a masthead, he had the look of a man who believed himself better than the orders he followed. His black bandanna clung wet to his brow, his voice cutting like a whip.

"Tell me, lads — what manner of fool sails us straight into this, all for debts he can't even name? And when it's done — when the sea's finished with us — what then? What pension waits? What dock will have us when our knees give out and our hands can't hold a line?"

Every man on this deck knew the score. The privateering days were done — Queen Anne's war over, letters of marque expired, a thousand sailors thrown to the wind without so much as a coin for their trouble. Some grumbled agreement, fists tightening on ropes and cutlasses. Others glanced toward Elias Tidewell, the Bosun, who stood firm at the starboard rail, hair plastered to his brow, his massive arms locked on the lines.

“Hold your tongue, Rafe!” Elias’s voice rang clear. Solid and broad as the beams beneath their feet, he hauled a line to secure the foresail with hands thick with rope burns and a calm that anchored the men nearest to him. “The Captain’s brought us safe through worse than this. Question him, and you question your own chance at seeing land again.”

Rafe’s mouth twisted. “Worse? Aye, we’ve weathered storms, and still we’re poorer than dock rats. How many years now has Slamyrbach promised ‘one last voyage’? Yet here we are — half drowned and bound for Nassau, where every cutthroat waits to slit us open. For what? To pay a debt that ain’t ours?” He jerked his thumb toward the dark water where the rigger had gone. “Ask him what his pension looks like.”

The words fell among the crew like sparks in a powder room. A few men muttered their agreement, shifting uneasily at their posts.

Elias dropped the line and stepped closer, his bulk filling the narrow space between crewmen. “You forget yourself, Rafe. The Captain bears the debt, not us. He takes the weight so we may all eat, so we may all have a ship beneath our boots. If you’ve no stomach for it, say it plain. But don’t poison the rest of us with your bile.”

A crack of thunder shook the deck, and for a moment it seemed nature itself held its breath. The sea rolled the ship hard to starboard, and every man grabbed for the nearest hold. When the Providence righted herself, Rafe was still standing, still staring, his eyes narrowed to slits.

“Plain enough, then. I’ll follow the sea before I follow a man chasing shadows. And mark me — others here think the same.”

He” swept his gaze across the deck, daring any to contradict him. Several men lowered their eyes, unwilling to stand in open defiance, yet equally unwilling to side with Elias. The divide was as clear as the lightning above — and just as dangerous. A ship could survive a cracked mast. A cracked crew was another matter.

Slamyrbach had not spoken a word, but he had heard every syllable. His hand clenched the wheel tighter, knuckles white. He let the silence build until it had weight — until even the storm seemed to lean in to listen — and then his voice cut through, deep and measured as the toll of a ship's bell.

"Rafe."

The crew froze. Even the rain seemed to soften.

"You mistake my silence for weakness. But I hear your words, and I reckon you mean them. So I'll give you this — if you think me unfit to lead, you may step ashore at Nassau and find a new master. But so long as you stand upon the Providence, you will not sow division. You'll haul rope, trim sail, and keep your tongue behind your teeth."

His eyes — lit by a lash of lightning that turned the blue to white fire — fixed on the mutineer.

"And if you cannot, then the sea will be your judge, not I."

The deck held still, the crew caught between fear and admiration. It was not bluster in the Captain's words. They had all seen him cast men overboard before, though never without cause. And in this moment, soaked and storm-lit, his figure filling the space between wheel and sky, he looked less like a man and more like something the ocean itself had carved and decided to keep.

Rafe dipped his head just enough to avoid open defiance. But the look he shot Elias was a promise, sharp as a knife's edge: this isn't finished.

As the crew returned to their labor, Elias caught the Captain's gaze. No words passed between them, but the understanding was there — old, deep, forged in storms that predated this one. Twenty years of shared watches and unspoken reckonings. Elias would stand loyal. He always had. But the storm on deck would prove as dangerous as any storm at sea.

Then Slamyrbach did something the newer men had never seen. He released the wheel to Gideon with a nod — and as his hands left the spokes, his right shoulder dropped a fraction, the weight of the wheel suddenly gone and the weight of his body suddenly present. He straightened before anyone could notice, but Elias could read it. Stepping to the quarterdeck rail, he called down to the men — not with anger, not with command, but with something older. A ritual. A gathering.

"Eyes steady."

His voice carried through the rain like a bell across water. For a moment nothing happened. Then Elias straightened at the starboard rail and answered, low and sure:

"Blades sharp."

A beat. Two. Then from the rigging, from the deck, from the galley hatch where Ortiz stood with his cleaver still in hand, the rest of the crew murmured the final words together — some loud, some barely a whisper, but all of them:

"Hearts true."

It was neither a cheer nor a prayer but something between — a thing this crew had learned in waters most men never sailed, a call that meant: we are still here, we are still together, and we have not yet begun to break.

Slamyrbach held the silence that followed, letting it settle over the deck like a balm. Then he took back the wheel from Gideon, and the ship sailed on.

Rafe stood apart, arms folded, his mouth a thin line. The words had not crossed his lips. But he had heard them. His jaw tightened.

***

In the flash of the next lightning strike, something pulsed against Slamyrbach's chest — faint, almost imperceptible, like a second heartbeat pressed to his own. The parchment in his breast pocket. He didn't need to unfold it. The words were branded into his memory as surely as the mark at the back of his neck:

Five hundred and eighty-nine pieces of eight.

The debt. The noose. The sum that bound him to Cornelius Vark like a hound to its chain. Not six hundred. Not five hundred. But precisely five hundred and eighty-nine — an odd sum, chosen by Vark himself. Some numbers count. This one summoned.

A jolt seared through the nape of his neck. He winced, free hand flying up as if swatting away a biting insect. For a fleeting moment, the hidden brand burned beneath his wet hair — one he had no memory of receiving — seared into his flesh like a brand of ownership. Whether the heat was real or remembered, he could never tell. The scar did not care about the difference. He pressed his palm against it, breathing hard. The heat felt alive — pulsing in rhythm with the lightning, as if the storm and the mark shared a language he could feel but not translate.

Marked. Cursed. Or perhaps worse — watched.

Vark never left things to chance. Every figure, every ledger, every debt was a chain forged with purpose. And until that exact sum was repaid — that precise, maddening, deliberate number — he was bound.

One last voyage. One last storm. One last debt.

***

Gideon lingered near the quarterdeck, his hands busy with a line but his eyes on the men. He had his father's blue gaze, though softer, not yet sharpened by the years that had honed the Captain's into something that could cut. He saw the crew's weariness, their hunger for coin, their longing for rest. And in his own heart stirred an ache he dared not speak aloud. How long must a man live chained to salt and timber? How many years lost before he might find a hearth to warm him, a gentle hand to hold? He had known no other life than this — the creak of rigging, the smell of tar, the endless horizon that promised everything and delivered only more horizon.

His duty was to his father — 'Captain' in the open, 'Papa' in the quiet of their cabin. He would not leave him. Not yet. But he dreamed of a life someday beyond the sea, and the dreaming was getting louder.

His hand rose to the silver earring in his lobe, the twin to his father's, and he whispered only to himself: 'And I you, Papa.'

***

A flicker of movement broke the tension's hold.

From beneath a coil of rope slinked the ship's stowaway: a wiry calico cat, her patched fur — black and orange and white — plastered by the rain. She padded across the planks with unhurried grace, tail flicking, utterly unimpressed by the storm. She paused to lap rainwater from a puddle, then sat, blinking solemnly at the men as if they were the spectacle and not the gale that raged around them.

From below burst a roar thick as rum. Manuel Ortiz, the ship's cook, charged from the galley hatch. He was a short, barrel-bellied Spaniard with a mustache bristling like a broom and an apron that bore the history of a hundred meals. In one hand gleamed his meat cleaver, in the other a hunk of dried cod with a bite missing. At his feet the calico darted, a strip of the cod clamped in her jaws like a trophy.

"Ladrón! Thief!" Ortiz bellowed, and with a flick of his wrist hurled the cleaver. It struck sparks from the deck, slicing the very tip of the cat's tail before burying itself in the salt-pork barrel with a thock that shivered the handle like a tuning fork. The cat did not look back. She did not need to. She had won, and she knew it. The rigging received her like a cathedral receives a sinner — without judgment and with plenty of shadows.

The men gasped, then laughed — real, belly-deep laughter that rolled across the deck, cracking the tension like thunder splitting clouds. For a moment every man on the Providence was the same man: wet, exhausted, alive, and grateful for the absurdity of a cat that feared nothing and a cook who could not abide theft. Even Slamyrbach, at the wheel, allowed himself the ghost of a smile.

Ortiz wrenched his cleaver from the barrel, tested the edge with his thumb, and roared louder than the storm. "Run, gatita! You live — but now you carry my mark! Next time, I take the ears!"

The laughter lingered in the timbers like warmth after a fire, and for a breath the ship felt whole again.

***

The storm eased by dawn.

It didn't end so much as lose interest — pulling back its claws, lowering its voice, turning its vast attention elsewhere as if the Providence had passed some test it had not known it was taking. Streaks of light broke through the thinning clouds, pale and tentative, touching the deck like fingers testing a wound. The sea heaved in tired swells, and the ship rode them with the weary patience of an old creature that had outlasted worse and expected worse again.

Men moved slower now, wringing out cloth, checking lines, cataloguing damage with the grim arithmetic of survival. A torn sail. A cracked spar. A man with a gash across his forearm who sat quietly while another stitched it shut with sailmaker's thread. And one man fewer than yesterday, unspoken, a name that would not be called at the next muster. The cost of the night, tallied in cloth and blood and wood. But another storm — of men, of loyalty, of betrayal — was only beginning to gather.

In the rigging above, the calico shook herself dry and stretched with the luxurious indifference of a creature that had never once doubted her place in the world. She surveyed the deck below with proprietary calm, her shortened tail twitching like a metronome counting time that only cats could hear. Somewhere below, one of the younger sailors muttered a half-rhyme they'd heard whispered in Nassau taverns. His voice was thin, half-swallowed by the morning wind, but it carried:

"Five hundred and eighty-nine pieces of eight, / Pay them up or seal your fate..."

The words drifted across the wet planks and up through the rigging, where the wind caught them and carried them out to sea — out past the horizon, where things listened that had no name and no mercy and all the time in the world.

Slamyrbach heard. His hand found the parchment in his breast pocket and pressed it flat against his chest. At the back of his neck, the mark throbbed once — faint as a coal before ash — then fell still.

He turned his gaze to the horizon where the dawn was drawing a line between what had been survived and what was yet to come. His thumb found the thin gold band on his right small finger and turned it once, slowly, the way a man turns a key in a lock he is not yet ready to open.

And below, in the shadows, Rafe sharpened his knife.

CHAPTER TWO

Song of the Doldrums

The sea lay flat as hammered pewter, its surface broken only by the lazy slap of waves against the hull. After the storm's fury, the stillness felt unnatural — a silence that pressed against the men's ears until even the creak of timbers seemed loud as cannon fire. The Providence drifted listless in the grip of the doldrums, her sails limp against the masts, and the sky above had gone white and featureless, as though someone had drawn a sheet over the world.

Two nights ago the ocean had raged and tested them. Now it offered nothing at all. No wind. No current. No sign that it remembered the violence of two nights past, or cared.

Men sat in patches of shade and talked about the things men talk about when the horizon offers nothing: women they'd left, coin they'd lost, the rigger who'd gone over the rail. No one said his name. Saying it made it real, and 'real' was too close to 'next'.

"What's waiting for us, then?" one of the older hands muttered, picking at a splinter in his palm. "Nassau? Another port, another debt. And after Nassau — what? My knees are shot. My back's no better. Twenty years of hauling line and I'll die on a dock with nothing but the clothes I'm wearing."

No one answered him. No one needed to. Every man on the deck had done the same calculations and arrived at the same answer.

***

In his cabin, the Captain sat alone, stripped of his heavy coat. His linen shirt clung to him in the humid air, the sleeves rolled to his elbows revealed the scarred muscles of his forearms and the various tattoos that mapped a life lived at the edges of the world. His scabbard still hung at his hip, always within reach. The cabin was chaos, but an organized chaos that bore the marks of a lifetime at sea. Shelves lined with books in half a dozen languages. A cracked compass, its needle trembling with age. A brass sextant polished bright by use. A painting of a log cabin among the mountains, the lines soft, almost feminine — by a woman's hand. A gold amulet hung from a nail near the stern windows — a vertical rectangle on a chain, its surface dark with handling. And at the center, on the Captain's desk, lay the parchment, curled like a serpent, its faint ink whispering that accursed number: 589 pieces of eight.

On his fingers, the light caught something else. Seven rings — silver thumb rings worn smooth, bands of black onyx flecked with gold on the middle fingers, a gold band with milled edges on the left small finger, and on the right, two: a thin band of gold, plain, unremarkable except for its stubborn presence — Lianor's ring, placed there the morning he sailed and never removed — and beside it, a ring whose red markings had faded to a language only his skin remembered. They glinted in the flickering lamplight, tokens of a story untold. No one knew their meaning. Not the crew. Not even Gideon.

He traced the edge of the scroll with a finger, the metal of his rings cool against the parchment. The touch yielded no answers, only silence. The curse was not merely debt. It was a weight in his bones. And always, when he thought of it, he thought of her. Lianor. The woman who had tamed him when he was young, whose faith had never wavered even when he deserved none of it. Without her, he would have been nothing more than a brute with a ship. With her, he had found purpose — and the ache of longing now was sharper than any cutlass. He could see her in his mind: standing in the cabin doorway of their mountain home, fireweed blooming in the foothills and the mountains still carrying snow on their shoulders. He longed for that life, the quiet one she had always believed he could live.

"Soon," he whispered softly.

His hand brushed the back of his neck, where the brand burned faintly even in calm. He pressed his palm against the mark — Thresh's mark, Vark's mark, whoever had put it there while he lay drugged and helpless in a port he could no longer name. 'Not yours... Never yours'.

He had said it before — to the dark, to the sea, to no one. It was not a prayer. It was a line drawn in the soul, the place where a man decides what belongs to him and what does not. They could mark his skin, chain him with numbers. But the thing beneath — the thing that loved Lianor, that raised Gideon, that still believed a man could sail home — that was his, and no brand would claim it.

He sat a moment longer, then rose and crossed to the sea chest that stood beneath the stern windows. It was older than the ship — older than his captaincy — a thing of oak and iron that had followed him from his home on the French coast, to the southern seas, and all the way to the northern mountains where Lianor was waiting. He lifted the lid. The smell of cedar and salt rose to meet him, and beneath it something fainter: the ghost of lavender, pressed between pages long ago.

The chest was heavier than a sea chest had any right to be, and heavier still for reasons the crew did not need to know. But that was a weight for another day. Today his hands wanted only the one thing they always wanted when the sea went quiet and the cabin walls pressed close.

Under the charts, beneath the rolled leather of a spare scabbard and a pouch of navigational tools, his hands found it. A small book, no larger than a hymnal, bound in cloth that had once been green and was now the color of sea-foam left too long in the sun. Its spine was soft from handling. Its corners were rounded by years of being held, set down, and held again.

He knew every page without opening it — the drawings by a child's hand, a girl's hand, tracing the arc of a life he had watched from the wrong side of a distance he had built himself. Birthdays he had not attended. A confirmation dress he had not seen in person. A wedding where he stood in the back row and left before the dancing. And on the last page, written in a woman's steady hand was a single line he had read so many times the ink should have worn away from the looking:

'For my father. So you can see what you missed, and know I turned out fine.'

He held the book the way a man holds a wound — gently, with both hands, the weight of it far greater than cloth and paper could account for.

After a time he placed the book back beneath the charts, closed the lid, and pressed both palms flat against the chest as though sealing a covenant. Then he returned to his desk, squared the parchment, and turned his gaze toward the painting of the mountain cabin, where fireweed bloomed like a promise that the world still kept such things for men who had the courage to go home.

***

On deck, the men grew restless. The ship's stowaway calico — wiry, tail freshly shortened — had resumed her rounds with the lordly disdain of a creature that considered the entire vessel a personal estate, and its crew merely the help. She darted into the galley, a flash of patched fur and brazen hunger.

"¡Dios mío!" roared Manuel Ortiz, sweat glistening on his bald pate. He caught sight of the cat with a strip of dried cod clamped in her jaws and snapped the wet towel with the wrist of a man who'd been cracking linens since before he could shave. It sounded like a pistol shot and caught the cat square on the hindquarters. The beast let out a yowl of pure outrage and vanished into the rigging with her prize.

Ortiz squinted up at her with a mixture of fury and grudging admiration. "You," he announced, pointing his ladle at the calico, "are Cajun. That is your name now. Because you are nothing but spice and trouble."

The cat blinked once, slowly, in the manner of a creature accepting a title she had always known was her due.

Yet as Ortiz turned back to his galley, he caught sight of something that twisted his smile. Rafe Cutler, with darting eyes, uncorked the water cask and took a long, secret pull before corking it again. Ortiz said nothing. He only folded the towel over his shoulder and kept his counsel. A man who steals water in the doldrums is already telling you who he is.

***

Gideon stood near the rail, watching the horizon. The sea mirrored the sky so perfectly it felt as though the ship floated in air, suspended between two pale infinities. His mind wandered — not to mutiny, nor to Nassau, but to a memory.

He was a boy again, standing on the docks beside his father. The smells of pitch and brine filled the air. Merchants shouted prices, gulls shrieked overhead. At a stall, his father paused, his eyes catching on a pair of simple silver earrings. He bought them without haggling, then handed one to Gideon.

"So I can always hear you when you call," Wry said, with a grin that belonged to a younger man, one who still believed the sea would give back more than it took.

They paused at a leatherwork stall. Wry picked up an awl, snatched a bottle of rum from a passing drunk, and poured it onto the point. "It's a difficult journey from being a boy to a man," he said, and guided Gideon to a post. The awl went through his earlobe in one clean push. Gideon winced but did not cry out.

"And I will always hear you, Papa!" Gideon said solemnly, his boy's voice carrying more weight than he understood.

Wry cleaned the awl again, tilted his head, and drove the point through his own left lobe without flinching. The second silver hoop slid home. He crouched to Gideon's height and turned his head so the boy could see them both — father and son, matched in silver.

"Now we match," he said. Then he grinned, ruffled the boy's hair, and wrapped his muscular arm around Gideon. "Let's go make some noise!"

And the two pressed into the crowd, laughing, the silver catching the light between them like a signal only they could read.

The memory warmed him now, even as sweat trickled down his brow. He tugged lightly on the earring, a private gesture of loyalty — a bond that storms and debts could not sever.

***

Below, Elias sat at a rough-hewn table with Ortiz, who gnawed on a crust of bread between gulps of ale. The two men spoke quietly, their words drowned by the murmur of the crew.

“You’ve eyes,” Elias said. “You saw Cutler with the water.”

Ortiz shrugged. “Si. I saw. But a man who steals water in the doldrums is already dying. No need for me to put the rope on his neck. Not yet.”

Elias studied him for a long moment, then nodded once. He tore a piece from the bread, chewed it slowly, and looked at his hands — the hands that had reached for the rigger in the storm and come back empty.

“I had him,” Elias said. Not to Ortiz. To the table, to the bread, to the space where the words needed to go. “Fingers touched. Then the wave.”

Ortiz was about to drink, then instead, set down his ale. He knew better than to offer comfort to a man like Elias, who would treat it the way a wound treats salt. Instead he pushed the bread across the table — the whole loaf, not a piece — and said, “Eat. The dead don’t need it. You do.”

Elias looked at the loaf. A weight settled behind his eyes — not grief, exactly, but the acknowledgment of grief’s address, the knowledge of where it lived and that he’d be visiting it for a while. He tore off another piece.

“Twenty years I’ve sailed with that man,” Elias said, quieter now, nodding toward the Captain’s cabin. “Twenty years of watching him carry a debt that would have broken three men. He doesn’t bend. Doesn’t complain. Just holds the wheel and holds the wheel and holds the wheel.” He paused. “But I see what it costs. His back’s worse than he lets on. The Orient took something out of his spine that the sea’s been collecting on ever since.”

Ortiz said nothing. He waited. Elias was not a man who spoke often so interrupting him was like interrupting a glacier — pointless and possibly dangerous.

“I stay because he’s worth staying for,” Elias said. “Not because he asks. He never asks. That’s the whole problem with good men — they carry everything alone and call it strength.”

He finished the bread. “Someone’s got to check the joinery. Make sure the ship holds while the captain pretends he’s fine.”

Above them, through the deck boards, shouting and clanking mugs rolled across the main deck. The Captain had ordered rum distributed — better to drown mutiny in drink than let it fester in silence.

***

Dusk settled over the Providence like a hand laid gently on a feverish brow. The work was done — what little the doldrums offered — and the men had earned their rest. They sprawled across the main deck in the amber light: draped over crates, leaning against the lashed cannon, sitting on coils of rope with their backs to the gunwales. Lanterns were being lit, one by one, their small flames catching and steadying as the sky above them turned from white to copper to a deep, bleeding crimson that spread across the western horizon like a wound the day had been hiding.

Ortiz had brought up a pot of something hot and thick, and the smell of it — pepper, salt pork, ship’s biscuit softened in broth — cut through the salt air and drew men from every corner of the deck. Mugs of rum passed hand to hand.

One of the crew with fair skin and tattooed arms, the one who hummed a tune after the storm, leaped up on a crate. The full lyrics remembered now, he raised his voice without accompaniment. His tenor voice carried, clear as glass, through the still air.

‘Drink to the storms we’ve survived / And the doldrums that nearly took our lives...’

The men quieted. They listened. Then someone pulled a mandolin from a sea chest, its strings worn but true. Another brought forth a small accordion. Ortiz banged his wooden spoons on a barrel, laughing as he found the rhythm. The song swelled, instruments weaving into the lyrics that were clearly calling out for everyone to join in. At the chorus, the whole crew thundered in unison:

‘Five hundred and eighty-nine pieces of eight, / Pay them up, or seal your fate...’

The sound shook the timbers, laughter mixing with song. By the second verse, they were shouting the lines about the stowaway cat and Ortiz's flying cleaver. Even Cajun poked her head from the rigging, tail twitching in indignation at her sudden fame.

When the third verse began, a figure appeared at the top of the companionway. The crimson sunset poured through the hatch behind him, and for a moment he was nothing but silhouette — broad shoulders, the shape of the fur mantle, one hand on the frame — cut from the dying light like a figure stamped on a coin. Then he stepped forward and became a man again, and the men cheered.

Gideon, grinning, brought him a mug of rum. Their eyes met — father and son, bound by more than blood — and the same piercing blue shone in both their eyes, the father's tempered by decades, and the son's still bright with becoming.

Gideon tugged his earring. Wry grinned back, took the rum, and together they pushed through the cheering men.

Arm in arm, they sang the last chorus, bellowing with the crew:

'Five hundred and eighty-nine pieces of eight, / Pay them up, before it's too late...'

The Providence rang with their voices, rolling across the water, echoing into the darkening sky. And somewhere, in the shadows of the deep, unseen forces listened — smiling, perhaps, at the chorus of men who thought their song was only jest.

***

That night, as the men slept uneasy in hammocks, Slamyrbach stood alone at the rail. The sea was so calm it seemed to hold its breath. Then the mark at his neck flared again. No lightning, no storm. Just heat, sharp and biting. He gritted his teeth, one hand clutching the wood.

Cajun arched her back and hissed at nothing, staring wide-eyed into the horizon where no ship sailed and no gull flew. Slamyrbach followed the cat's gaze. For a heartbeat, he thought he saw eyes — vast, shadowed, watching — in the clouds. But when he blinked, the sky was empty.

Still, the weight of them lingered. He whispered Lianor's name into the silence, the vow heavy in his chest: 'Survive. Return. Never fail her again.'

Below, in a pocket of dark that kept its own counsel, Rafe drew a whetstone down his knife in slow, deliberate strokes. The sound carried no further than the shadows it was born in.

And the sea, flat and patient, held whatever it held, and gave nothing away.

CHAPTER THREE

The Weight of the Wheel

The wind held for three days after the doldrums broke. The Providence ran with it, her canvas fat and pulling, her wake a white road unrolling behind them into blue distance. Men's spirits lifted the way they always did when the ship was making way — there was less time to think, less silence to fill, and the horizon moved instead of staring back.

On the fourth morning the sky changed its mind.

It began at the edges — a yellowing of the light, a thickening of the air that pressed against the skin like damp cloth. The barometer in the Captain's cabin dropped three lines before noon, and Wry stood studying it with the expression of a man reading a letter he'd hoped wouldn't come. He tapped the glass once. The needle didn't move. He tapped it again. It dropped another line.

He climbed to the quarterdeck and studied the sky the way he studied everything — without hurry, reading what it was hiding behind what it was showing. The clouds to the south were stacked in a wall that leaned forward at the top, as though something behind them was pushing. The sea beneath had gone an ugly green, the kind of green that meant depth and trouble and water that remembered being violent.

"Bosun," he said.

Elias was already there. He'd read the same sky and arrived at the same conclusion.

"Aye, Captain."

"All hands. Reef the topsails. Strike the topgallants. Double-lash the guns and anything that moves. And get the men fed — there won't be time later."

Elias moved. When Elias moved, the ship moved with him — not because he shouted, but because men who had sailed with him understood that when the Bosun's pace changed, the world was about to change with it. Within minutes the deck was a controlled fury of men hauling, tying, battening. Ortiz fed them biscuit and cold salt pork from a bucket, shoving food into hands that didn't stop working.

Gideon was everywhere. He checked the foresail lashings, tested the anchor lashing, inspected the bilge pump, and drove the men with an energy that was half his father's steadiness and half something of his own — quicker, sharper, more urgent. He'd been through storms before, but something about this one sat wrong in his gut. He kept looking south, where the cloud wall was eating the sky.

"She's coming fast," he said to Elias as they crossed paths near the mainmast.

Elias glanced south. "Aye. Captain's seen it."

"Has he?" The question came out with an edge that surprised them both. Gideon caught it, swallowed it, and moved on. But Elias had heard it, and filed it without expression.

***

The storm hit at the change of the afternoon watch.

It was not like the first storm. The first had been a brawl — wild, chaotic, the sea throwing punches from every direction. This one was a siege. The wind came from the south in a single sustained wall of force that laid the Providence over fifteen degrees to starboard and held her there, groaning, while the rain arrived horizontal and the sea stacked itself into long gray rollers that marched with the discipline of an army.

Wry stood at the wheel. His hands knew their place. His back protested — the old injury firing along the spine in sharp, rhythmic pulses that matched the waves hitting the hull — but his hands knew their place, and that was enough. He held the heading: north by northeast, angling into the storm's shoulder rather than running before it.

Gideon saw the heading and felt it in his feet — the angle of the deck, the direction of the bow, the relationship between wind and course. And it was wrong. He was sure of it. Running before the storm — south to north, wind at their backs — was the textbook move. It kept the waves behind them, reduced the stress on the rigging, and used the storm's own power to push them toward Nassau. Every sailor learned it. Every instinct screamed it. And his father was ignoring it.

Wry was sailing across the storm. Into its shoulder. The Providence was taking waves broadside-to-quartering, each one slamming the hull and sending men staggering. The rigging screamed at angles it wasn't designed for. Water poured over the starboard gunwale in sheets.

Gideon climbed to the quarterdeck. The rain hit his face like gravel. He grabbed the rail and leaned close to his father's ear — or meant to. What came out was louder than he intended.

"You're killing us! We should be running south to north — wind at our backs!"

Wry's eyes didn't leave the horizon. "No."

"The rigging can't take this angle! We're shipping water on every wave — the bilge pump is already falling behind!"

"I said no."

Men heard. Of course they heard — the wind was loud but the argument was louder, and men on a ship in a storm have ears tuned to the frequency of command, because command is what stands between them and the water. Faces turned. Hands slowed on lines. Elias, at the foresail, looked up.

"Papa —"

The word came out before Gideon could stop it, the wrong word, the private word, spoken in the public storm. He caught himself. "Captain. The safe course is before the wind. Every man on this ship knows it."

Wry's jaw tightened. His knuckles shifted on the spokes but his heading did not change. When he spoke, his voice carried the flat authority of a man who has no time to explain and no intention of trying.

"I've sailed thirty years, son. Get off my quarterdeck and tend the foresail."

The words landed like a door slammed shut. Gideon stood in the rain, his face a map of everything he was feeling — anger, humiliation, and something hotter he couldn't name. He opened his mouth. Closed it. His hand went to his earring — the silver one, the bond — and for a moment the gesture looked less like loyalty and more like a man testing whether a rope still held.

He turned and went down the steps to the main deck. Elias watched him go. Then he looked at the Captain. Wry's eyes were still on the horizon. His face had shifted — a tightening around the mouth that had nothing to do with wind or water.

***

Two hours later, the storm proved the Captain right.

The weather shifted — as he'd known it would, as thirty years of reading the sky had told him it would — and the sustained southerly broke apart into a confused crosswind that would have caught a ship running before it broadside and rolled her. The Providence, already angled into the storm's shoulder, absorbed the shift without crisis. Her heading barely changed. A shift that would have been catastrophic for a ship running south-to-north was, for Wry's chosen course, barely a shudder. The men felt it. Some understood it. Others simply noticed that they were still alive and the ship was still upright and the Captain was still at the wheel, blue eyes fixed forward, hands sure, as though the storm had been a conversation and he'd simply waited for the other party to finish speaking.

Gideon felt it too. He was at the foresail, soaked through, arms burning from two hours of hauling line against wind that wanted to tear it from his hands. He felt the shift. He felt the ship settle into the new wind like a horse finding its stride. And he understood — in the bones, not the brain — that his father had been sailing toward this moment the entire time. Not reacting to the storm.

Anticipating it. Reading something in the sky or the water or the decades of storms behind him that Gideon's young years could not yet see.

***

The storm passed by evening, leaving the sea heavy and tired and the sky washed clean to a pale violet that faded to black. Men moved through the aftermath checking lines, pumping bilge, wringing out cloth. No one had been lost. The Providence had held.

Gideon worked alongside them, saying nothing, doing everything. He threw himself into the labor the way men do when they can't face the conversation waiting for them — harder, faster, longer, as though rope and canvas could absorb what words couldn't.

Elias found him at the foremast, coiling a line that was already coiled. The Bosun stood beside him and said nothing for a while, which was his way of saying I'm here.

"He was right," Gideon said, not looking up.

"Aye."

"I knew the textbook answer. He knew the real one."

"Aye."

Gideon finished the coil. Set it down. Picked it up and started again. "I called him Papa. In front of the men."

Elias let a breath pass. "I heard."

"He'll want to see me."

"He will."

Gideon set the coil down for the last time and looked at Elias. In the dark, the older man's face was unreadable. But his voice, when it came, was not what the face promised. It was something older and softer.

"Your father doesn't need you to be right, lad. He needs you to be steady. There's time enough to be right when you've got the wheel. But if you crack the crew's faith in the hand that holds it —" He paused. "A ship can survive a wrong heading. She can't survive two captains."

Gideon nodded. He touched his earring once, and went below.

***

The Captain's cabin was lit by a single lamp. Charts were spread on the desk but Wry wasn't looking at them. He was leaning back in his chair, eyes closed, letting his spine unknot from the hours at the wheel. The fur mantle was off. The scabbard hung on the chair back instead of his hip. He looked smaller without them. Older. A man in a linen shirt with a bad back and a son who'd just called him out in front of his crew.

Gideon closed the door behind him. The cabin was small enough that the silence filled it immediately, pressing against the bulkheads.

The Father in him let the silence do its work — the same technique he'd used on Rafe in the first storm, but different here, because this silence was not for the crew. This silence was for the two of them, and it carried a weight that had nothing to do with authority and everything to do with love.

"Sit down," Wry said.

Gideon sat.

More silence. The lamp swung with the ship's gentle roll, sending shadows back and forth across the desk like a slow conversation between the light and the dark.

"You were wrong about the heading," Wry said. "You know that now."

"Yes, sir."

"But that's not why we're here." Wry looked up. His eyes met Gideon's matching blue eyes and held them. "You challenged me on the quarterdeck in front of the men. In a storm. While I was holding the wheel."

Gideon opened his mouth. Wry raised one finger — not a command, just a pause — and Gideon closed it.

"A ship has one captain. Not because the captain is always right. I'm not always right. I've made calls that nearly killed us — you were too young to remember the Banks, but Elias wasn't, and he'll tell you I turned us into the teeth of a nor'easter that should have sunk us. I was wrong... but I was wrong from the wheel."

He paused. "If I'd been wrong today, we'd have lived — because the crew trusted the heading. If they'd seen two men fighting for the wheel in that storm, we'd have died — even if one of them was right."

Gideon's throat worked. His hands were resting on the edge of the desk as he tried to dab at the open blisters with a rag, blisters that didn't want to stop bleeding.

"I understand."

"I don't think you do. Not yet." Wry's voice softened — "One day you'll hold this wheel. You'll make calls that men question. You'll be wrong sometimes and right sometimes and you won't always know which until afterward. What you need — what these men need — is not a captain who's never wrong. It's a captain whose hands don't shake while they're deciding."

He reached across the desk and gripped Gideon's forearm — the grip of a sailor, wrist to wrist, the hold that keeps a man from going over the side.

"You have the mind for it. You have the eyes. But the wheel doesn't care about talent, son. It cares about stillness. And you weren't still today. You were loud."

Gideon looked at his father's hand on his arm. The thin gold band. The scarred fingers. The grip that had held the wheel through two storms and thirty years and a back that was breaking by degrees.

"I'm sorry," he said, looking deep into his father's eyes, "for being loud. And for challenging your authority and experience."

Wry held the grip a moment longer. Then he released it, sat back, and his face softened — not quite a smile, but close enough to warm the room.

"Your mother would have said the same thing. She'd have said it quieter, and it would have hurt more."

Gideon laughed. It was small and raw and unexpected, and it cracked the silence the way Ortiz's laughter cracked tension on the deck.

Wry reached for a bottle and two tin cups. He poured rum into both and pushed one across the desk. Father and son drank in a quiet that was no longer silence but the sound of a rift being mended. Together.

"Eyes steady," Wry said.

"Blades sharp," Gideon answered.

And below them the Providence sailed on, her timbers moaning, her crew sleeping, her heading true.

CHAPTER FOUR

The Scar and the Shadows

The wind laid a cautious hand into the slack sails until canvas sighed, billowed, and took hold. The Providence leaned with relief. Lines groaned. Blocks creaked. Men stretched as the blood returned to numb limbs. After the second storm and the days of dead air that preceded it, even a small wind felt like salvation.

By midmorning the sea had turned from pewter to a deeper blue-green, ruffled with cat's paws that stitched the water into moving lace. Gulls appeared first — white flashes banking, crying for scraps — and then the scent came: distant smoke, sweet rot from mangroves, a hint of fruit crushed underfoot. Nassau, somewhere beyond the haze, called to them like a rumor made of heat.

Captain Wry Slamyrbach watched the horizon, hands easy on the rail, one thumb worrying the leather of his scabbard as if it were a rosary. The crew moved with a lightness that wasn't joy so much as reprieve. Rafe Cutler walked the deck with a lean predator's grace, his black bandanna drawn low, eyes measuring, weighing. He spoke softly into corners, shoulders turned with men who pretended to share a joke. Elias matched him without mirroring — where Rafe slithered, the Bosun simply stood where he was needed, tying true lines, checking lashings, steadying. The men noticed both.

Gideon worked the deck with a quietness that was new. Since the cabin, since the rum and the two words that mended what the storm had cracked, he moved differently — not subdued, but settled. He deferred to Elias on rigging matters he would have handled himself a week ago. When he passed his father at the rail, they exchanged a look that carried the weight of two men who have fought and forgiven and are still learning what comes after.

Cajun, having fully recovered her dignity after the towel affair, resumed her rounds with a queen's unconcern: prowling coils of rope, examining buckets, pausing to stare at nothing in particular with an intensity that made sailors superstitious. Ortiz swatted at her with a rag and missed, then tossed her a gristle-end for good behavior. The cat accepted like royalty receiving tribute.

By noon they sighted brown-backed frigatebirds and a curve of low cloud anchored in the east — the kind that clung to islands. A murmur rippled the deck. Men spat and smiled in the same breath. Nassau meant coin and knives and women and traps. Nassau meant temptation.

***

In the Captain's cabin the air lay warm and heavy, smelling of tallow and paper and sun-baked wood. Wry set out his instruments with ritual care: dividers, worn charts, the old sextant that had saved his life more than once. His scabbard lay across the desk, never beyond reach.

He turned his hands palm-down on the desk. The thumb rings caught the lamplight — Grace on the left, Harmony on the right, the silver worn smooth by years of wear but the names still sharp in his memory. The master's voice, quiet as water over stone: You try with force. Force is a young man's answer to an old question. He remembered the weeks of training with Grace alone — the left hand learning stillness while the right hand flailed. Then Harmony alone — the right hand learning flow while the left hand starved. Neither ring worked by itself. Both together was something else entirely. The master had smiled only once, the morning Wry's hands finally moved as a single instrument, and said: Now you are ready to hold something worth holding.

The memory slid into another — unbidden, unwelcome, sharp as a slap.

Not sequences. Flashes. A lantern guttering in a low room. The sweet-sour taste of laudanum and rum, thick enough to coat the throat and slow the world to honey. A laugh like seawater poured over steel. And then Morcant Thresh, bending close, breath honeyed and rotten.

"Marks are for men who think they belong to no one," Thresh had murmured. With a fistful of hair Thresh wrenched his head forward, exposing the bare skin at the nape of his neck. The stench of burning hair and flesh. A sting that went deeper than skin — a brand pressed to the base of the skull with deliberate, unhurried precision. He had tried to rise. His arms had not obeyed. He had tried to speak. His tongue had thickened to a dead thing in his mouth. And Thresh had laughed again, soft, as if gentleness and cruelty were the same instrument played at different volumes.

The memory slipped like a fish. He couldn't hold it, only feel where it had been. He brushed the nape of his neck and felt, for an instant, heat under the skin, as if the mark remembered on his behalf.

He closed his fist over the thin gold band, the smallest ring. 'Not yours. Never yours.' Quieter this time. Less a declaration than a fact.

To ground himself he turned to the painting of the mountain cabin — fireweed blanketing the foothills, the highlands rising green and steep into the late summer sun — and held it with his eyes until the memory of Thresh's laugh faded. Then he turned back to his charts and began plotting the approach to Nassau harbor.

***

On deck, the day wore thin. The wind held. The men worked in rhythms, this was not storm-work, it was arrival-work, the kind that fills hands but leaves the mind free to wander.

Ortiz looked up from gutting a grouper and caught Rafe at the water cask again, quick-handed as a pickpocket. The cook's face did not change. He dabbed his knife on a rag, took two careful steps forward, and said quietly, "Careful you don't drink more than your shadow, amigo. Men who drink their shadow get followed by something else."

Rafe's smile showed the canines. "Old woman's talk, Manuel."

Ortiz returned to his fish. "Sí. Old women live long. Men who spit at them do not always." He set his knife down, blade toward himself, a sign men recognized without admitting they did.

Elias arrived with two coils of line on his shoulder, watching the exchange by not watching it. He set a coil down, looked at Rafe as one looks at weather: a fact to be accounted for. "We'll be in soundings by dusk."

Rafe shrugged and let his eyes roam the horizon as though he'd been considering only that. "Soundings, sure enough. And then what? We pay a debt by chasing the ghost that set it? Nassau takes debts and multiplies them."

"We recover what was taken and return what is owed," Elias said simply. "We keep the men safe."

"Safe." Rafe tasted the word like a bad fruit. "Safe doesn't fill a purse. And safe doesn't put a roof over your head when the sea spits you out. Ask the lads on the Exeter what 'safe' bought them — begging on the Kingston docks, every last man."

"Neither does a knife in your ribs," Elias said, and turned away to tie a line, his hands working the knot with calm precision.

***

Deep night. Hammocks swayed like cocoons in a drift of snores and mutterings. Lanterns burned low to embers, throwing slow-turning shadows across beams. The air below decks smelled of tar, sweat, and the stale sweetness of rum breathed out in sleep.

It had started earlier that evening, when Cajun discovered an open jar of rum left carelessly near a gun port. Ortiz had spotted the cat lapping at the jar and swatted gently, but the damage was done. Cajun's eyes had gone wide and glassy, her walk a sailor's roll that would have earned her laughter if anyone had been watching. She had climbed to the rafters above the gun deck with the exaggerated care of a drunkard ascending a cathedral staircase, settled herself along a joist, and fallen asleep with her shortened tail ticking to a tune that existed only for cats and fools.

Now the rum betrayed her. Sleep took her with a sudden sag of muscle. She rolled. For a breath she was a patch of falling darkness. Then a bundle of claws, fur, and startled yowl landed square across Rafe Cutler's face.

There is a speed to rage that outpaces reason. Rafe came awake with a roar and a flail, hands flashing to tear the thing off him. Claw met cheek. Skin parted. A bright line sprang from jaw to temple — a scar cut by accident and finished by anger.

Hammocks snapped as men jackknifed, curses fell like hail, a lantern swung wild and threw a theater of madness across canvas and faces.

Cajun, having rediscovered gravity with an insult, launched herself. She bounced off a bulkhead, ricocheted from a sling, and vanished into barrels with the speed of a blasphemy. In her wake: a single tuft of calico fur, drifting like evidence at a crime scene.

For a heartbeat there was silence. And then, because men are men and ships are ships, laughter erupted — hard, helpless, belly-grabbing laughter, the kind that catches your ribs and refuses to let go. Ortiz's laugh rose above the rest like a cannon, tears streaking the creases of his face.

"¡Mira!" he wheezed, pointing. "The cat gives him a captain's stripe!"

Rafe stood rigid, blood bright on his cheek, chest heaving. A dozen jests flew and died as they hit the wall of his stare. He wiped the blood with the heel of his hand and looked at it as though it were a prophecy written in a language he was only beginning to understand.

Elias moved without hurry, the only man not drawn into the current of hilarity. He stepped close enough to be heard and no closer. "Go to the galley. Ortiz will clean it."

Rafe did not move. The laugh tide swallowed the order for a moment, then ebbed as men realized what Elias had done — given Rafe a way to walk away without losing face. Rafe turned on a heel and left a trail of red drops behind him.

Ortiz met him at the hatch with clean water, strong liquor, and hands that were deft when they were not murderous. He cleaned the gash with a tenderness that was half insult, half priestly. "There," he said, patting Rafe's shoulder when he'd bound it. "Now you look distinguished. Like a gentleman who lost a duel to a cat."

Rafe's mouth did not smile. His eyes did not change. He threw the blood-stained rag he was holding onto the floor, and with a look of disgust, not gratitude, left Ortiz who was trying to hold back a chuckle.

By the time the hammocks settled again, the story had already grown a tail of its own — Cajun had leapt from the Royal Yard with a cry like a trumpet and carved her name upon Rafe's face; Ortiz had thrown his cleaver to save the cat and sliced off Rafe's ear instead (untrue, though Ortiz praised the version); the Captain himself had laughed (he had not, though he'd smiled in the dark where no one could see). The ship slept eventually, the way storms end – when there's no more wind.

***

Gideon took the middle watch, as often he chose to; he liked the hour when stars seem nearest and the sea sounds like breathing. He walked the deck with a blanket over his shoulders and touched the earring in his lobe — less a question and more an answer.

He found his father at the rail, where the quarterdeck met the night, where captains stand when they cannot sleep for thinking.

"Tomorrow," Gideon said.

Wry nodded. His profile was all angles and quiet, his eyes dimmed to something deeper by the dark. "Tomorrow. We walk among cutthroats, thieves, and worse. Keep your blade sharp, your ears open, and your faith tighter still."

Gideon grinned despite the solemnity. He tugged his earring with two fingers. "Aye, Captain."

"Papa will do," Wry said, so quiet no one but Gideon could have heard it. The words hung different now — after the storm, after the quarterdeck, after the cabin and the rum. Papa was not a slip anymore. It was a door left open on purpose.

They stood a while in silence, quietly building a bridge made of trust.

***

Dawn lifted like a blade from its scabbard, the edge of light sliding across a sea as smooth as hammered bronze. The Providence slipped over it, quiet for once, breathing easy after a hard run.

Before the day could burn the haze away, a shadow ship wrote itself upon the horizon — sleek, unfamiliar, her canvas cut into three triangular sails that bit the sky at sharp angles. She moved the way a cipher moves through a crowded room: unseen until you've already read it.

A ragged squawk tore free of the cipher-ship's lines. The Captain raised a looking glass in the direction of the noise. A mottled parrot, green and gold like tarnished coins, broke from the dark web of rigging and leapt into the morning. For a breath it hovered between the two ships, wings beating the air to paper, then was drawn to the Providence like iron to a lodestone.

"Pieces of eight! Pieces of eight!" it shrieked, skimming the foremast and perching on the larboard rail with the arrogance of a lord.

Cajun hissed from a coil of rope, hair up along her spine, the shortened whip of her tail twitching like a spiteful metronome. The parrot cocked his head and looked — not at the cat, not at the crew — but at Captain Wry Slamyrbach. Its beak clicked. Its eye glittered.

Then the voice came, unmistakable, sing-song and cruel:

"Five hundred and eighty-nine pieces of eight! Pay them up — or seal your fate!"

Silence rippled out from the words, a cold draft through warm breath. Men crossed themselves or spat over the side to break the hex. Rafe's new scar — Cajun's gift — pulled tight as he smirked. Elias's jaw locked like a vise. Ortiz lifted his ladle half in jest and waggled it at the bird.

"Another mouth for supper?" he boomed.

The bird shrieked laughter, flared its wings, and launched itself into the rigging where it settled above Cajun's favorite perch with the deliberate provocation of a new tenant. The cat glared upward.

The parrot preened. An ancient war had begun, and neither combatant intended to lose.

The triangular-sailed cipher-ship slid away along another path, swallowed by haze. No one hailed her. No one waved. She passed like a thought the sea had decided not to finish.

Wry said nothing. He felt the brand at the nape of his neck grow warm, then hotter, as if the bird's words were a striker and his flesh the flint. He let no wince show. He kept his eyes forward, where the haze was beginning to thin.

***

What followed was the longest kind of day — destination visible but refusing to arrive. Nassau sat on the horizon like a smudge of charcoal, growing so slowly that men swore it was retreating. The wind held but held gently, pushing the Providence at a pace that mocked urgency. There was nothing to do but wait, and watch, and think.

The crew had split along lines drawn in the first storm and deepened in every silence since. It was not open — no man declared himself for Rafe or for the Captain — but it was visible in the way men grouped, the way conversations stalled when certain boots approached. Rafe's men gathered near the foremast — the younger hands mostly, the ones with no savings and no prospects. The Captain's men held the quarterdeck and the stern — the older sailors, the ones who'd survived things younger men only talked about. Between the two camps, a handful drifted, and both sides watched *them*, most carefully.

Elias moved among all of them. That was the Bosun's gift — he belonged to no faction because he belonged to the ship. He checked lashings with Rafe's men and shared tobacco with the Captain's. He said little, but noticed everything.

***

In the early afternoon, Nassau was now a definite shape — green hills, a smear of buildings, the dark jut of the fort. Gideon found his father in the cabin. Wry was studying the harbor chart, marking depths with a stub of pencil, but his hands were still and the pencil hadn't moved in some time.

"May I?" Gideon said from the doorway.

Wry gestured to the chair. Gideon sat. The cabin was close and warm, the lamp unlit — enough light came through the stern windows to read by, a soft amber that made the charts look older than they were.

For a while neither spoke. The ship creaked. The parrot, somewhere above, muttered to himself in a language that was not quite speech, not quite song.

"I've been thinking about Elias," Gideon said.

Wry looked up.

"Twenty years he's sailed with you. He's stronger than half the crew combined. He reads the sea as well as any man I've met. He could captain a ship. Any ship. And he's never once reached for the wheel."

"No," Wry said. "He hasn't."

"Why?"

Wry set the pencil down and leaned back. The chair protested. His back protested harder, but he'd long since stopped distinguishing between the two.

"Because Elias understands something most men don't. There's more than one way to hold a ship together. The captain holds the wheel. The bosun holds the crew. Take away either one, and the ship goes down. But they're not the same job, and a man who's built for one will break himself trying to do the other."

"And Elias is built for the crew."

"Elias is built for the truth. He tests every idea for weak joinery. He doesn't need to stand at the wheel to know if the heading is sound — he feels it in the lines, in whether the ship is sailing or just being pushed." Wry paused. "I've made decisions that should have killed us. Elias knew it before I did. But he didn't grab the wheel.

He strengthened the rigging and made sure the ship could survive my mistake. That's not following. That's a different kind of leading."

The words sat between them.

"I don't know if I want the wheel," Gideon said. The words came out like a confession drawn from a deep well — honest and cold and surprised to see daylight. "I know you expect me to take it. I know the crew expects it. And I can do it — the storms proved that, even if I proved it badly." A ghost of a smile. "But wanting it is different from being able to do it."

Wry studied his son. His eyes found Gideon's and held — with the careful attention of a man hearing something important for the first time.

"There's honor in any choice that's made honestly," Wry said. "But I'll tell you something, and I want you to hear it without arguing." He waited. Gideon nodded.

"You're not Elias. Elias is the iron — he holds the shape. You're the fire — you make the shape. A man can choose not to lead, but a fire can't choose not to burn. It just is."

"And if the fire burns the ship?"

"Then the bosun puts it out." A half-smile now, matching his son's. "That's what Elias is for."

Gideon looked at the chart on the desk — Nassau harbor, depths marked in fathoms, the channel narrow and the shallows wide.

"When we leave Nassau," Gideon said. "If we leave Nassau. Will you teach me the approach? Not the chart — I can read the chart. The other thing. The thing you did in the storm, when you read the sky and knew the wind would shift before it shifted."

Wry's hand found the gold band. He turned it once. "That's not something I can teach. It's something you learn by being wrong enough times to start being right. But I can stand beside you while you learn it."

“Grace and Harmony,” Gideon said quietly, and when Wry’s eyes sharpened he added, “I’ve seen you touch the thumb rings when you’re thinking. I’ve always wondered what they meant.”

“They mean that nothing works alone,” Wry said. “Not even a captain.”

The afternoon light shifted. The chart glowed. Gideon did not look away.

***

Dusk came like a held breath slowly released. The sky turned from amber to copper to a deep violet that bled into the sea until there was no line between them. Nassau resolved itself from smudge, to shape, to substance — the green of the hills darkening, the white of the buildings catching the last light, the harbor opening before them like a hungry mouth.

The lead came up smelling of mud and shell, the sea’s bottom announcing itself with a tang like a cellar door opened. They were in soundings. The anchor was readied. Men moved to their stations with the tension of sailors about to make landfall in a place that might welcome them or swallow them whole.

Lights pricked the eastern dark — a chain of sparks that became lanterns, then a scatter of star-echoes that were not stars at all but taverns and windows and fires. The island breathed in the end of another day, restless, hungry, waiting. The wind carried the unmistakable scent of Nassau — woodsmoke and cane sugar and something sour beneath, the smell of a place that lived by night and lied by day.

The Providence swung gently toward harbor, her timbers settling into the sounds that come before a thing begins. Below, men dreamed of coin and rum and women who would remember their names for exactly as long as they could pay. Above, the rigging hummed a single note that might have been wind or might have been warning.

The parrot — whom the crew had already taken to calling Cipher, after the ghost-ship that delivered him — tucked his head beneath a wing and slept on a yardarm he had chosen with the certainty of a creature that knows exactly where it belongs.

Rafe sat in the shadows of the lower deck, his new scar still raw, his knife still in his hand. But for once he was not sharpening it. He was looking toward the glow on the horizon with an expression that, in better light, might have been hunger — or recognition, as if Nassau were a mirror and he did not like the face it showed him.

The Captain, of course, saw none of this. His eyes were forward, where the island waited. His hand rested on the rail, unhurried. Beside him, Gideon stood — not behind, not ahead, but beside.

Nassau. Where debts came due and men discovered what they were made of. The Providence held her breath, and the night leaned in to listen.

From the yardarm, in the dark, Cipher stirred. He did not repeat the old chant. Instead he murmured something new — low, almost conversational, as if trying out words he had overheard and was deciding which ones to keep. In the morning, the men who heard them in their half-sleep would remember only a feeling. A feeling that the bird had been listening to everything, and was learning, and that whatever it was assembling from the pieces of their voices was not yet finished.

CHAPTER FIVE

The Blue Anchor

The harbor unfolded like a fan stained by too many hands. Docks jutted out from the shore, as crooked as collapsed ladders; shanties leaned together like drunkards swapping secrets. Smoke lifted from cook fires — sweet cane, bitter coffee, meat fat hissing in iron pots. Tar and oakum scented the air with shipyard musk; brine rode under everything; somewhere limes were being cut and their bright oil flashed up like golden raindrops caught by the morning sun. The sound was a rope of voices plaited tight: hawkers crying wares in English and Spanish and patois; a saw whining through wet timber; gulls strafing the water with insults; a dog barking at a crab; a woman laughing in a doorway, low and dangerous. Color struck like thrown paint — scarlet kerchiefs, yellow spice sacks, indigo-dyed shirts from distant lands.

And beneath all of it, the heat. Not just warmth — weight. The air pressed against the skin like a damp hand, thick with moisture and the sweetness of rot. Heat that makes men short-tempered and women sharp-tongued and dogs too lazy to chase the crabs they bark at.

Nassau didn't welcome you. It appraised you. It checked your pockets and your teeth and decided how much you were worth before you'd stepped off the gangplank.

"God's teeth," Elias said, folding his arms. "A nest of knives."

"A nest where sharp men hatch," Rafe murmured, "...if they've a mind to."

Lines coiled, sails went to sleep, boots boomed on planks as the Providence kissed a dock that groaned as if remembering better ships. Wry stood at the top of the gangplank and surveyed the harbor without hurry. He set the watch: four men to stay with the Providence, armed and sober, rotating every six hours. He gave Elias the order to secure the cargo holds and chain the powder locker. He told Ortiz to fill the water casks from the harbor spring and buy fresh provisions — fruit, salt, hardtack, and whatever meat could be trusted not to kill them.

"And rum?" Ortiz asked, already knowing the answer.

"And rum. But not from the first man who offers it."

The crew dispersed along the dock in knots of two and three. Rafe disappeared into the crowd within minutes, his lean frame swallowed by the market's noise like a man born in it. Wry watched him go and said nothing.

Gideon stood beside his father. "Where do we start?"

"We listen," Wry said. "This island talks more than it thinks it does."

***

And then the boy appeared.

No herald, no fanfare. Just motion. He came down the wharf like water under pressure: wiry, barefoot, fast. Sun-cured skin. Eyes like bottle glass — bright, mischief lit from inside. His flaming red hair stuck where salt wanted it. His shirt was laundry that had lost the argument; his breeches belonged to a larger ghost. A piece of string hung from his back pocket, one end trailing like a tail.

He didn't slow. He vaulted a coil of hemp, slid between two arguing porters, and skimmed the lip of a fishmonger's cart without touching it. A vendor swung a ladle at him too late; the boy's laugh came back like a thrown stone.

He cut across a food stall where pyramids of bruised fruit leaned into the shade. His hand blurred. Two apples vanished — one into his mouth, one into his left hand. He bit into the first, juice running down his chin, and in the same motion twisted mid-leap like a cat and tossed the second to a child crouched in the alley's mouth — a child smaller than hunger, eyes stunned wide. The apple hit palms and stuck. The child bit as if rescued from a well.

The boy didn't watch. He knew what hunger looked like because he wore it under his grin the way other boys wore bruises under their shirts — always there, never shown, part of the architecture of staying alive. The giving wasn't charity. It was instinct. A thing he did the way he breathed, because somewhere beneath the performance there was a boy who couldn't walk past the thing he'd been.

He landed light, wiped the juice from his chin with the back of his wrist, and came to a stop near the Providence's gangplank — not at the foot of it, but close enough to study the men. He pulled the string from his pocket and his hands began to work it immediately, knotting and unknotting with the restless precision of fingers that could not afford to be still.

Ortiz, who had been readying a bark about thieves, shut his mouth around a laugh that surprised him. "¡Mira, pájaro sin alas! A bird with no wings," he said. "What do we call you, pequeño?"

The boy pocketed the string and cocked his head like Cipher had. "Kipp," he said. The name snapped like twine. "An' I know which tavern cheats softest, which alley cuts deepest, an' who sells news worth buyin'."

His accent was Irish — a sing-song that made even threat sound like a tune half-remembered from somebody else's childhood.

Rafe, who had reappeared from the crowd as quietly as he'd vanished, curled his lip. "Dock rats sell lies that cost as much as truth."

Kipp grinned, chipped tooth flashing in the sun. "A lie told right'll save yer hide twice, master. Once from a knife, once from a fool."

Wry had been watching from the rail — the apple, the child in the alley, the hands that couldn't stop moving. He came down the gangplank slowly, the dock boards creaking under his weight, and stood where the boy could see him full. He spoke to Gideon, pitching his voice so the boy could hear.

"We need a guide who knows the streets. Someone who knows where questions are safe to ask and where they'll get a knife for an answer."

Kipp's grin sharpened. He knew an audition when he heard one.

Gideon stepped forward, standing where the boy could meet his eyes without craning. "We're looking for someone, Kipp. Not a tavern. Not a fight." He paused, wondering if he was falling into a trap. "A woman taken where she didn't choose to go."

Kipp's grin turned sharp. "Ye look like men who've lost the piece o' the map that was drawn in the dark. Name?"

"Seraphine Vark," Wry said, his voice enough to turn heads for fifty feet. "And mind your tongue when you say it."

Kipp's grin faded to alertness. He glanced left and right, quick as a gull. "Then ye'll want The Blue Anchor. Not for her — she's no kind to sit in rooms reekin' o' spilled rum. But for the men paid to watch fer them that ask."

Elias studied him. "Paid by whom?"

Kipp shrugged with studied care, too casual to be careless. "By men who don't see the daylight. Men who take their breakfast at Vark's countin'-house, an' their supper where the docks drown."

Rafe's scar pulled taut as he spat. "Cats may like you, boy, but rats are all you'll ever be."

The boy's grin turned thin and sharp. "Rats survive, master. Lions get mounted on walls."

Wry's deep blue eyes locked on him across the wharf — the quieter blue, the one that measured rather than cut — and Kipp held the gaze as if it were a challenge. Then his grin flickered back, bright and reckless. "Let's all live through lunch, eh?"

He turned and started up the quay, threading the crowd with the ease of a needle through familiar cloth. The crew followed — Gideon first, then Elias, then the Captain. Ortiz brought up the rear, already collecting the names of spice vendors he intended to revisit. Rafe followed at his own pace, keeping his distance, watching the crowd with the flat attention of someone who had already decided where to cross.

And for three steps, when no one was watching — between the fishmonger's cart and the shade of a sail loft's awning — Kipp's grin dropped.

It didn't fall to sadness. It fell to nothing. The face beneath was younger than the performance, and older than the years. It was the face of a boy who had been running so long that stopping felt like falling, and falling was the one thing Nassau didn't forgive.

Then, uninvited, the way it always came — his mother's voice. Not a memory, exactly. More like a groove worn into the floor of his mind by years of hearing her say it, the words arriving whether he wanted them or not:

The Lord is close to the brokenhearted. He saves those who are crushed in spirit.

She had said it every night. Hands on his head, his red hair wild even then, her voice even the way only a voice can be even when everything else is shaking. He didn't pray anymore — hadn't since the alley became home — but the words prayed themselves, rising through him like water through a crack in stone.

Then the grin came back. It always came back. Not because the boy was brave — though he was — but because the grin was the door he kept between himself and the dark, and if he let it close he wasn't sure he could open it again.

He quickened his pace. The string resumed its dance — the same patient knotting his mother's hands had made with wool and hook, sitting by the fire, making something whole out of a single thread.

And behind him, Wry watched the boy's back with an expression that no one on the crew had ever seen on the Captain's face .

***

The Blue Anchor announced itself with a sign that had seen better anchors, better blue, and perhaps better gods. Inside was heat and noise and the smell of wood that had drunk as much as men. Sawdust tried to pretend it kept the floor clean. A fiddler sawed at a jig with murderous joy; dice clattered; a man fell into a laugh that became a cough.

Cipher's voice threaded the din from somewhere outside, as if the bird were a town crier who hated his parish:

"Five hundred and eighty-nine pieces of eight — pay them up — or seal your fate!"

It ducked and surfaced in the hubbub like a dolphin, sometimes near, sometimes far, always where you couldn't quite lay hands on it.

"Wait here," Kipp told Ortiz. "Or ye'll be sold to a baker for yer lard." He slid past two card players and through a back arch, Gideon on his heels, Elias a step behind. Rafe lingered in the doorway like smoke. Men who smelled of blubber oil and gun grease lifted their chins at him; he gave one nod to a man whose left ear was an absence. Words didn't pass. The knowledge that they could was enough.

At the bar, Ortiz made a friend in the time it takes to pour a drink and insult a cousin. His laugh rolled easy. He watched the room with his third eye, the one cooks need more than sailors.

Wry took a place where he could see the street through the open door and the room in the mirror behind the rum bottles. The brand at his neck had gone quiet since they'd made landfall — not cooled, just waiting, the way embers wait. Cajun had followed them ashore with the insolent ownership of cats and queens, and now sat in the Blue Anchor's doorway, tail curled around her paws, watching the room with the expression of a creature compiling a list of everyone who owed her something.

***

A soft, melodic voice behind him drew Wry from his reflection as a mug of brandy was placed before him.

"Hello, Wry. It's been a while."

"It was meant to be," the Captain replied without turning around, his gaze finding her in the mirror behind the bar.

There she stood — a slender, middle-aged woman with golden skin that hid her age well. Long, raven black curls hung around her shoulders and down her back, small flowers braided into the curls. Her emerald green eyes scanned the Captain's face in the mirror, looking for something she used to know. She held an empty tray tucked under one arm while her other hand fingered a silver clasp that hung on a necklace around her neck. Her accent, when it came, carried the ghost of somewhere far south — the Cape, perhaps. She had lived in Nassau long enough to sound like Nassau, but underneath there was always that other music, faint and warm.

Wry turned around. Her eyes searched his the way they always had — not for what was on the surface, but for what he kept underneath. For a moment neither of them spoke. The tavern noise filled the space where words might have gone, and that was enough.

"Brandy," the Captain said, returning her gaze. "I didn't expect to see you here. It's been a long time."

In one smooth motion she slapped the tray on the table, spun a chair around, and mounted it like a knight preparing for battle. Facing Wry with arms crossed on the back of the chair, she leaned in close enough that the scent of lilacs braided into her hair reached him before her words did.

"You didn't say goodbye."

The words carried no anger. They carried the quiet weight of a woman who has had years to distill a hurt into its purest form, and has arrived at a single sentence that says everything.

Wry's gaze fell down to his mug cupped in his hands and he shifted in his chair. He took a long draft and said, "I don't like long goodbyes. I didn't know if I'd ever be back. I didn't want to give you false hope."

"Hope is what keeps one alive on this island," she said.

Then she saw the small gold band on his finger.

The silence was not empty. It was full — full of the years between them, the ports they'd shared, the Orient where they'd met, the fire that had burned between them and the morning Wry had walked away without looking back. All of it lived in the small space between her eyes and his hand, and neither of them pretended it didn't.

She reached for his right hand. Her fingers hovered near the gold band without touching it, as though it were a wound she didn't want to reopen.

"What's her name?"

"Lianor," the Captain said without looking up.

"She must be very special," she whispered.

"She is."

Brandy's hand withdrew. She straightened on the chair, and her face rearranged itself — not the collapse of hope, but the quiet reorganization that happens when a woman decides to set down a thing she's been carrying and discovers she's lighter without it. The emerald eyes didn't dim. They sharpened.

"You look tired, Wry. Not sea-tired. Bone-tired. The kind that sleep doesn't fix."

"It's been a long voyage."

"It's been a long life." She studied him — the silver in his beard that hadn't been there, the way he held his back too carefully, the rings that told a story she'd only heard the first chapter of. "You're here for the debt."

It wasn't a question.

"I'm here for a woman named Seraphine Vark. The debt is the chain that brought me, but she's the reason I can't leave without cutting it."

Brandy's expression changed again — a flicker, quick as a card turned and turned back. "I know Seraphine. Not well. But I know what she's doing, and I know who's watching her do it." She leaned forward. "And I know things about your debt that you don't, Wry. Things that will change what you think you're carrying."

The fiddler sawed into a new tune. Dice clattered. Someone won or lost. The Blue Anchor kept its noise going, indifferent to the quiet storm gathering at a corner table.

"Tell me," Wry said.

Brandy glanced at the room — a quick sweep, professional. "Not here. Not now. There's a place — the Red Mercy, near the old battery. I'll take you tomorrow, when the men who watch have drunk enough to stop watching." She paused. "But Wry — what I have to tell you about the debt, about whose name is really on it — you're not going to like it."

Their eyes met. Something passed between them that the Blue Anchor's noise couldn't touch — the quiet recognition of two people who had once shared a fire and learned, separately, that fire alone isn't enough to build a life on. Brandy's fingers found the silver clasp at her throat.

"You still wear it," Wry said.

"I still wear it."

She stood, took the tray, and became a barmaid again — the transformation so smooth it was like watching a door close.

"Get your men settled. Feed the boy — he's skin and bone and fire and he'll burn out by nightfall if someone doesn't put food in him. And Wry —"

She turned back. The emerald eyes held his.

"Go home after. Love that woman. Before you forget how."

She didn't wait for an answer. She moved into the crowd, the tray already collecting empties, the flowers in her hair catching lamplight as she went. Within seconds she was the Blue Anchor's barmaid and nothing more — invisible in the way that women who know too much learn to be invisible.

Wry sat alone at the table with his mug and his rings and the weight of a sentence he hadn't expected to hear from the woman he'd left without saying goodbye. Go home. Love that woman. It sounded like Lianor, like the green book, like every promise he'd made and not yet kept.

***

Outside, Cipher had found a perch on the Blue Anchor's sign — settling into the crook of the rusted iron with the proprietary calm of a creature that intended to stay. Cajun, from the doorway, glared upward with the focused hatred that only cats and old enemies can sustain.

Kipp sat on an overturned crate near the alley mouth, legs drawn up, chin on his knees. Gideon had brought him a plate — bread, cheese, a strip of dried meat — and the boy had eaten with the careful speed of someone who knew that food left unguarded didn't stay around for long.

Now his hands were busy again — but not with the string. He'd found a chunk of charcoal from a dead cook fire and a scrap of parchment blown against the alley wall, and he was drawing. His fingers moved with the same restless precision they gave the string, but here the precision had a different purpose — not comfort, but vision. The charcoal moved in quick, certain strokes, and a picture took shape on the parchment: a broad-shouldered man with a fur mantle and piercing eyes, Cipher perched on one shoulder, Cajun curled in the crook of his opposite arm. Both animals looked outward with identical expressions of arrogant disdain, as though they had agreed on nothing except their mutual superiority.

Gideon watched over his shoulder. "That's good," he said. "That's actually very good."

Kipp shrugged, but his fingers kept moving — adding the rings on the man's fingers, the earring in his lobe, the lines of a face that had been carved by weather into something the boy couldn't name but recognized.

Wry came out of the Blue Anchor and stopped when he saw the drawing. Kipp held it up without ceremony.

Wry looked at it for a long moment. Then he laughed — a real laugh, short and surprised, the sound of a man caught off guard by something that wasn't pain. "The bird and the cat. Together. On me." He shook his head. "They'd tear each other apart in seconds."

"Maybe," Kipp said, tucking the drawing inside his shirt. "Maybe not. Stranger things happen when someone's holdin' 'em both."

The Captain's laugh faded to something quieter. He looked at the boy — the charcoal-stained fingers, the chipped tooth, the eyes that held more than they showed — and whatever he saw there, he kept it to himself.

"Keep it safe," Wry said. "We'll see if you're right."

The Blue Anchor's sign creaked in the evening wind. Nassau settled into its nightly business of sin and survival. And somewhere in the streets beyond, the name Morcant Thresh moved through whispers the way smoke moves through a room — touching everything, owned by nothing, impossible to hold.

Tomorrow, the Red Mercy. And the truth about the debt.

But tonight, bread and charcoal and a boy whose hands could not stop making things, because making was the only prayer he had left.

CHAPTER SIX

Red Mercy House

Morning came to Nassau the way hangovers come to drunkards — slowly, with regret, and without any intention of being gentle about it. The sun hit the rooftops and turned the harbor into a sheet of hammered brass. Dogs stretched in doorways. Vendors dragged carts to their marks. The smell of coffee and cane smoke braided through the air, chasing the last of the night's rum-breath into the alleys where it belonged.

Brandy met them at the corner of Harbor Street and the lane that led uphill toward the old battery. She'd traded the barmaid's tray for a shawl that covered her hair and most of her face — the practical disguise of a woman who knew that being recognized on this walk would cost more than being invisible.

"Stay close," she said. "And let the boy lead. He knows the teeth in these streets better than I do."

Kipp was already ahead of them, the string between his fingers, his bare feet finding the cobbles with the confidence of a creature that had memorized every crack and slope. He didn't look back. He didn't need to. He knew who was following and how fast they walked and where they'd hesitate, because knowing these things was how you stayed alive when you weighed ninety pounds and owned nothing but a piece of string and a chipped tooth.

Wry walked behind him with Elias at his shoulder. Gideon brought up the rear. Ortiz had been left at the Blue Anchor — "Someone needs to guard the rum, and my feet are not built for hills," he'd said, though the cleaver tucked under his apron told a different story. Rafe had not been invited, and had not asked to be.

The alleys narrowed as they climbed. The buildings pressed closer, shutters drawn against the heat, laundry strung between balconies like surrender flags. The noise of the harbor faded, replaced by the quieter sounds of a neighborhood that lived on secrets: a door closing too quickly, a whisper cut short, the scratch of a quill behind a shuttered window.

Somewhere above them, Cipher's chant drifted like a thread unwinding:

"Five hundred and eighty-nine pieces of eight..."

It was fainter here, as if even the bird knew that some streets were not for shouting.

***

They rounded a blind corner where the alley narrowed to single file, and nearly walked into a wall of man.

He filled the passage — bare-armed, bare-chested, tattooed from collar to belt with serpents and anchors and skulls that writhed in the shadows like living things. Between his shoulder blades, raised and ridged where the iron had done its work, three digits scarred the skin: 587. He was enormous — barrel-chested, thick-necked, the kind of man who didn't need a weapon because he was one. He leaned against the stone, picking his teeth with a splinter, watching the alley.

Kipp didn't hesitate. He launched himself sideways onto a barrel, used the momentum to vault upward, and somersaulted clean over the giant's head — the knotted string snapping out mid-air and catching the big man across the left eye with a crack like a green branch breaking. Kipp landed on both feet behind him, grinning, already waving the others through with an urgent flick of his hand.

The man bellowed, staggering, one massive paw clamped over his eye. By the time he'd turned around, the alley was empty.

"Move," Gideon said, and they moved — past the staggering bulk, through the gap, into a parallel lane where Kipp waited, breathing hard, grinning harder.

"Thresh's," Kipp said, jerking his thumb back toward the groaning man. "Watches this stretch for anyone headed where we're headed. He'll have a shiner by sundown."

Wry studied the boy. "You've done that before."

"Aye. He's slow and I'm not. That's the whole trick." Kipp wound the string back around his fist, the same string that had been a cat's cradle and a comfort object and was now, without any change in material, a weapon. "We go left here."

Elias looked back the way they'd come, listening. No pursuit. The big man's cursing faded behind them like weather moving off. But the Bosun's face carried the expression of a man filing a threat.

***

They came up beneath the lee of a plaster wall blotched with sea-salt blooms. From there, Red Mercy's doors and balconies presented themselves like a stage. The old battery above it was a broken tooth of stone, its cannons rusting in their emplacements, the embrasures choked with bougainvillea and heat. The house itself stood at the turn of Bay Lane where the slope climbed toward the ridge — a coral-lime facade the color of faded bruises, shutters the red of dried hibiscus. Laughter slipped through the shutters and so did music, the lazy pulse of a drum, the metallic twang of a stringed thing plucked with rings.

"Eyes steady," Wry said.

"Blades sharp," Gideon answered.

A beat. Two. And then Kipp, who had never heard the words before, who had no right to them and no invitation — Kipp looked from one man to the other, read the rhythm the way a street musician reads a song he's never played, and said:

"Hearts true."

Wry looked at him. The boy met the look without flinching. He didn't know if he'd guessed right or wrong, and his face said he didn't much care — he'd felt the shape of the thing and filled it, because that's what you did when you'd survived twelve years by reading patterns faster than the men who made them.

"How did you know that?" Gideon asked.

Kipp shrugged. "Two out of three's a rhythm. A rhythm wants finishing. Even I know that."

The boy had earned his place in the chant by being there when it mattered and not waiting to be asked.

***

Inside, the Red Mercy was amber light and low noise. The air smelled of incense, lime oil, and the particular sweetness of rum that's been poured too many times in the same room. Women moved between tables with trays and smiles that were part of the furniture. Men sat in clusters, speaking in voices calibrated to carry no further than the nearest ear.

Brandy led them to a table in the back, beneath a balcony where the shadows pooled deep enough to hide in. She ordered drinks — not rum but coffee, thick and bitter, the kind that keeps a man's wits where his fists want to be.

Kipp had mapped every exit before his backside hit the chair. Kitchen door, left. Street door, behind them. Window to the yard, right, shuttered but not locked. A ladder in the yard, missing a rung two from the top. Roof hatch above, locked from the inside but not by anyone who cared. He mentioned all of this to Wry in a voice no louder than the coffee's steam, and Wry listened the way he listened to weather reports — as information that might save lives.

And then Brandy leaned forward, and the room around her seemed to pull back like a tide.

"You don't owe, Wry."

Four words. The table went still.

Her voice was low, urgent, stripped of everything that had made it melodic at the Blue Anchor. Her hand went to the silver clasp at her throat and held it — not for comfort, but for anchor.

"I couldn't say it with ears in every wall. Not at the Anchor. Not where his men drink." She swallowed. "My brother. He borrowed your name when the lamps were low and the ink was wet. Vark took the name because it was easier than the man. A signature on a ledger — what does it matter whose hand held the quill when the debt is owed to a man who doesn't care about hands, only numbers?"

She paused. The clasp caught the light.

"I let it stand." Her voice didn't break. The break was in the tray she'd left at the bar, in the steadiness of her hands that cost her everything to maintain. "I let it stand because my brother was dying and the debt would have killed him faster, and because you were gone and the sea is large and I thought — I thought you'd never come back. The debt was never yours, Wry. My brother signed your name to a ledger in the dark, and Vark has been collecting on it ever since — not the sum itself, but the interest, the fees, the penalties he invents to keep the chain tight. Twenty years of payments, and the number never shrinks, because Vark doesn't want it paid. He wants it owed."

Silence. Not the silence of a room — the room kept its noise, its music, its laughter — but the silence of five people at a table who have just heard a truth that rearranges everything.

Elias shifted. His jaw worked. His arms unfolded for the first time since they'd sat down. Twenty years he'd watched the Captain hand over coin at every port — interest payments, docking levies, fees that arrived in Vark's name with the regularity of tides — and the balance never moved. Now he knew why.

Gideon's eyes moved from Brandy to his father and back, recalculating a debt he'd carried his whole life. Every storm. Every voyage. Every "one last time." All of it built on a number that didn't belong to them.

And Wry.

Wry didn't move. His hands were wrapped around his mug, knuckles tight. Then, slowly, he set the mug aside and pressed both palms flat on the table, as if the wood could steady what the words had tilted. After a moment, his thumbs began to tap — Grace on the left, Harmony on the right, alternating, the silver clicking softly against the wood. Left, right. Left, right. The body's way of thinking when the mind has been struck dumb.

The back of his neck went cold. Not the familiar heat of the scar — something else entirely. A trickle of ice, like meltwater off the cabin roof in the territory, the kind that catches you at the nape of the neck when you're not quick enough through the doorway. It ran down his spine and settled at the base, where the old injury lived. His body knew what his mind was still assembling: twenty years of payments made on a debt that had never been his.

He thought of the bargain. Vark's voice, oiled and certain, delivered through an intermediary in a port whose name he'd forgotten: 'Bring me my daughter. Return Seraphine to Nassau, and the debt is cleared. Your name struck from the ledger.'

That was the mission — the one last voyage. Bring Vark his daughter and walk free. He had believed it because the alternative was that there was no end, and a man cannot sail forever toward a horizon that never arrives.

And now this. The debt was a forgery. The mission was built on a lie. And the woman he'd crossed an ocean to deliver to her father was sitting upstairs in a house of secrets.

He thought of the storms. He thought of the men he'd lost — the rigger who went over the rail, whose name no one said. He thought of the years at sea when he could have been home, when Lianor stood in the cabin doorway and the fireweed bloomed in the foothills. Five hundred and eighty-nine pieces of eight. The original sum, untouched, immovable, while twenty years of interest payments bled him dry at every port. A daughter's green book. A wife's patience that should have broken and didn't. A son who'd grown up on salt water because his father believed he owed a debt that could never be paid — because it was never meant to be paid.

He said nothing for a time that stretched, then shortened, then became an answer all its own.

"We'll leave this where it is until we're past knives," he said.

His voice was level. His eyes were not. Behind the piercing blue, something had cracked — not broken, cracked — and through the crack poured a light that was either rage or grief.

"There's more," Brandy said. "But it needs another voice to tell it. Not mine."

***

Brandy led them up the stair with the gait of a woman who knew which boards creaked and which didn't. At the landing the air changed: less rum, more perfume; less laughter, more hush. A woman with a laugh like rain leaned where Brandy said she would, twirling a ribbon around two fingers. Brandy murmured something that made the laugh roll like summer thunder, and the watcher's eyes followed, as planned, as hoped.

At the cracked door Brandy paused, hand on the frame. "I sent word ahead. She knows your name and your business. Don't waste time pretending to be anyone else."

Wry found the door with a cracked hinge and pushed inside.

The room was dressed like a chapel to deceit. Red screens softened the light to wine. A couch, a pair of chairs, a bowl of cut limes sweating oil into the air. And a woman who sat writing, her head turning at his entrance as though she had known he was there all along.

Seraphine Vark.

She was younger than rumor made her. Hair the color of straw fell straight and long, past her shoulders, past her waist — lighter than it should have been, the roots showing a shade darker where the lye hadn't reached. The kind of hair a woman keeps because it is the one thing in her life no one else controls. Her skin was pale where Nassau's sun had not claimed it. Her dress — cut low like the others in this house — was costume, not confession; she wore it the way a soldier wears a disguise, with visible discomfort and perfect execution. Her hands were the thing you noticed second — long-fingered, ink-stained at the tips, a pencil callus on the right middle finger. Hands that worked. Her gray-blue eyes met Wry's and did not waver. In her lap sat a leather-bound ledger, its spine cracked from use, its pages thick with figures. She held it the way another woman might hold a weapon she had spent years sharpening.

"You are Captain Slamyrbach," she said. Not a question, but a measure. Her voice carried the Dutch lilt of another shore — precise, unhurried, the voice of a woman accustomed to being the smartest person in any room and polite enough not to say so. "Brandy described you. She left out the rings."

"I am."

"And you came to Nassau to bring me back to my father. To return the wayward daughter and clear your debt." The words were flat. Not accusation — inventory. She was listing facts as her ledger listed figures: without emotion, because emotion made the numbers lie.

Wry met her eyes. "That was the bargain."

"There is no bargain. There never was. My father does not release men from debts, Captain. He releases them from hope." She gestured to the chair with grace that seemed learned in another life. "Sit. And let me show you what you've actually walked into."

Wry sat. Behind him, Elias filled the doorframe. Kipp crouched by the window, string in hand, watching the yard below with the professional attention of a boy who knew that conversations like this one tended to be interrupted by men with blades.

And Gideon stepped into the room.

Seraphine's eyes moved to him — a quick assessment, measuring worth the way her ledger measured coin. The assessment slowed. Her gaze held on his face a beat longer than calculation required. She saw his eyes — the same blue as the Captain's, but younger, warmer, lit with something that hadn't yet been spent. She saw the way he stood — not behind his father but beside the door, balanced between protection and readiness. She saw his hands — a sailor's hands, scarred and competent, but also a young man's hands, still capable of gentleness.

The assessment took perhaps two seconds. She returned her eyes to Wry. But the return was a fraction too quick — the correction of a person caught looking at something they didn't expect to find.

Gideon had seen it. He'd felt something shift in his chest that had nothing to do with storms or debts or his father's war. It was smaller than that and larger than that.

He said nothing. He moved to the wall and stood with his arms at his sides, and if his hand went to his earring it was only the old habit, the private gesture, and it meant nothing new.

Except that it did.

Seraphine opened the ledger.

"Your debt is a fiction, Captain. But the system that created it is not. My father — Cornelius Vark — operates a web of false ledgers, forged signatures, and phantom debts that binds half the merchants in Nassau and a quarter of the captains who sail these waters. You are not the only man carrying a number that was never his. You are simply the only one who came back to pay it."

She turned the ledger toward him. Columns of figures, names, dates — a cartography of corruption rendered in ink and arithmetic.

"I have been documenting his system for three years. Every false entry. Every forged mark. Every coin that moved from a real pocket to a phantom account." She met his eyes. "I am his daughter, Captain. And I am building the instrument of his destruction."

Wry looked at the ledger. He looked at the woman. He looked at the numbers that told a story of rot so deep it had become the architecture of an entire island's commerce.

"Why?" he said. "He's your father."

Seraphine's jaw tightened — the first crack in her composure, brief as a match-strike.

"Because churches burn, Captain. Ledgers survive. And the only thing more powerful than a corrupt system is an honest record of how it works."

Wry heard them, and in them he heard something he hadn't expected to find in Nassau — not just an ally, but a mind. A weapon sharper than any cutlass. A woman who had taken her father's own instrument and was turning it against him with the patience of a siege and the precision of a surgeon.

He looked at his hands — the rings, the scars, the gold band — and felt, for the first time in twenty years, the lightness of a stone set down and the heaviness of what replaced it.

“Tell me everything,” he said.

And Seraphine began to speak.

CHAPTER SEVEN

Two Women in the Dark

The message came by way of a girl with a bruised wrist and a level voice. She appeared at the Blue Anchor near midnight, slipping through the kitchen entrance like smoke under a door, and found Brandy clearing tables in the lamplight. The girl whispered three sentences. Brandy set down her tray.

"Thresh knows the Captain came. The watchers sent word an hour ago. They'll move Seraphine before dawn — not to another room — to the counting house." If that happened, everything Seraphine had built for three years would disappear.

The girl left as quietly as she'd come. Brandy stood in the kitchen with the smell of cold grease and lime peel around her, and made a decision that took no longer than a heartbeat because the heart had been making it for years.

There was no time for men who needed plans before they could move. There was only the dark, and the alleys she'd memorized by instinct and necessity, and a woman upstairs at the Red Mercy who had three years of truth in a leather binding and no idea that the walls were closing in.

Brandy pulled the shawl over her hair, drew the small carved-handle knife from the drawer where it had lived for twenty years, and tucked it into the sash at her waist. The teacher had given it to her the morning they left the mountain. She had carried it across oceans and never once had to use it for the thing it was made to do. Tonight, perhaps, would be the first. She walked into the Nassau night.

***

The Red Mercy's kitchen gate was exactly where Kipp had said it would be — near to falling of its own good nature. Brandy eased it open with two fingers and a hip, and crossed the yard in the dark. The ladder was there. The missing rung was where the boy had promised. She climbed by feel, her hands seeing for her in the dim light.

The roof hatch opened with a twist and a tug and she muffled the sound with the heel of her hand. She dropped into the upper hallway, where the air was thick with perfume and low music and the silence of a house that was always listening.

She found Seraphine's room by the crack in the hinge.

The woman was awake. She was always awake — Brandy had learned this in the handful of conversations they'd shared, passed in the Red Mercy's hallways like notes between prisoners. Seraphine slept the way birds sleep, with one eye open and the other calculating the distance to the nearest exit.

"We leave now," Brandy said from the doorway.

Seraphine looked at her. The gray-blue eyes measured, weighed, decided. She asked nothing. She reached for the ledger — always the ledger first — and tucked it inside her dress against her ribs, where the binding pressed against her skin like a second heartbeat.

"The dress," Brandy said. "It marks you. Here." She pulled a spare shawl from under her own and tossed it. Seraphine wrapped it over the low-cut neckline and became, in an instant, a different woman — a market vendor, a laundress, anyone who wasn't a girl from the Red Mercy.

"Stay behind me," Brandy said. "Step where I step. When I stop, you stop. And if I tell you to run —"

"I don't run," Seraphine said. Her voice was steady, the Dutch lilt precise. "I have never run from anything in my life."

Brandy looked at her — this pale, composed woman clutching a ledger against her ribs in a house that sold what she refused to sell — and a grimace that was half smile crossed her face. "Then walk fast. And if I tell you to hit someone, don't ask who."

***

Using a tall chair, they went out through the roof hatch, down the ladder, across the yard, and into the alley that ran behind Bay

Lane like a scar behind an ear. The night was close and hot, the air thick with the smell of jasmine and drains and the distant sweetness of sugarcane being crushed somewhere in the dark. The moon was a sliver — enough to see shapes, not enough to see faces. A small mercy. There would not be many tonight.

Brandy moved through the alleys without hesitation. She knew which turns were dead ends, where the drunks collected, and the pickpockets worked. And she also knew where Thresh's men stood watch in the small hours when honest people slept and dishonest people did business.

Seraphine followed. She was quieter than Brandy expected — her steps careful, her breathing controlled, her eyes scanning every shadow with systematic attention. Where Brandy moved by instinct, Seraphine moved by observation. Where Brandy felt the alley, Seraphine read it.

They made good time. Four blocks. Five. The harbor smell grew stronger, which meant the Providence was close, and that meant safety was close. Brandy allowed herself a breath that was almost relief.

The breath was premature.

***

They came around a corner where two alleys crossed — a junction she knew, and was usually empty at this hour — and found four men.

Sailors. Not Thresh's men — that was the first thing Brandy read, and the reading took less than a second. These were merchantmen, off some vessel in the harbor, deep in their cups and looking for trouble the way drunks look for trouble with the menace of men who have nothing to lose and just enough rum to believe they're invincible.

They blocked the junction. One leaned against a wall, bottle in hand. Two sat on a crate, legs stretched across the alley. The fourth stood in the center, swaying gently, a large man with small eyes and a grin that had nothing friendly in it.

"Well now," the large one said. "Two ladies walking alone. In the dark. Must be looking for company." His voice was English, thick with drink.

"We're not," Brandy said. Her voice was flat. No fear, no invitation, no room. "Step aside."

"That's not very friendly." The man with the bottle pushed off the wall. "Come on, love. Sit with us. Have a drink. We're celebrating."

"Celebrating what?" Brandy kept her voice even, kept moving forward, kept the angle so that the wall was at their backs and the wider alley was to the left — the escape route, if it came to that.

"Being alive," the large man said. "Same thing everyone celebrates in this godforsaken place."

The two on the crate rose. The junction tightened. Four men, two women, and a distance between them that was shrinking.

Brandy's hand found the carved handle at her sash. She didn't draw it. Drawing the teacher's knife on four drunk sailors was an escalation that worked only if you were willing to use it, and using it on four men was mathematics she didn't like — the blade was small, and she had twenty years of not between herself and the thing it was made for. What she needed was a distraction, a confusion, something that broke the group's momentum long enough for the gap to open.

Seraphine stepped forward.

The move surprised Brandy. It surprised the sailors more. The woman who had been hidden behind a shawl stepped into the thin moonlight, and her posture changed. She straightened. She let the shawl slip from one shoulder. She smiled.

"Mijnheren," she said, and the Dutch turned the word into something that sounded like an invitation wrapped in silk. "You are celebrating. We are lost. Perhaps you can help us."

She stepped toward the large man — not away, toward — and the sailor's grin widened because his rum-soaked brain read the approach as surrender.

Seraphine turned suddenly and looked toward the harbor, drawing the large man's gaze. Her right hand found the bottle in the younger sailor's grip — the one who was closest, leaning forward to hear the pretty Dutch woman speak — and she took it from his fingers with the smooth authority of a woman who didn't hesitate to to take what she needed to accomplish a goal.

In a single motion, she swung the bottle against the side of the large man's head. The sound was extraordinary — a heavy, wet crack that belonged in a cooperage, not an alley. The man's eyes crossed. His knees buckled. He went down like a mast in a storm, slowly at first, then all at once, and hit the cobblestones with a weight that shook dust from the walls.

Silence. One full second of it.

Brandy moved. She was already moving before the bottle connected, because she'd seen the geometry the moment Seraphine stepped forward — the distraction, the approach, the transfer of the bottle from one hand to another — and she understood that the second the large man fell, the other three would either freeze or attack, and the window between the two was exactly wide enough to escape through.

"Now," Brandy said.

They ran. Not blindly — Brandy led, Seraphine followed, their feet finding the cobbles in rhythm, the shawls flying behind them like dark wings. The three remaining sailors stood over their fallen companion, too stunned or too drunk to give chase. By the time the rum reassembled their courage, the alley was empty, the women were gone, and the large man was snoring on the cobblestones with a bruise forming on his temple. The three men looked toward the empty alley, looked at their companion, looked at each other, and burst out laughing.

***

They stopped three blocks later, in a doorway deep enough to hold them both. Brandy leaned against the wall, breathing hard, her hand still on the carved handle she hadn't needed to draw. Seraphine stood beside her, the ledger pressed against her ribs, her breathing controlled, her gray-blue eyes wide but held.

"Where did you learn that?" Brandy asked.

Seraphine looked at the hand that had held the bottle. It was shaking — the first tremor Brandy had seen from her, a crack in the composure that made her more real than all the poise and ledger-craft that had come before.

"A woman who is not looked at can do anything."

Brandy stared at her. Then she laughed — a laugh that started low and climbed, half relief and half recognition, the sound of one survivor discovering another. "You are terrifying," Brandy said. "In the best possible way."

"I am practical," Seraphine said. But the corner of her mouth betrayed a half-smile — the acknowledgment that practical and terrifying were, in her case, the same thing.

They stood in the doorway until their breathing steadied. The night sounds of Nassau wrapped around them — distant music, a dog's bark, the creak of ship rigging from the harbor. The moon had moved. The alley was empty.

"The Providence," Brandy said. "The Captain's ship. It's at the harbor. You'll be safe there — Elias will see to it."

"I am not looking for safety," Seraphine said. "I am looking for a platform. My ledger can end Vark's hold on this island, but only if it reaches the right hands. Your captain has a ship, a crew, and a name that Vark has been hunting for twenty years. That makes him either my greatest ally or my greatest liability."

"He's both," Brandy said. "Most good men are."

They walked the rest of the way in silence — two women moving through the dark with the confidence of people who have just proven they don't need permission to save themselves. Brandy's street knowledge guided their feet. Seraphine's eyes watched the shadows.

The harbor opened before them, the Providence's masts dark lines against the stars. The watch lantern burned on the quarterdeck, and the shape of a man — Elias, who seemed to neither sleep nor require sleep — stood at the rail, his silhouette as solid and immovable as the ship itself.

He saw them coming. He didn't call out. He simply moved to the gangplank and stood aside, and when the two women climbed aboard he nodded once, as though women arriving at midnight from the alleys of Nassau was precisely the sort of thing he'd expected.

"Captain's below," he said.

"She's out," Brandy said, nodding toward Seraphine. "Thresh was moving to take her before dawn. We didn't wait."

Elias looked at Seraphine, then at Brandy, and his expression shifted — the quiet recalibration of a man adjusting his count.

"Aye," he said. "He'll wanna know."

***

In the Captain's cabin, the lamp was lit. Wry sat at his desk with the charts spread before him, but his eyes were on the painting. He turned when the door opened, and his face changed — not at Brandy, but at who stood behind her.

Seraphine stepped into the cabin. Her eyes swept the room — the books, the compass, the painting — and landed on the man.

"You said you wouldn't leave," Wry said.

"Thresh decided for me," Seraphine said. She held the ledger out. "Your ship. My numbers. Together we can do what neither of us can do alone."

Wry looked at the ledger. He looked at Brandy, who leaned against the doorframe with her arms crossed and the teacher's knife still at her sash.

"How did you get here?" he asked.

"We walked," Brandy said.

"Through Nassau. At night. Alone."

Seraphine met his eyes. "We were not alone, Captain. We had each other. That was sufficient."

Admiration crossed Wry's face — or the recognition that the women standing in his cabin were more dangerous than half his crew, and that this was exactly the kind of danger he needed.

"Sit down," he said. "Both of you. Tell me what plan."

Outside, Cipher dozed on the yardarm. Cajun slept beneath a coil of rope. The harbor held its breath, and the night — which had tried its best to stop two women from walking where they chose — settled back into the dark, nursing its bruises.

CHAPTER EIGHT

Two Tables

The night split itself in two, as Nassau nights do — one half lit by lamps and rum, the other by lanterns and purpose. Two tables. Two arguments. Two visions for the same crew's future.

THE FIRST TABLE

The tavern had no name. It sat at the back of a lane that smelled of tar and dog and the sweetness of rum spilled so many times the wood had given up trying to dry. A curtain of sailcloth served as a door. The lamp inside was tallow, not oil, and it threw a light the color of old teeth.

Rafe Cutler sat at the head of a table that had been a door in a previous life. Around him: Harkin, the wiry Bristolman who'd taken to echoing his phrases. Dench, a gunner whose knees cracked when he climbed the ratlines. Two brothers from Plymouth who'd signed on at the same port and intended to die at the same one. A young Dane who spoke little English but understood coin in every language. And three others — quiet men, men who'd said nothing during the doldrums but had listened to everything.

Nine men. Not a mutiny. Not yet. But the table was set for one.

Rafe stayed seated, voice low. He spoke the way fire speaks to dry wood — low, warm, patient, and the wood had no chance.

"You know what's waiting for you. All of you. Not the ones who think they don't — I mean the ones who've done the arithmetic." He looked at Dench. "How old are you?"

"Forty-three."

"And your knees?"

Dench said nothing. His knees said it for him every morning.

"Forty-three, and you climb the ratlines because you have to, and one day your knee gives out on the way up and you fall, and the sea takes you or the deck takes you, and either way you're gone. What pension waits? What savings? You've sailed fifteen years, Dench. What 'ave ya got?"

"The clothes I'm wearing," Dench said. "And the boots. Mostly."

"That's the whole of it. That's the whole of it for every man at this table and every man on that ship." Rafe let the silence work.

He turned and pulled the collar of his shirt down. At the base of his neck the skin was raised and pale where a hot iron had burned three digits into the flesh — 588. Vark's brand. Every man in the room had one somewhere.

"I was fourteen," he said. "Vark's men held me down. I was told the mark meant I belonged somewhere." He let the collar fall. "It meant I was owned."

He looked at Dench. "The Captain's a good man. I'll say that and mean it. But a good man with a forged debt and a broken back and a plan that changes every time a woman hands him a ledger — that's not a future. That's a gamble."

"My father was a good man. By all accounts. Told my mother he'd be back before the tide turned. Twenty years of tides. The door stayed shut." His voice carried no heat. It was worse for that — the flatness of a wound so old it had stopped bleeding and simply become part of the landscape. "I've seen what happens to men who gamble on 'good' men. They die loyal and they die poor. I won't build my life on another man's promise. Not again."

Harkin nodded. The Plymouth brothers exchanged a glance. The Dane understood enough.

"What I'm offering is simple," Rafe said. "Simple. No revolution, no sermon about how the world should work. Just the truth: the letters of marque are gone. The Queen's war is over. Every privateer in the Caribbean is either hanging or begging. The age of men like us is finished, and the only question is whether you finish it on your feet or on your knees."

He paused. He poured rum — not from the tavern's supply but from a bottle he'd brought, good rum, the kind that costs — and pushed the cups across the table.

"We take the ship. Not by blood — I'm not asking for blood. The Captain and his boy and the Bosun can have a longboat and a fair wind. We sell the cargo at Tortuga. We split the coin nine ways — equal shares, no captain's double, no owner's take. And we scatter. New names. New ports. A man with his share of a cargo and no debt on his back can start fresh anywhere."

The rum sat in the cups. The men looked at it.

"And the woman?" one of the quiet men asked. "The one with the ledger?"

Rafe's expression didn't change, but the pause before he spoke was a fraction too long — "The woman has her own plans. They're not ours. Her father runs this island, and she thinks a book of numbers will bring him down. Maybe it will. Maybe the moon will fall into the harbor. Either way, it's not our fight."

Dench picked up his cup. Harkin picked up his. The Plymouth brothers followed. The Dane drank.

Rafe watched them drink. Because it was the truth. That was the thing about Rafe Cutler that made him dangerous — he didn't lie. He didn't need to. The world was hard enough without embellishment, and the men at his table knew it, and the rum was good, and the future he was offering was the only one that added up.

He drank last. The scar on his cheek — Cajun's gift — caught the tallow light and turned it into a line of shadow that made his face look older than it was. Older and sharper.

THE SECOND TABLE

On the Providence, Ortiz had cleared the galley table and covered it with a cloth that had once been white and was now the color of a life well used. He'd set out bread, cheese, dried fish, sliced mango, and a pot of something that smelled of pepper and patience. He'd placed a plate at every seat — eight of them, evenly spaced, each with the same portion.

It was not a meal. It was an argument.

They gathered: Wry at the head. Elias standing. Brandy near the galley hatch, shawl over her shoulders, emerald eyes watching. Ortiz at his station, ladle in hand, Cajun weaving between his ankles. Kipp on the floor with his string, cross-legged, making a net that looked like it might actually catch something. And Seraphine, at the center of the table, the ledger open before her. And Gideon, across from her.

"Nassau is a machine," she said. Her voice carried the clarity of someone who had rehearsed this in her mind a thousand times and was now, at last, speaking it aloud to people who might listen. "It takes in men, grain, rum, and timber. It produces debt, violence, and profit — but only for the men who built the machine." She tapped a column. "Vark takes forty percent of every transaction that passes through his counting-house. The merchants pay it because they have no alternative. The sailors pay it because the merchants pass the cost. The women pay it because the sailors have nothing left."

Gideon leaned forward. He was reading the columns — not skimming, reading, the way his father read weather, looking for the pattern beneath the numbers. "These aren't just records," he said. "You've built projections. Here — if the tax dropped to fifteen percent, the market volume doubles within a season." He looked up at her. "How do you know that?"

"Because I've been counting for three years," Seraphine said. "Counting what comes in, what goes out, and what disappears. The numbers don't lie, monsieur. People lie. Ledgers do not."

Their eyes met across the table. The moment lasted no longer than it should have — two people discussing arithmetic, nothing more — except that Gideon's finger had stopped on the page where her finger had been a moment before, close enough that neither of them could pretend not to notice, and neither of them moved.

Seraphine looked away first. She turned a page.

"The machine can be rebuilt. Not destroyed — rebuilt. A ledger that is open. A market where prices are set by agreement, not by one man's greed. A system where every transaction is recorded and visible to all." She paused. "And a provision — here —" she turned to a page at the back, where the columns changed from debts to something else entirely, "for the men who do the work."

Wry leaned in. The page showed a simple structure: a percentage of every voyage's earnings held back in a common fund, managed by the crew, disbursed to men who were injured, to the families of men lost at sea, and to men who had served long enough to step ashore and live.

"A pension," Wry said.

"A shared security," Seraphine corrected. "Pensions are given by masters to servants. This is owned by the men who earn it. Every man sees the ledger. Every man knows his share. No captain can take it. No merchant can tax it. It belongs to the crew."

The table went quiet.

Ortiz cleared his throat. The room turned to him.

"Three days ago," Ortiz said, stroking Cajun's head, "I went to the market. Bread at one stall cost three coins. The same bread, same flour, same baker — one coin at the stall around the corner. Why? Because the first baker pays Vark's tax and the second doesn't. Yet."

He held up a thick finger. "I bought from the second. I told the first why. The first baker dropped his price to two coins by afternoon. No violence. No threats. Just information."

He held up a second finger. "I found the waterman who sells fresh water from the spring above the ridge. He charged four coins a barrel. The ships' captains had no choice — there's one spring. I told him I'd found a second spring, half a mile east. His price dropped to two coins before I'd finished the sentence."

He set Cajun down. The cat protested briefly, then found a new lap — Gideon's — and settled without apology.

"Numbers," Ortiz said, "are only recipes written in a different hand. You combine them right, people eat. You combine them wrong, people starve. This one —" he nodded at Seraphine "— she knows how to cook."

Seraphine turned the ledger to face the full table. "Every debt Vark holds in Nassau. Every name. Every sum. Every date." She let the weight of it sit. "If this ledger is made public — if every man can see what every other man owes and to whom — the machine breaks. Not with cannons. With daylight."

Elias studied the columns. His arms were folded but his eyes were not — they moved across the numbers with the attention of a man checking joinery, testing every joint for the crack that would bring the whole structure down. He found none. His eyebrows rose a fraction, which for Elias was the equivalent of applause.

"And Thresh?" he said. "He won't sit still while you dismantle his master's engine."

"No," Seraphine said. "Which is why I need your ship, your crew, and your captain's reputation. A name that Vark has been hunting for twenty years carries weight. If that name stands behind the ledger, the merchants will listen. If they listen, they'll act. And if they act —"

"The machine stops," Gideon said. He was still looking at the numbers. Or he was looking at the woman who had written them. The lamplight made it difficult to tell, and perhaps that was the point.

Seraphine met his eyes again. This time she didn't look away.

"The machine stops," she said. "And something better takes its place."

"My name is already borrowed by men who didn't ask," Wry said.

The room felt Brandy shift. The confession from the Red Mercy hung in the air, unresolved.

"Then take it back," Seraphine said. "A name reclaimed is worth more than a name that was never stolen."

***

The cabin emptied one by one. Elias to the watch. Brandy to the dock, where she'd slip back to the Blue Anchor before dawn — her absence would be noticed, and noticed was dangerous. Ortiz to his galley, humming, Cajun at his heels. Kipp to a hammock he'd claimed in the bow, the string still in his fingers, his eyes closing on a day that had given him more belonging than any day before it.

Seraphine stayed at the table, organizing her ledger, making notes in the margins. Gideon stayed too — not sitting, standing near the bulkhead, arms at his sides, as though he hadn't quite decided whether to leave.

"You understood the projections," Seraphine said without looking up. "Most men look at the numbers and see ink. You saw what they meant."

"My father taught me to read weather," Gideon said. "Patterns in the sky, patterns in the water. Numbers are just patterns on a page."

She looked up. The gray-blue eyes found the deep blue, and the air between them held — a chord waiting to resolve.

"You have your father's eyes," she said. "But not his weight. Not yet. That's not an insult — it's a mercy. Weight comes soon enough."

"Is that what the ledger is? Weight?"

"The ledger is proof that weight can be shared." She closed the book. Her hand rested on the cover. "Goodnight, monsieur."

"Gideon," he said. "Not monsieur."

The held note resolved — not into harmony, not yet, but into the promise that harmony was possible. She allowed herself the edge of a smile.

"Goodnight, Gideon."

She turned and headed to a bunk prepared for her, the ledger tucked under her arm where it had spent every night for three years. In its pages lived a future that was not yet real but was, for the first time, possible.

***

Rafe returned to the Providence in the gray hour before the crew woke. He came aboard quietly, the way a man comes home when he isn't sure it is one.

Light from the galley. The smell of coffee, of bread already in the pan. Ortiz was up early, as Ortiz always was — moving between stove and table with the unhurried economy of a man who has done this ten thousand mornings. Cajun was at his heels, fully awake, supervising.

The table was set. Eight places. The same cloth, the same careful spacing. Eight plates, each with the same portion — bread, dried fish, a wedge of hard cheese. Not last night's argument. This morning's. The same argument, made again, before anyone had asked for it.

And beside the plates: a single page in Ortiz's hand, copied from the ledger in the night — eight names, eight equal shares, the columns ruled with the patience of a man making a point without saying it.

He stood in the doorway. Ortiz glanced up, said nothing, and went back to the galley. Cajun regarded him from beside the stove with the flat assessment of a creature that has already decided and is simply waiting for him to catch up.

Rafe looked at the table. He looked at the page copied from the ledger. And for a moment his face opened. Recognition. The recognition of a man who has seen a door he could walk through and a room that might hold him and a table with a plate set for him, the same size as every other plate.

Then the moment was gone. Whatever had opened in his face closed again — carefully, deliberately, like a door pulled shut from the inside.

And once in his hammock below, the whetstone came out. The blade found it. Slow, deliberate strokes in the dark. And the two tables — the one in the nameless tavern and the one in the galley of the Providence — sat empty in the small hours, holding nothing but the ghost of two arguments that would, before Nassau was done with them, tear a crew in half or make it whole.

CHAPTER NINE

A Dead Man's Chain

The Providence settled into Nassau's harbor like a horse in an unfamiliar stable — alert, uneasy, one ear always turned toward the door. Two days since landfall. Two days of revelations that had rearranged the architecture of twenty years. The debt was forged. The mission was a trap. Seraphine was aboard with a ledger that could burn an empire. And somewhere in Nassau's web of alleys and counting houses, a man named Thresh was sharpening whatever he intended to send next.

The crew felt it. They didn't know the specifics — Wry had kept the debt revelation close, sharing it only with Elias, Gideon, and Ortiz — but sailors read their captain the way they read the sky, and the sky had changed. Men who'd been restless in the doldrums were now restless in a different key, the restlessness of a crew that senses something coming and can't decide whether to face it or flee.

Rafe's men kept their distance. Not openly — but the geometry of the deck had shifted. Men who ate together a week ago now ate apart. Conversations died when certain ears might be listening.

Elias watched all of it. That was his job — not just the lashings and the lines, but the human rigging, the tensions and loyalties that held a crew together or tore it apart. He watched and he waited and he kept his counsel, because counsel given too early is advice, but counsel given at the right moment is wisdom.

***

The harbor was quiet except for the slap of water against hulls. From the streets came the distant sound of Nassau doing what Nassau did after dark — drinking, fighting, singing, dying, all of it at once, all of it tangled together like rope that had given up on being coiled.

Brandy sat across the table from Wry in the Captain's cabin. She'd come back from the Blue Anchor an hour ago, slipping aboard with the ease of a woman since she was old enough to know why. The lantern swung slow overhead, throwing their shadows against the bulkhead in long distortions.

A mug of something dark sat between her hands. Wry had pulled the rye from the locker behind the chart drawer — a squat green bottle he'd carried since a port whose name he no longer trusted himself to pronounce, brought out only when the night called for something rye and the moment called for something serious. Neither of them was drinking.

"You always did this," she said.

"Did what?"

"Fought storms by tidying the table." She nodded at his hands. He'd been squaring the charts, aligning the dividers, setting the sextant in its box.

He stopped, looked at his hands, then at her.

"You watched close," he said.

"I watched everything. That was my mistake." She took a drink. "You were easy to watch and hard to hold. I was the same. Two fires in the same hearth — we burned the house down."

"We were young."

"We were stupid. There's a difference, but it's thin." She set the mug down. "Lianor. Is she good?"

"She's better than good. She's the reason I'm still here."

Brandy nodded. No jealousy. No bitterness. The emerald eyes held. The silver clasp caught the lamplight.

"Then get home to her, Wry. Settle the debt — or what's left of it — and go home."

"That's the plan."

"Plans die in Nassau."

"So do debts."

He reached across the table and set his hand, palm down, beside hers. Not touching. Close enough to mean something. Close enough that the warmth of his skin and the warmth of hers shared the same stretch of scarred oak, and what remained between them was both nothing and everything.

"Thank you," he said. "For the truth at Red Mercy."

She looked at his hand beside hers. "I owed you that much."

"You owed me nothing."

"Then I gave it free." She didn't move her hand. Neither did he. The lantern swung. The shadows traded places on the wall. And in the quiet between two people who had once been young and stupid and on fire, something settled — the finished shape of a thing that had been broken and had found, over years and distance, a way to be whole without being repaired.

Then Brandy's face changed. It happened the way weather changes on open water — not gradually, but all at once. She withdrew her hand. She wrapped both around the mug. She looked at the table instead of at him, and when she spoke, her voice carried something it hadn't carried before — not guilt, which she'd already confessed, but the thing that lived beneath the guilt, the thing she'd been carrying longer and heavier.

"There's more, Wry. And it's worse."

He waited. He was good at waiting. The sea teaches patience to the men it doesn't kill.

"The brother who stole your name." She paused. Her throat worked. "He's dead."

The cabin went very still.

"Vark killed him. Not with a blade — Vark doesn't soil his hands. He simply called the debt. Sent Thresh. My brother couldn't pay what he'd signed for, because the signature was yours and the debt was built for a captain's earnings, not a clerk's. Thresh didn't explain. Her voice was level now, the way a surgeon's hands are level. "They found him in the harbor. The magistrate called it drowning. Everyone knew what drowning meant."

Wry's hands were wrapped around his mug. He hadn't touched the rye. His face hadn't moved. But the understanding shifted into place — a man had died for a chain locked around the wrong neck, and the woman sitting across from him had lived with that knowledge for years.

"When?" he said.

"Twenty years ago. Twenty years I've known, and couldn't tell you, because you were on the other side of the world chasing a number that was written in a dead man's hand."

A dead man's chain. That's what it was now.

"You carried this alone," Wry said.

"Who was I going to tell? The sea? The bar?" Her laugh was short and hard, the sound of something hitting stone. "I told the clasp." She touched the silver at her throat. "Every night. I told it your name and his name and I asked it to forgive me for both."

"Brandy —"

"Don't." The word was quiet but it closed a door. "Don't forgive me. Not yet. Forgiveness given too fast is just another way of not hearing what someone said."

She stood, left the mug, and walked to the door.

"He was a good man, my brother. Weak with money. Strong with love. He took your name because he was drowning and your name was the only rope he could reach." She turned her head — not all the way, just enough for her profile to catch the lamplight. "He would have paid it back. He was that kind of stupid."

She stepped through the doorway. Then she stopped.

Her hands went to her throat. The silver clasp — the one she had worn every day since Nassau, the one she had whispered names to in the dark, the one that had carried the weight of a confession for twenty years — came free with a small click. She held it for a moment in her palm. Then she turned back into the cabin, not looking at him, and crossed to the bulkhead near the stern windows where a gold amulet hung from a nail. It was a vertical rectangle on a chain, its face carved with a skull set in filigree, the metal patinated by years of salt air and lamp-smoke. She had given it to him the morning before he sailed. He had never moved it. She lifted it from the nail and turned it once in her palm — front, then back — and her fingers paused for a breath on the reverse before she drew the chain over her head and settled the amulet against her throat. In its place she hung the silver — his gift, returned to where it belonged. She walked to the door with her head down, and was gone.

***

Brandy came down the gangplank and did not turn toward the Blue Anchor. She turned the other way. Along the quay, past the chandler's warehouse where the crates stood stacked in moonlight, past the dry dock where a sloop sat on its cradle with its hull stripped bare. The night air carried the harbor's permanent smell — tar, salt, and brine.

She walked without hurry. The streets knew her feet and her feet knew the streets, and tonight she was not walking to arrive. She was walking to leave.

The fish market was closed, its stalls shuttered and locked, the cobblestones still wet from the afternoon's wash. She stopped. This was where she had stood on her first morning in Nassau — nineteen years old, free for the first time in her life. She had nothing but the clothes from the merchant's stall and a knife the teacher had given her and no idea what freedom was supposed to feel like when it wasn't a word anymore, but a fact. She had stood here and watched the fishermen shout their prices and the women haggle and the cats circle and the whole loud mess of a market doing what markets do, and she had thought: I will learn this place. I will make it mine. And she had.

She let the memory sit for a moment. Then she let it go.

The corner where Harbor Street met the road uphill — where she had stood the morning she watched him sail years ago. The first leaving. She had come to the corner before dawn because she could not watch from the dock — the crew did not know what she was to him, and knowing would have changed the way they looked at both of them. So she had stood at the corner, high enough to see the harbor mouth, and she had watched the ship shrink until it was a shape, and then a suggestion... and then nothing at all. She had stood there a long time because walking away from nothing was harder than watching something leave.

She stood at the corner now. The harbor was dark. The Providence was there — she could see its shape at the mooring, its lanterns, the silhouette of its masts against the stars. He was in there. In the cabin. With the lamp and the charts and the ghosts of everything she had just told him. She had given him the last of it tonight — the brother, the death, the chain. There was nothing left to carry.

She closed that door. Not with anger or grief, but with the quiet finality of a woman who has spent years holding something open, and has finally found the strength to let it close. The hinges didn't creak. The latch didn't stick. It closed cleanly, like it was built for it.

She turned from the corner and walked toward the Blue Anchor. The streets were nearly empty now. A dog trotted past with something in its mouth. A lantern flickered in an upstairs window and went out. And somewhere in the walk — she could not have said where — the weight she'd been carrying settled into something lighter. Not gone, but rearranged. The way a room looks different after you move the heaviest piece of furniture, even if the room is the same.

She reached the Blue Anchor. The sign creaked on its hooks. She stood beneath it for a moment, her hand on the door, the gold amulet at her throat catching the last of the moonlight.

Without looking back at the harbor, she went inside.

***

Wry sat alone. His thumb found the gold band and turned it once — the old gesture, the private covenant. But tonight the gesture carried something new: the weight of a man he'd never met, whose desperation had cost twenty years and whose death had cost more, and whose sister had just walked out of a cabin with a grief that Wry couldn't fix and she and she was struggling set down.

He turned and looked at the painting of the cabin in the mountains, and thought of the life that was waiting if he could find his way through the wreckage of a debt that had never been his, and a death that should never have happened.

He turned the lamp down. The cabin went dark. The Providence creaked in the harbor, and the night held its secrets the way Nassau always held its secrets — close, and with no intention of letting go.

***

On the dock, a shadow watched.

He was easy to miss if you didn't know what you were looking for, because he was the size of a thing that should have been impossible to miss. That contradiction — the enormity of him hiding in plain sight — said something about how long he'd been doing it. He stood behind a stack of crates near the chandler's warehouse, motionless, the way stone is motionless. He watched the Providence with his one good eye. The other eye — the one a boy's knotted string had closed two days ago — was swollen to a slit of purple and yellow that throbbed in time with his pulse.

Thresh had sent him. "Watch the ship. Count the men. Note who comes and goes. Report back before dawn." Simple orders for a simple man — that's what Thresh believed, because Thresh had never looked at the man he'd branded and seen anything more than a weapon with legs.

So he watched. He counted. He noted.

He noted that the cook came out at intervals to dump scraps over the side, and that each time he did, he paused to look at the stars and mutter something that might have been a prayer or might have been a recipe. He noted that the Bosun walked the deck in a pattern that covered every angle, every shadow. He noted that the woman with the ledger sat in a circle of lamplight near the galley hatch, writing, always writing.

And he noted the boy.

The boy came out after midnight. Red hair catching the harbor's reflected light. Barefoot. The string in his hands, knotting and unknotting. He sat on the gangplank with his legs dangling over the water, and for a while he just sat — no grin, no performance, just a boy at the edge of a ship looking at the dark.

Then the boy looked directly at the crates where the shadow stood.

The man didn't move. He'd been looked at before and not seen — his size worked 'against' him in alleys, but 'for' him in darkness, where the brain refuses to believe that something that large could be hiding. The boy would look away. They always looked away.

The boy didn't look away.

He reached into the pocket of his too-large breeches and pulled out something wrapped in cloth. He unwrapped it. Bread. A chunk of the same bread Ortiz had baked that morning, dense and warm and real.

The boy looked at the crates. He looked at the bread. And then he set it on the edge of the dock, carefully, the way you set a plate for someone you can't see but know is hungry, and went back to the gangplank without a word.

The man stood behind his crates for a long time.

He was not a man who thought in words. Thresh had beaten words out of him years ago, replacing them with obedience and the dull grammar of fists. But something moved in him — older than Thresh, older than the brand, older than the violence that had been his only language. It moved the way water moves under ice: invisible, but present, and strong enough to crack anything that tried to hold it still.

He could not understand it. It was the wrong shape for the world he knew.

He reached down and picked up the bread. He ate it in the dark, slowly — as though remembering that food could be given instead of taken.

Before dawn, he went to give his report. He told Thresh everything he'd seen — the cook, the Bosun, the woman with the ledger, the comings and goings, the watch rotation.

He did not mention the boy, or the bread.

It was the first secret he had ever kept from the man who owned him, and he carried it as he'd carried the bread. He was not sure yet what it meant, but was unwilling to let it go.

CHAPTER TEN

The Counting House

Amsterdam in November was a city that had learned to make money from the cold. The canals ran dark and still beneath a sky the color of spent pewter, and the wind off the Zuiderzee cut through wool and linen and flesh with the democratic efficiency of a thing that did not care who you were or what you owned. Merchants hurried along the Herengracht with their collars turned up and their ledgers tucked against their chests. The Exchange hummed behind its grand facade. Thousands of transactions passed through its halls in the time it took a man to drink his coffee. Each one recorded, each one taxed, each one feeding a system so vast and so invisible that the men it enriched and the men it crushed walked the same streets, drank at the same inns, and never understood they were playing different games.

The counting house of Cornelius Vark stood on the Keizersgracht, three doors west of the church whose congregation included half the men who owed him money and all of the men who pretended they didn't. It was a narrow building — four stories, brick, with a gabled roof and a hoist beam jutting from the top floor like a finger pointing at the sky. It looked like every other merchant house on the canal. This was the point.

Inside, the ground floor held twelve clerks. They sat at identical desks arranged in two rows of six, working identical ledgers with identical pens, their collars buttoned against the chill. The clerks worked in silence. Speaking was permitted only to request ink or to report an error. Errors were reported in writing, on forms designed for the purpose, because Vark believed that a man who must write down his mistake is less likely to make it twice.

The scratching of nibs on parchment was the counting house's heartbeat — relentless, the sound of an organism that processed the labor of thousands of men on three continents and reduced it to columns of figures that fit on a single page. Cargo from the East Indies. Sugar from the Caribbean. Slaves from the African coast, recorded not as men but as units, because the ledger did not have a column for humanity and Vark had not seen fit to add one. Debts owed by captains, merchants, plantation owners, colonial governors — every name a number, every number a chain leading back to this room, these desks, this building on the Keizersgracht where the canal water reflected the gray sky and gave nothing away.

The fourth floor held records. Thousands of ledgers, bound in leather, shelved by year and by region. A man could walk these shelves and read the financial biography of half the Atlantic world — who owed what, who paid what, who defaulted, who prospered, and at what cost. The ledgers did not judge. They recorded. And in the recording, they did something more powerful than any navy or any army. They made the world legible to the men who could read them, and invisible to the men who couldn't.

Vark's office was on the third floor. It was not large. It did not need to be. A desk — mahogany, purchased from a governor who could no longer afford it. A chair — leather, high-backed, positioned so that the window behind it cast the occupant's face in shadow while illuminating the face of anyone who sat across the desk. A map of the Atlantic on the wall, pinned with small flags that marked the positions of ships, ports, and debts.

And Cornelius Vark, sitting behind the desk, reading a letter that had arrived that morning on a packet ship from the Caribbean.

He was not what men expected. Small — not short, but compact, built for efficiency rather than display. Gray hair cropped close. A narrow, clean-shaven face and brown eyes that were remarkable only for their steadiness. They did not dart. They rested on what they regarded with the patience of a scale waiting to be tipped.

He dressed plainly; dark coat, white shirt, no jewelry. In a city where merchants wore their wealth like armor, Vark's plainness was its own authority.

***

It was not the first letter about his daughter.

Two years ago, a captain named Brouwer — reliable, unimaginative, the kind of man whose reports read like cargo manifests — had written from Havana. He had seen a young woman matching a description Vark had circulated among his more trusted captains: the right age, the right bearing, booking passage toward Nassau. Brouwer had not approached her. He had been instructed not to. He had written a letter, sealed it, and sent it on a merchant brig bound for Cadiz, where it would transfer to a Dutch packet for Amsterdam.

The letter never arrived. Somewhere off the coast of Spain — storm, piracy, incompetence, it did not matter — the brig was lost with all cargo and correspondence. Vark did not learn this for months. He waited. He verified shipping schedules, cross-referenced manifests, ran the numbers the way he ran every number. When the silence stretched past any reasonable delay, he accepted the loss and filed it as he filed all losses: as a cost, not a grief.

Two years. No confirmation. No second sighting. Vark was not a man who acted on single sources, but neither was he a man who ignored a pattern. His daughter had vanished from Amsterdam at fourteen with a head full of numbers and a knowledge of his methods that no outsider possessed. If she had gone to Nassau — and Nassau was where the desperate and the clever both washed up — then she would not be easy to find. She was his daughter. She would know how to disappear.

He had considered tasking Thresh. But Thresh was in Nassau to expand the counting house's reach — opening new lines with colonial merchants, establishing branch ledgers in Curaçao and Bridgetown, the slow conversion of suspicion into dependency that was Thresh's particular talent. Diverting him to search for a girl on the strength of a two-year-old rumor from a lost letter would pull him from work that was producing revenue and confirm nothing. Thresh was not a bloodhound. He was an architect. Vark did not waste architects on errands.

So he had sent the captain instead. Slamyrbach. A man who owed him, who could move through Nassau without attracting the kind of attention Thresh attracted, and who could be pointed at a problem without being told what the problem was. Vark had given him just enough — a name, a location, a task — and let the man's own debts do the rest of the work.

Three weeks after Slamyrbach sailed, a second letter arrived. From Brouwer. The captain had written again, this time from Kingston, and his tone carried the faint irritation of a man who has done his job and been ignored. He referenced his earlier report — the woman in Havana, the passage to Nassau — and noted that he had received no reply and no further instructions. He assumed the information had been useful. He hoped Vark would confirm receipt of this letter, at least, as he had begun to wonder if he was writing to a wall.

Vark read Brouwer's second letter and understood two things at once. The first letter had been lost. And his daughter was in Nassau. Not a rumor or a hunch. Confirmed, by a man who had now seen her twice and taken the trouble to write about it twice.

He had already sent Slamyrbach. Good. But now he had confirmation, and confirmation changed the calculation.

He wrote to Thresh that evening. A short letter — the girl may be in Nassau, confirm and hold, recover the secondary ledger if possible, do not neglect the expansion work. He sent it on the next packet. But packets were slow, and the sea was indifferent to urgency. The letter would not reach Thresh for weeks — and by the time it arrived, Slamyrbach would already be on the ground.

What Vark did not know — could not know — was that his daughter had prepared for the possibility of being found. She had taken lye to her hair in the manner of the island women, lightening it until it bore no resemblance to the dark fall that Brouwer had described. She worked under a different name. She kept to the back rooms of the Red Mercy and spoke to no one about Amsterdam. Thresh, when the letter finally reached him, would have nothing to work from but a description that no longer matched and a name she no longer used. He had never seen her. All he had were dock rumors — enough to set a man named Cael to watching, not enough to act.

***

Now, weeks later, Vark sat with a different letter — from Thresh this time, written in the abbreviated code they used for correspondence that might be intercepted. Ship names replaced with numbers, people replaced with commodities, actions replaced with trade terms. Translated, it read:

The asset is now aboard the captain's vessel with the secondary ledger. The captain has been informed of the signature's origin. The crew is divided — a faction led by a hungry one may be useful. The local enforcer's man was seen near the dock but his report was incomplete. Awaiting instructions.

Vark read the letter twice. He set it on the desk. He placed his hands flat on the mahogany — a gesture his daughter would have recognized, because she had inherited it, along with his mind for numbers and his talent for patience.

The asset. His daughter. Seraphine.

He permitted himself a moment of something that, in a man who allowed himself emotions, might have been called admiration. She had taken three years of his education — the mathematics, the accounting, the systematic thinking he had paid tutors to install in her mind — and turned it into a weapon aimed at the machine he had built. She had done exactly what he would have done in her position, which was the problem. He had built her too well. He had given her the tools and the intelligence and the education, and he had neglected to install the one component that would have made her safe: loyalty.

Loyalty was not teachable, he knew this. He had tried — with Thresh, with the clerks, with the captains and merchants who owed him. What he had learned was that loyalty was either purchased or coerced, and that the purchased kind lasted only until someone offered more, and the coerced kind lasted only until the coercion failed. His daughter had been neither purchased nor coerced. She had been raised. And raising, it turned out, was the least reliable method of all.

He rose and walked to the map. Nassau sat on the wall like a thumbprint, small and dark, at the edge of a web of trade routes that connected three continents. He had built that web. Not with ships — he owned no ships — but with paper. With ledgers. With the understanding that the man who controls the record of a transaction controls the transaction itself, and that the man who controls enough transactions controls the world.

His daughter understood this, and that was what made her dangerous. She hadn't taken his money or his ships or his men. She had taken his method. She had built a counter-ledger — a transparent record that, if made public, would expose the gap between what his ledgers said and what was true. And the gap between what a ledger says and what is true is the gap where profit lives. If that gap closed, the machine stopped.

He returned to the desk. He took a fresh sheet of parchment — heavy cotton stock, watermarked with the counting house's seal — and began his reply.

His instructions were precise. They always were.

Recover the secondary ledger. Priority above all else. Direct the hungry one. Offer the ship and passage with cargo. Acceptable cost. The captain: use the son or the woman. His choice. Make him choose. If he cannot be controlled, remove him. Publicly. The girl returns to Amsterdam. Fourth floor. Indefinite.

Six lines. No explanations, no reasoning, no rhetoric. Thresh would understand because understanding was what Vark paid him for.

He signed the letter with the counting house's seal — a pressed wax circle bearing no image, only 'His' number. The number that sat at the top of every ledger in the building. The number that was not a name but served as one, because Cornelius Vark had learned long ago that names are personal and numbers are permanent, and permanence was the only currency he trusted.

He folded the letter and sealed it, then rang the bell on his desk. Soon a clerk appeared — silent, eyes on the floor.

"The next packet to Nassau," Vark said. "Priority."

The clerk took the letter and left. The door closed. The nib-scratching resumed below.

Vark returned to his ledger. The column he'd been working on before the letter arrived — an indigo shipment, a penalty clause, a warehouse that would change hands by week's end. The column waited for him like a sentence waiting to be finished. He picked up his pen and resumed the line.

Twelve clerks scratched below him. The Exchange hummed three streets away. And in Nassau, twelve days away by the fastest packet, his daughter sat on a ship with a ledger that contained the truth about every figure in his columns.

The pen scratched. The counting house kept counting.

CHAPTER ELEVEN

The Old Man on the Corner

Wry found Gideon standing at the rail late at night when Nassau's activities took on a new flavor. He had sensed an unasked question for years in this boy that had become a man, and the time was ripe for an answer.

"I was younger than you," he began. "And stupider, which is saying something."

Gideon didn't smile. He listened. That was enough.

***

The village had no name worth remembering — a fishing settlement on the French coast where the houses leaned into the wind and the wind leaned back. Wry had grown up there the way boys grow up in places where the sea is the only employer, the only entertainment, and the only way out. He was restless, hungry, and full of energy that had nowhere useful to go. He was good at everything and master of nothing. Carpentry. Smithing. Navigation. Swordplay with sticks against the harbor wall. Each one held him never longer for a week or a month, and rarely, a season.

He wanted to be a privateer. This was the dream — the naive, dream of a boy who'd heard stories in taverns and believed them. He would sail under letters of marque. He would amass wealth. And then — the part that made the dream different from every other boy's dream of piracy and glory — he would stop. He would take his fortune to a mountain, build a cabin, and live in quiet solitude, far from the chaos that had paid for it. Endure the storm to earn the calm.

He had married young. His childhood sweetheart — steady where he was wild, patient where he was restless. She was a niece to the local priest. They married because that's what you did in a French fishing village when you loved a girl and she loved you back and neither of you had the imagination yet to see how different you were. They had a daughter.

He didn't tell Gideon much about this. He said the marriage was real and the love was real and the leaving was his fault. He said that the same restless energy that couldn't settle on one thing long enough to master it had made him a poor husband and a worse father. He said he left a woman and a baby girl in a village on the French coast and went looking for something he couldn't name. And that the leaving was the first great failure of his life, and that every failure after it carried the shape of that one inside it.

"She sent me a book," he told Gideon. "My daughter. A green book. She wrote in it — her thoughts, her faith, her life. She sent it across the ocean to a father who left before she could walk, and every page of it was a grace I didn't earn."

He did not say more. Gideon did not ask about the wife, because his father's face made it clear that the story was about the daughter, and that the daughter was the wound that mattered.

"So there I was," Wry said, after a moment. "Twenty-four. A wife I couldn't be still for. A daughter I couldn't stay for. Good at everything, master of nothing, and burning through every day like it owed me something." He turned the gold band on his finger. "And then I met the man who changed it."

The old man on the corner.

He was not old in the way that stories make old men old — no beard to the belt, no staff, no riddles. He was old in the ordinary way: bent, sparse-haired, sun-damaged, with hands that had done one thing for fifty years and showed every day of it. He repaired nets. He sat on the same stone at the same corner every morning, his fingers working the mesh with a speed that made young men's hands look like they were moving through water. He spoke to no one unless spoken to, and when spoken to, he said less than expected and meant more.

Wry spoke to him because he'd exhausted every other conversation in the village.

"You're fast," the old man said, watching Wry's hands attempt a net repair that was falling apart as quickly as he made it. "Fast and impatient. Two things that look the same and aren't."

"I learn quick."

"You start quick. Learning is what happens after the starting gets boring."

The old man's fingers didn't pause. The net grew under his hands the way coral grows — slowly, invisibly, perfectly.

"You want to be a privateer."

"I want to be free."

"Same thing, to a boy. Different thing, to a man." He tied off a knot without looking at it. "There's a place. East. Far east — past the ports you've heard of, past the routes the merchantmen sail. A man lives there who teaches the thing you need."

"What thing?"

"The thing that comes after fast." He looked up. His eyes were the color of the sea on a day when the sea is not performing for anyone. "Stillness. The kind that has teeth."

He told Wry three things: a direction, a name, and a warning. The direction was east. The name Wry would keep to himself for the rest of his life, speaking it only to the rings and to Lianor. The warning was simple: "He will not teach you what you want. He will teach you what you need. They are not the same thing, and the distance between them is where most men quit."

***

Wry paused. He leaned on the rail and let the telling settle.

Below them, Nassau was doing what Nassau did at night — performing itself for anyone willing to watch. Lanterns swung on their hooks along the quay, throwing long orange scars across the water. Music came from somewhere near the Blue Anchor, a fiddle and a drum that couldn't agree on the tempo. The smell of cook-fires mixed with the harbor's permanent stink of tar and rotting rope and the low, sweet undertone of rum that hung over the town like a second atmosphere.

On the foredeck, Elias was making his rounds. They could see his shape moving between the guns — unhurried, deliberate. He paused at the starboard rail, looked out at the harbor for a moment, then moved on.

Cipher sat on the capstan, head tucked, one eye open. Cajun lay coiled on a rope locker three feet away, her tail flicking in the slow rhythm of a creature that is not asleep and wants Cipher to know it. Neither moved further. The truce they maintained at night was not peace — it was the mutual acknowledgment that hostilities would resume at dawn and that rest, in the interim, was a tactical decision.

Somewhere below, a hammock creaked. Kipp. The boy should have been asleep hours ago, but the creaking had the rhythm of someone who was awake and working — the small, repetitive sound of string being pulled through string, and a faint clicking sound they hadn't heard before.

Gideon heard it too. He glanced toward the hatch, then back at his father. "Go on," he said.

***

The journey took the better part of a year. Wry worked his passage on merchant vessels — scrubbing decks, hauling cargo, mending sails — through the Mediterranean, around the Cape. He sailed into waters where the trade routes frayed into threads that led to places the maps didn't bother naming. He was seasick. He was robbed twice. He was nearly killed once, in a port dispute over a crate of nutmeg that turned out to be someone else's crate of nutmeg. He learned all the sailing skills fast, except patience. He learned patience only because the sea refused to offer an alternative.

He arrived at the base of a mountain in a country he couldn't pronounce, carrying everything he owned in a canvas sack and wearing boots that had given up pretending they were waterproof.

The path up the mountain took two days. It was not marked because it didn't want to be found. Wry found it anyway, because the old man's directions were precise — no wasted words, no ambiguity, every turn exactly where it was promised.

The teacher's compound was a clearing near the summit — a stone house, a forge, a training ground of packed earth, and a view that stretched to the sea. The air was thin and clean and carried the scent of cedar and sandalwood.

The teacher was waiting. Not because he knew Wry was coming — or perhaps because he did. He was a lean man, neither young nor old, with hands that belonged to a craftsman and eyes that belonged to a priest. He wore plain clothes and carried no weapon. He looked at Wry the way a carpenter looks at a plank.

"You are fast," the teacher said.

"So I've been told."

"Fast is the first thing I will take from you. Sit."

Wry sat. The teacher sat across from him. Between them, the packed earth of the training ground held nothing — no weapons, no tools, no tests. Just dirt.

"Why are you here?"

"To learn to fight."

"No. Why are you here?"

The honest answer was harder than the easy one, and harder still because the teacher's eyes were the kind that made dishonesty feel like wearing wet clothes — possible, but unbearable.

"Because I can't be still," Wry said. "And I think the stillness is where the thing I need lives."

The teacher regarded him for a long time. Then he nodded — not approval, but acceptance.

"Three rules," the teacher said. "First: you do nothing without my instruction. Second: you master nothing until I say you have. Third: you leave when I say, not when you decide."

"And if I break them?"

"Then you will learn something. But not what you came here to learn."

***

The training began without weapons. It began with breathing, with sitting. It began with the maddening, excruciating discipline of doing nothing — sitting on the packed earth while the sun moved and the shadows moved and the birds moved and everything in the world moved except Wry Slamyrbach, who was not permitted to move until the teacher said he could.

He hated it. His muscles cramped. His mind screamed. His pride informed him daily that this was a waste and the old man on the corner was a fool and the teacher was a fraud and the mountain was a prison designed by someone who hated joy.

He sat anyway. Because the alternative was quitting, and quitting meant going back to the village and the nets and the half-finished everything, and he'd rather sit on dirt for a hundred years than admit that 'fast' was all he was.

Weeks passed. The sitting grew easier. Not because his body stopped complaining, but because the space behind his eyes shifted. The racing slowed. Not stopped — it would never stop — but it slowed enough that he could see the individual thoughts instead of the blur. The way a man on a fast horse can see the landscape only when the horse walks.

Then the weapons came out.

The forge held a dozen blades — swords, daggers, spears, curved things and straight things, weapons from traditions Wry couldn't name. The teacher laid them on the ground in a line and told Wry to choose.

"Choose the weapon you will master. Not the weapon you admire. The weapon that fits the hand you have, not the hand you wish you had."

Wry walked the line. He picked up a curved sword — too light, too quick, a weapon for a man who wanted to dance. He picked up a broadsword — too heavy, too slow, a weapon for a man who wanted to crush. He picked up a rapier — elegant but thin, a weapon for a man who wanted to prove something.

He picked up the cutlass.

It was not elegant or beautiful. It was a working blade — heavy enough to cut, short enough to move in close quarters, balanced so that the weight sat forward where a sailor's instinct put it. It was a tool that did not pretend to be anything other than what it was.

"This one," Wry said.

The teacher looked at the cutlass, then at the boy.

"Good," the teacher said. "Now put it down. You will not touch it again for three months."

***

A squawk from Cipher caught their attention and they looked up at the rigging, but they couldn't make out what Cipher was trying to say. Wry rolled his shoulders — the left one first, then the right, the way he always did when his back was tightening from standing too long. The rail was not a kind place for a damaged spine, and the telling had kept him in one position longer than the body wanted.

The harbor had quieted. The fiddle was done. The lanterns still burned, but the spaces between them had darkened as the taverns closed their shutters one by one. The tide had shifted — Gideon could feel it in the way the Providence moved at her mooring.

Elias appeared at the top of the companionway. He saw them at the rail and stopped — not intruding, just noting. His eyes found Wry's stance, read the stiffness in his back, filed it. He gave a single nod — everything's quiet below — and went back down without a word.

Cipher had moved to the shrouds. He hung upside down by one foot, an arrangement that looked like an accident but was, Gideon suspected, deliberate. Below him, Cajun sat at the base of the mast, looking up with the patience of a cat who has done this math before and knows the bird will come down eventually.

"Three months," Gideon said. "No blade."

"Three months. I thought I'd go mad. Turns out that was the point."

CHAPTER TWELVE

Grace and Harmony

Very late the next evening, Wry came below expecting an empty cabin, a nip of rum, and the particular silence that belongs to a man alone with his own thoughts after a long day. Instead he found Gideon, sitting across from the desk with the lamp already lit.

With a grin on his face Gideon couldn't read, Wry chuckled softly, "I'm guessing you're wanting the second half of the story?" He half filled two tin cups, then poured himself into his chair, unable to tell which groaned louder — his back or the chair. He glanced out the stern windows with a far away look in his eyes and began.

The night training started. It came after the regular sessions ended, when the mountain was dark and the body was tired but the mind — the racing mind, the mind that had never fully surrendered — whispered that the teacher was going too slow. That the forms could be pushed further. That a man who trained in secret, after hours, could advance beyond the pace the teacher set and arrive at mastery faster than the path allowed.

Wry listened to the whisper. He knew better, but he listened anyway.

He began training alone after dark. Extra forms. Harder drills. Faster combinations. He pushed the blade through movements the teacher hadn't taught yet — movements he'd watched from a distance. But those movements were meant for a body that had been prepared for them, and a spine that had been strengthened to hold them.

His spine had not been strengthened to hold them.

He felt it first as a tightness — a band of heat across his lower back that came during the private sessions and faded by morning. He ignored it the way young men ignore the body's warnings, because the body is conservative and the will is not, and the will was winning. The tightness became a catch. The catch became a pain.

The pain became a thing that lived in his spine like a wire pulled too tight, humming at frequencies he could feel but not name.

He said nothing. He hid it. He adjusted his stance to compensate, shifted his weight to spare the place that hurt, and continued the private training because stopping would mean admitting that he'd broken the first rule — you do nothing without my instruction — and the admission would cost more than the pain.

The teacher saw it, of course. But he said nothing, because some lessons cannot be taught by warning. They can only be taught by consequence.

Wry stopped speaking for a moment. On the deck above, a boot scraped — Elias, making his rounds. The Bosun's tread was as much a part of the ship's night sounds as the water against the hull.

Wry reached for the rum and topped up their cups — not much, just enough to mark the pause. The lamp had burned low and the cabin had taken on the amber closeness of a space that has held too many words and needs air.

He stood. The chair protested. His back protested louder. He moved to the stern windows and opened one, and Nassau came in — not the night version, which was music and smoke, but the early-morning version, which was gulls and the slap of water against the hull and the distant sound of someone arguing about the price of salt fish on the quay.

Dawn was coming. They had talked through the night.

On deck above them, the ship was stirring. Boots on planking. The scrape of a bucket being filled. Elias's voice, low and level, directing the morning watch. The anchor watch reported — nothing moved in the night, nothing needed moving.

Through the open window they could hear Kipp. He was up early, perched somewhere on the bowsprit from the sound of it, talking to Cipher in the one-sided conversation he maintained with the bird each morning — a stream of observations, complaints, and questions that Cipher answered with silence or a tilt of the head, which Kipp seemed to find sufficient.

Wry watched the harbor lighten. The water was turning from black to gray to the pale green it would hold until the sun finished climbing. A fishing boat was heading out, its sail catching the first of the offshore breeze.

He turned from the window. Gideon hadn't moved.

"The rings," Wry said, sitting back down. "That's the next part."

***

The teacher waited until the pain had taught what it could. Then he brought out the rings.

They came in a wooden box — plain, unvarnished, the kind of box a craftsman makes when the contents matter more than the container. The teacher set it on the ground between them and opened the lid.

Two rings. Silver, thick-banded, identical. Around the center of each ring ran a band of etching with neither letters nor pictures, but rather shapes that the eye wanted to read as language but the mind could not translate. They were the same size, the same weight, the same in every visible way.

"They are identical," the teacher said. "But they are not interchangeable. One is Grace. One is Harmony. Worn correctly, they complete the instrument. Worn on the wrong hands, they work against the bearer — a blade pulled in two directions instead of one."

"How do I know which is which?"

"You don't. Not yet. That is part of what you must learn. And once you have learned it — once you have bonded with them — no other man can wear them in the same manner. To anyone else, they are pretty pieces of metal. To you, they will be something more."

"Grace," the teacher said, lifting the left ring. "For the hand that steadies." He set it on the ground in front of Wry, to his left.

"Harmony," he said, lifting the right. "For the hand that acts." He set it beside the other, to Wry's right.

"Apart, they are jewelry. Together, with the blade, they are something else." He looked at Wry. "But only if the man who wears them is something else first."

Wry reached for them. The teacher's hand stopped his — not with force, but with placement. A palm laid flat covering each of the rings.

"You tried to advance without instruction. Your spine carries the cost. Do you understand why I did not stop you?"

"Because I needed to learn it myself."

"Because the cost is the teacher. You knew the first rule. Knowing a rule and believing it are not the same. You would have obeyed the warning for a week, a month — then the impatience would have returned, and you would have trained in secret again, and the damage would have been worse. The body teaches what the mouth cannot."

He removed his hands. "Now. The rings."

***

The training with Grace and Harmony was unlike anything that had come before. The rings connected the blade to the man's center — not the center of his body, but the center of his intent.

The teacher demonstrated once. He put the rings on his own thumbs — the last time they would answer to him —took the cutlass, and moved through a form that Wry had been practicing for months. The movements were the same. The blade followed the same arcs, the same geometry of attack and retreat. But something was different. The air around the blade was different. The sound was different — not the whistle of steel through air, but something beneath it, a hum that lived in the frequency between hearing and feeling.

"The rings respond to stillness," the teacher said. "Not the stillness of the body — the stillness of the motive. A man who draws the blade in anger will find the rings are dead metal. A man who draws in vanity, in revenge, in fear — dead metal. They serve only the clean draw."

"Clean how?"

"Free of self. A blade drawn to protect is clean. A blade drawn to punish is not. A blade drawn because there is no other choice is the cleanest of all." He set the cutlass down. "The rings are not a weapon, boy. They are a question. Every time you reach for the blade, they will ask: why? And if the answer is true, they will amplify what the blade can do. If the answer is false, you will fight with steel alone — which is sufficient for most men, but not for the man you are becoming."

Wry put on the rings. Grace on the left thumb. Harmony on the right. They fit as though they had been made for his hands — which perhaps they had, or perhaps the training had shaped his hands to receive them, which amounted to the same thing.

He lifted the cutlass. He moved through the form.

Nothing happened. The rings sat on his thumbs like rings. The blade moved like a blade. The hum was absent.

"Again," the teacher said.

He tried again. And again. And again. For days he tried, and for days the rings remained jewelry and the blade remained steel and the thing the teacher had demonstrated refused to appear.

From below, through the deck boards, the faint clicking sound came again — Kipp, awake in his hammock, working at something with his hands in the dark. Gideon glanced toward the hatch. Wry waited. The clicking settled into rhythm, and the telling resumed.

One day the teacher standing in the doorway said quietly, "You are trying with force. Force is a young man's answer to an old question."

"What's the question?"

"Who are you when no one is watching?"

Wry didn't have an answer. He sat with the question the way he'd sat on the packed earth in his first weeks — without comfort, without progress, with only the stubborn refusal to leave.

***

The answer came one day that seemed like any other day, there was a light scent of plumeria on a gentle breeze, but otherwise, it was quite unremarkable. Answers arrive when they're ready, not when one tries to will them into being — and today, the answer was ready.

He was moving through the form — the same form, the hundredth repetition — and his mind, for the first time, had gone quiet. No rings. No hum. No thought of mastery or progress or the teacher's approval.

It was thinking about the village. About the old man on the corner. About the nets that grew under the old man's fingers — slowly, invisibly, perfectly — not because the old man was trying to make a net, but because he had made so many nets that the making had become part of his breathing, part of his being. The net was not a product. It was an expression of a man who had given his life to one thing and found in that giving, that one thing was enough.

The rings woke.

It was not dramatic. It was a warmth — gentle, the warmth of a hand held by someone who means it. Grace hummed on his left thumb. Harmony hummed on his right. The cutlass moved through the form, and the air around it shifted — not visibly, not audibly, but in the way that the air shifts when a note is played in tune after hours of playing it wrong. Something locked into place. Something that had been waiting.

Wry finished the form. He stood in the clearing with the blade at his side and the rings warm on his thumbs. The mountain was quiet. His mind was quiet. And he understood — not in his head, but in his body, in the damaged spine that was still the truest part of him — that the rings had not changed. He had.

The teacher watched from the doorway of the stone house. He did not speak; he did not need to.

***

The stern windows were still dark, but the darkness had thinned — the harbor shifting from black toward a gray that was not yet dawn but had stopped pretending to be night. Gideon leaned back in his chair. The cabin was close now, warm with the lamp and the hours and the weight of everything that had been said. He looked at his father's hands. The rings sat on Wry's thumbs — Grace, and Harmony — the same way they had for as long as Gideon could remember. He had grown up seeing them. He had never known what they were, not really. Silver bands with copper etching. His father's hands would not have looked right without them.

"Can I —" He stopped.

"Ask."

"Can you feel them? Now, I mean. Right now."

Wry turned the rings slowly. "Not the way you'd feel a hot coal or a cold wind. It's quieter than that. Like the difference between a room where someone is present and a room where no one is. You can't point to the difference. But you know."

Above them, the morning watch changed. They could hear the shuffle of it — men coming up, men going down, the small negotiations of a crew finding its rhythm in port.

But beneath the normal sounds there was something else — an absence. Rafe's voice was not among them. Since Nassau, since the crew had scattered to the taverns and the gaming houses and the places where men go to forget they are sailors, Rafe had kept his distance from the ship. He came and went, but the coming was late and the going was early, and the men who had listened to him in the storm were listening to him still, only now the listening happened ashore where the Captain could not hear it.

Wry heard the absence. Gideon saw him hear it — the slight tilt of the head, the way his eyes moved to the overhead as if he could see through the planking to the deck above.

"Rafe?" Gideon said.

"Later. We're not finished."

Wry turned the rings once more, then settled back in the chair.

***

Every week, down the mountain, through the valley, to the merchant town at the base. The teacher called it endurance training. Wry called it errands.

He told it with a half-smile — the smile of a man looking back at his own ignorance with the particular tenderness that only distance provides.

The supply runs were a day down the mountain and two days back — the descent quick through forest and scrubland, the return slow under a loaded pack. The town at the base sat at the junction of three trade routes and smelled of spice and dung and the particular optimism of people who believe that commerce will solve everything.

Wry carried a list. Rice, oil, salt, charcoal, the herbs the teacher used for medicines. He bartered with merchants who tried to cheat him and learned, through repetition, how to be cheated less.

The girl was not the point either. She was just there.

***

She was not what stories prepare you for. She was beautiful in the way that a well-made thing is beautiful, where the beauty lives in the precision and the purpose rather than the decoration. Long raven black curls, even then. Emerald green eyes with a twinkle in them that made you feel she knew something you didn't and found it funny. Golden skin warmed by a sun she hadn't been born under.

She was an indentured servant. The merchant who owned her contract — a thick man with soft hands and hard prices — had acquired it along with a shipment of ivory and indigo when her parents' vessel went down in a storm rounding the Cape. The parents drowned. The contract survived. The girl was twelve. She was now nineteen, and the indenture had three years left, and the merchant saw no reason to release her early because she was good with numbers and customers liked her face and indentured servants don't require wages.

Her name was not Brandy. That came later, in Nassau, when she chose a name that belonged to no one and therefore could not be taken from her. Her real name she gave to Wry on the third visit, and he carried it privately, permanently, spoken only to the people who had earned it — the same way he carried the teacher's name.

Wry was smitten. He did the stupid things. He carried her water casks when the merchant wasn't looking. He brought her wildflowers from the mountain that wilted in the heat before he reached the town. He attempted to juggle limes to make her laugh and dropped all three on a customer's foot. He tried to speak her language and produced sounds that made the cat leave.

She found it more than amusing. She found, in this sunburned, broad-shouldered, inarticulate boy who carried a cutlass and brought her dying flowers and couldn't juggle, something she had not found in seven years of indenture: someone who looked at her and saw not a servant or a contract or a face that was good for business, but a person. The looking was clumsy and obvious and entirely without strategy. The absence of strategy was the most honest thing she'd seen since her parents went into the water.

They talked. Over weeks, over months, in the stolen minutes between the merchant's errands and Wry's supply runs, they built a conversation that was also a bridge. She told him about the Cape — the light, the long farm road her mother walked, the sound of her mother's voice singing hymns in a kitchen where the windows faced a field of wild flowers. He told her about his village — the gray sea, the leaning houses, the old man on the corner who had sent him here. She told him she wanted to be free. He told her he wanted the same thing.

"Then we're the same," she said.

"We're not," he said. "You're stuck behind a counter. I'm stuck on a mountain. Mine's voluntary."

"That makes yours worse," she said. And smiled.

***

The plan to free her was Wry's. The execution required the teacher, though Wry didn't know this until the teacher told him.

“The merchant’s contract is a legal instrument,” the teacher said. “It can be satisfied by payment.”

“I don’t have money.”

“No. But you have labor. And labor has value. And value, properly documented, can satisfy a contract.” The teacher paused. “This is a lesson.”

“Everything is a lesson with you.”

“Yes. That is also a lesson.”

The negotiation took three weeks. Wry offered the merchant a season’s worth of labor. The merchant countered with two seasons. Wry countered with one season plus the repair of the merchant’s roof, which had been leaking since the monsoons and which the merchant had been too cheap to fix. The merchant accepted, because a dry roof was worth more than three years of a girl’s remaining contract, though he’d never have admitted it.

It was not dishonest. But it leaned hard against the fence. Wry knew the merchant’s roof was his weakness — knew the leak kept him awake, knew he’d been quoted three times the fair price by every tradesman in town. He offered to fix it knowing the merchant would value it far beyond its cost in labor. The contract was fair on paper. The leverage behind it was not.

Brandy saw it. She said nothing. But she saw it.

The merchant signed the release. Brandy walked out from behind the stall with nothing but the clothes she wore and a look on her face that Wry would carry in his memory for the rest of his life. It was a look not of joy, not relief, but with the particular expression of a person who has just discovered that the cage was real, and the man holding it open was real, and that the world contained a kind of goodness she had stopped believing in.

***

They left on a merchant ship bound for the western ports. The teacher saw them off at the base of the mountain. He gave Brandy a small knife with a carved handle. He gave Wry the box for the rings

— Grace and Harmony, now bonded to the only hands that would ever wear them. He gave them both a look that contained everything he would not say, because the things that mattered most were the things that language could not carry without dropping.

"Remember the question," he told Wry.

"Who am I when no one is watching."

"When no one is watching. When no one is counting. When the cost is higher than the reward." He looked at Brandy. "You have given him something I could not. The reason to be still."

They boarded the ship. The mountain shrank behind them. The sea opened ahead. Wry stood at the rail with Brandy beside him, his canvas sack, and the cutlass on his hip. He looked back at what he'd done — the negotiation, the bent rules, the deal that was not dishonest but close enough to feel like it. It wasn't pride, and it wasn't guilt, it was something else that made him wonder if it was something a man's character is made of.

He turned to Brandy. "I need to tell you something."

"You're going to tell me you feel guilty about the merchant?"

"I'm going to tell you I *almost* wasn't honest. And almost matters." He looked at the sea. "I've already failed once. I left a woman and a daughter in a village on the coast because I couldn't be still. I don't want to fail again. I want to make a vow. Not to you — to myself. That I will never again compromise who I am. That integrity isn't something I practice when it's convenient. It's something I choose, or it's nothing."

"That's a hard vow for a man going to sea."

"It's harder for a man who doesn't make it."

She didn't say anything for a while. The ship moved. The water divided and reformed. The mountain was gone.

"The golden rules," she said quietly. "My mother said them. Love God. Love others as yourself. Everything else is commentary."

***

“That’s how I got the rings,” Wry told Gideon. “And the blade. And the vow. And your mother’s predecessor, who turned out to be better at surviving Nassau than I ever was.”

They sat across the desk from each other with the lamp between them, the same way they had all night.

Gideon sat with his hands on his knees. He had not interrupted, in fact, he had not moved. He had listened the way his father had learned to sit on packed earth — without comfort, without impatience, with the stillness that has teeth.

“The back,” Gideon said. “The pain. That’s why.”

“That’s why.”

“And the rings — they only work when —”

“When the motive is clean. When I’ve examined why I’m drawing the blade and found the answer honest. They’re not magic, son. They’re a mirror. They show me who I am before I act, and if who I am is wrong, they let me fight with steel alone. Which is enough for most fights. But not all.”

He turned the rings on his thumbs, Grace and Harmony catching the lamplight. “I wear them always. Not just for the blade. Without them, I feel the pain in my back more — the old injury, the one I earned by impatience. They ease it. Not much, but enough. And I want to be ready. The unexpected doesn’t send word ahead.”

“And integrity.”

Wry was quiet for a moment. The lamp swung. Nassau murmured outside.

“Integrity is the thing I chose on that ship. And the thing I choose every morning. It’s not a trait — it’s a decision. You make it or you don’t. And the men who don’t —” He paused. His jaw tightened. “I have trouble with them. More trouble than I should. Your mother has told me this. She’s right. A man who lacks integrity isn’t necessarily evil. He may be desperate, or broken, or young. But I look at him and I see the choice he didn’t make, and it’s hard for me to see past it.”

"Rafe," Gideon said.

"Rafe," Wry agreed. "Rafe, who is not wrong about the math and not right about the method. And I can't forgive the method even when I understand it, and that's my failing, not his."

They sat in silence, father and son, with the lamp and the painting of the mountain cabin where a woman waited who had taught Wry what the teacher's rings could not — that integrity without love is just stubbornness, and love without integrity is just sentiment, and the two together are the only architecture that holds.

"Thank you," Gideon said. "For telling me."

"You asked."

"I didn't say a word."

"No," Wry said. "You didn't need to."

CHAPTER THIRTEEN

Nassau Days

Three days passed. Three days in which Nassau did what Nassau always did — ground men down and built them up and charged them for both. The Providence sat in the harbor, the ledger was being kept safe in Seraphine's cabin for the time being. As for the future..., well, that was still being calculated.

***

Ortiz went to the market at dawn. He went every day, because provisions needed replenishing. Also, it was in the market that the island's pulse was easiest to read. A man who buys bread hears what the baker is saying. A man who buys fish hears what the fisherman fears. And a man who visits the farthest corners of the market can hear the pulse of a community.

He moved through the stalls the way he moved through his galley — big, warm, unhurried — and people forgot to be suspicious of him. He sampled a mango and told the vendor it was the second best he'd ever tasted, which made the vendor want to know about the first. That led to a conversation about weather and shipping routes and the price of sugar, which led — as conversations in Nassau always led — to Vark.

"The counting house has been quiet," the vendor said. "Too quiet. When Vark's clerks stop collecting, it means something bigger is coming."

"What kind of bigger?"

The vendor shrugged with the eloquence of a man who had learned that specifics were dangerous. "The kind that makes men wish they'd paid when they had the chance."

Ortiz bought the mango. He bought salt and dried peppers and a sack of flour that was only slightly weevilled. He carried it back to the Providence and made breakfast for thirty men — the same portions at every plate, the same care in every bowl, because Ortiz believed that a man who eats well thinks well, and a man who eats equally begins to believe that equality is possible.

He also made a separate plate for the dock. He didn't explain it. He set it on the bollard nearest the gangplank — bread, cheese, a piece of dried fish — and went back to his galley. Kipp watched him do it and said nothing. The plate was empty by midmorning. Neither of them mentioned it. Above them, Cipher perched on the yardarm in silence — no chant or commentary. He watched the dock with one eye, and the alley with the other, as though he understood that some things were better witnessed than announced.

***

Gideon and Seraphine worked the ledger. They sat across from each other at the galley table and they worked. Not in silence and not in conversation, but somewhere closer to music — two minds at the same speed, finding a rhythm that doesn't need words.

Seraphine was building projections. If the open ledger system was adopted by even a quarter of Nassau's merchants, the effect on Vark's revenue would be catastrophic — not because the merchants would stop trading, but because the invisible tax that funded Vark's machine would become visible. And visible taxes have a way of becoming optional.

She needed someone who could look at a column of figures and see not the ink, but the current beneath it. Gideon could do this. He'd been reading patterns his whole life — wind, waves, the sky before a storm. He saw what she was building and understood it the way he understood a ship's rigging — not just the individual lines but the system, the tensions, the places where the load was carried and the places where it would fail.

"Here," he said, pointing to a column. "You've assumed the merchants will adopt at the same rate. They won't. The ones who owe Vark the least will move first. The ones who owe the most will move last, because they have the most to lose if Vark retaliates before the system is strong enough to protect them."

"So we need a phased approach."

"We need the first merchants to succeed visibly. The others will follow when they see the proof, not when they hear the argument."

Seraphine's pencil stopped. She was looking at the number, the one that had started everything, the one branded into the Captain's neck and chanted by Cipher across open water. Five hundred and eighty-nine.

"Gideon."

Something in her voice made him look up.

"Five times eight times nine." She wrote it on the margin of the page. "Three hundred and sixty."

He looked at the figures. Then he looked at her.

"A full circle," she said. "Three hundred and sixty degrees. The number was never arbitrary. My father chose it because the debt was designed to be inescapable — every payment brings you back to where you started. You sail the whole compass and arrive at the same point. That is what five hundred and eighty-nine means. It is not a sum. It is a sentence."

She looked at him. The gray-blue eyes held a quality he hadn't seen before — not admiration, but the specific pleasure of a mind that has found its match and doesn't have to slow down or explain.

Their heads bent toward the same page. His hand rested near hers on the table — not touching, not retreating, occupying the space that two people claim when they've stopped pretending they don't want to be close. Elias, passing the galley hatch on his rounds, saw it and kept walking. Some rigging you leave alone.

***

Kipp had his own Nassau.

It existed below the level where the crew walked — in the alleys behind the alleys, in the drainage channels, in the spaces between buildings where a boy could stand sideways and disappear. He knew every child who slept rough within half a mile of the harbor. He knew their names, their hiding spots, their injuries, their lies. He was their elder at twelve, not because he was the oldest but because he was the one who came back.

He'd been disappearing from the Providence for an hour each afternoon — slipping over the rail the way other boys slip through doors — without sound. He'd vanish into the streets, returning before the watch changed with nothing to show for it except dirty feet and a grin that was sometimes real, and sometimes not.

Gideon followed him once. Not to spy — to understand.

He found Kipp in a yard behind a chandler's warehouse, sitting on an overturned dory with four smaller children arranged around him like pupils at a very disreputable school. The children were filthy, half-starved, and riveted. Kipp had a piece of charcoal and a flat stone, and he was drawing — quick, certain strokes that turned the stone into a picture. A ship. The Providence. He was teaching them to recognize it.

"That's the one," Kipp was saying. "If ye see her flag, ye come to the dock. The cook — big man, laughs loud — he'll feed ye. Don't steal from the stalls near the gangplank or they'll chase ye off and then ye get nothing. Come quiet. Eat, and go."

One of the children — a girl, maybe eight, with a scar that ran from her ear to her chin — raised her hand. "What if the cook says no?"

"He won't. He's got a cat that eats better than any of us. If the cat eats, ye eat. That's the rule."

Gideon leaned against the wall and watched. The boy who had stolen apples and hit a giant in the eye and earned his place in a ship's chant was building something — not a network, not a system, but a web of children who knew where food was and how to get it without getting hit. It was Seraphine's ledger translated into the language of twelve-year-olds: information shared freely, resources distributed by need, the strong looking after the weak because someone had to and nobody else was.

He didn't interrupt. He went back to the Providence and told Ortiz to make the dock plate bigger.

***

Gideon didn't go back to the ledger that afternoon. He walked.

He needed streets that didn't expect anything from him. He walked the harbor road where the chandlers kept their shops, then turned uphill into the lanes where laundry hung between balconies and the air was thick with cook-smoke. He walked without purpose, which was itself a purpose. A man who has spent his whole life on ships rarely gets a chance to go nowhere, so this felt like a luxury.

He ended up at the market where the fish were sold in the morning and the flies were sold in the afternoon. He bought a lime because it was the cheapest thing he could hold, and he sat on a stone wall and ate it in quarters, and the sourness was good because it was simple.

He was thinking about Kipp.

Not the grin or the speed or the string or the stolen apples. He was thinking about the flat stone in the chandler's yard and the four children arranged around it and the charcoal picture of the Providence, drawn by a boy who was teaching other children how to eat. He was thinking about the girl with the scar who had raised her hand and asked what if the cook says no, and the certainty in Kipp's voice when he answered: he won't.

That certainty. It came from a boy who had been hungry long enough to know what hunger does to the mind, and who had decided — not learned, decided — that the answer to hunger was not to eat faster but to feed wider. It was the same instinct that drove Seraphine's ledger. Everyone should have the book. Everyone should have the plate.

The lime was gone. Gideon sat on the wall and watched Nassau pass.

***

He found Ortiz in the galley that evening, cleaning fish with the focused contentment of a man doing the one thing in the world he was built to do. Cajun sat three feet away, watching the scraps with the disciplined patience of a creature who had learned that Ortiz's generosity operated on a schedule and could not be rushed.

Gideon sat on the bench across the table. He didn't speak. Ortiz didn't look up. The knife moved through the fish — spine out, ribs out, skin peeled back — with the economy of ten thousand repetitions.

"You followed him," Ortiz said. Not a question.

"You knew?"

"I know when my dock plate gets bigger. And I know who tells me to make it bigger." He set the cleaned fish on the board and reached for the next. "What did you see?"

"He's teaching them. The harbor children. He draws the ship on a stone and tells them where to come for food. He's built a system — who's where, who's hurt, who hasn't eaten."

"Sí. He's been doing this since the second day."

"You knew."

"I feed the dock. He feeds the alleys. Between us, someone eats." Ortiz held up the fish. "This one has worms. You can see them near the spine — small, white, curled up like little questions. If you cook the fish, the worms die. If you eat it raw, the worms eat you. Most people on this island eat it raw because nobody showed them the difference." He set the wormy fish aside — not in the waste pile, but on a separate board. "I'll boil that one for the dock plate. Kills the worms. Fills a belly. No one needs to know."

Gideon watched him work. Ortiz named the thing he hadn't been able to frame.

"You watch him the way your father watches you."

Gideon looked up.

"Don't look at me like I've said something strange. I've cooked for men on six ships. I know what a father's eye looks like." He pointed the knife at Gideon, not threatening — punctuating. "Most men watch their crew the way they watch weather. Looking for trouble. You watch that boy the way a man watches something he's afraid to lose."

"He's not mine to lose."

"No. But he's yours to keep, if you choose it. And you've been choosing it since the day he hit a giant in the eye with a piece of string."

Ortiz went back to the fish. "The Captain sees it too. Why do you think the boy has a place at our table?"

Gideon said nothing. The galley was warm. The lamp swung. Cajun's tail flicked once, twice.

"He's twelve," Gideon said.

"Sí. He's twelve. And he's already built what most men never build. A thing where people eat." Ortiz set down the knife. He wiped his hands on his apron and looked at Gideon the way he looked at bread — testing the weight, checking the color, deciding if it was ready.

"You asked me once what I cook for. Not who. What."

"I remember."

"I cook for the table. Not the men — the table. Because the table is the thing that holds. Men come and go. They die, they leave, they get drunk and fall overboard. But the table stays. And if the table is set right — same plates, same portions, same place for every man — then the men who sit at it start to believe that the world can be fair. Not because it is. Because someone built a table that was."

He picked up the wormy fish and dropped it into the boiling pot. The water hissed. The worms died. The fish became food.

"That boy is building a table. He's doing it with charcoal and string in a yard behind a warehouse, for children who don't have a name for what he's giving them. But that's what it is. A table. And a table needs someone at the head of it."

Gideon sat with this for a while. The pot bubbled. Cajun's patience with the scraps finally broke and she launched herself at the cleaning board, was caught by the scruff of her neck mid-air by Ortiz's hand, and was deposited on the deck with the smooth authority of a man who had been deflecting cats since before Gideon was born.

"I'm not his father," Gideon said.

"No," Ortiz agreed. "You're not. You're the man who might become that. And you don't get there by sitting on a wall eating a lime. You get there by walking back to the ship."

Gideon stared at him. "How did you —"

"I was buying peppers. You were sitting on the wall, eating a lime, thinking." He shrugged. "I'm a cook. I notice what people eat and what they're chewing on when they're not eating."

***

The next afternoon Ortiz went to the market for salt and came back by way of the chandler's warehouse.

He appeared in the yard with a sack over his shoulder and a look on his face that said he'd been expecting to find what he found. Kipp had six children this time. They sat on crates and overturned buckets in a rough half-circle around the flat stone, which today showed a charcoal map of the harbor — the docks, the alleys, the stalls where food could be found, the corners to avoid.

Ortiz set down his sack. The children froze.

"Which of you washed your hands today?"

Silence. Kipp's eyes narrowed — not with suspicion but with the alert interest of a boy who recognized a performance when he saw one.

"Nobody? Dios mío." Ortiz lowered himself onto a crate that protested but held. He looked at the girl with the scar. "You. Show me your hands."

She held them out. They were filthy.

"You eat with these?"

She nodded.

"Then you eat everything your hands have touched. The dock. The mud. The fish guts. The rat droppings near the warehouse — yes, those are rat droppings, I can see it from here." He held up his own hands — thick, scarred, but clean. "A cook's hands are his tools. Dirty tools make bad food. Bad food makes a sick belly. A sick belly makes a child too weak to run, and a child in Nassau who can't run doesn't last."

He reached into the sack and pulled out a chunk of hard soap. He broke it into pieces and handed one to each child. "Every time. Before you eat. Rub the soap, rinse the hands, eat with clean fingers."

He looked at the girl. "You want to live past twelve?"

She nodded again. Harder this time.

"Then treat your hands like they matter. Because they're the only ones you've got."

He reached into the sack again and produced a cloth bundle. Inside: bread, dried fish, a wedge of hard cheese. Enough for six children and a boy with red hair. He set it on the flat stone beside the charcoal map. "Now wash. Then eat. In that order."

The children scrambled for the rain barrel. Soap appeared on grubby hands. Water splashed. The girl with the scar scrubbed with a ferocity that suggested she had taken the lesson not as advice but as a personal challenge.

Kipp hadn't moved. He sat on the overturned dory and looked at Ortiz with an expression the cook had never seen on the boy's face — not the grin, not the performance, not the sharp-eyed calculation. Something quieter. Something that lived beneath all of those things and had been waiting, perhaps, for a man to show up in a yard and hand out soap and call it survival instead of charity.

"The one with the blue eyes," Ortiz said, low enough for only Kipp to hear. "Gideon. He watches you."

"I know."

"Not the way a captain watches. The other way."

Kipp's fingers found the string. The knots began again — the patient motion, his mother's motion. "What other way?"

Ortiz stood. He picked up his sack. He looked at the children washing their hands, at the bread on the stone, at the charcoal map of a harbor drawn by a boy who had built a school out of nothing because nothing was what he'd been given and he'd decided it wasn't enough.

"Like a man watching something he's building a life around."

He left the yard. The children ate. Kipp sat on the dory with his string and his silence and a feeling in his chest he'd learned long ago not to trust — the feeling that someone was paying attention not because he was useful but because he was there.

His mother's voice came, quiet as breath: The Lord is close to the brokenhearted.

He let it stay. He let the children eat. And the afternoon passed with bread and soap and the slow, unmeasurable work of someone building a table where there wasn't one.

***

The next morning Gideon went to the market. Not for limes this time. He walked to a shop at the far end where a Dutch merchant sold paper and ink. He knew what he was looking for because he also liked to draw — quietly, privately, the way some men write poetry and tell no one. He had never been good enough to call it a talent, but he had been good enough to know what good looked like, and what he had seen on the flat stone in the chandler's yard was good.

He bought a small, leather-bound sketchbook, and a set of drawing charcoals graded from soft to hard wrapped in a cloth roll. He also bought a piece of white chalk for highlights.

He found Kipp on the foredeck that afternoon, cross-legged, working the string. He set the sketchbook and the charcoals on the deck beside the boy without ceremony — no speech, no explanation.

Kipp looked at the sketchbook. He looked at the charcoals, then at Gideon.

"For whatever you want. The stone. The ship. The children." Gideon paused. "You're drawing on scraps with cook-fire charcoal. These are better tools."

Kipp opened the sketchbook. He ran his thumb across the first page — feeling the texture. His fingers knew paper the way they knew string: by touch and by instinct. Despite his young age, he had learned that a material has its own language and the hand must learn to speak it before it can say anything worth hearing.

"The soft charcoal is for shading," Gideon said. "The hard for sharper lines. The white chalk lifts highlights if you lay the darks first."

Kipp looked up. The grin was gone. In its place was something rarer — the look of a boy who has just been seen.

"You draw," Kipp said. Not a question.

"I used to. Not well enough."

"Well enough to know what to buy."

Gideon didn't answer. He went back to the helm. Behind him, he heard the sketchbook open and the first charcoal touch the first page, and the sound was so small and so certain that it carried across the deck like a whisper that knew exactly who it was meant for.

***

It was Dench who moved first. The gunner with the cracking knees — the same man who'd sat at Rafe's table and drunk his rum — came to Elias one evening and asked a question that had been building in him for days.

"The woman's ledger. The pension thing. Would it cover a man's wife if he went over the side?"

Elias looked at him. "You've got a wife?"

"In Plymouth. Two boys. Haven't seen them in four years." Dench's voice was steady but his hands weren't. "If something happens to me, they get nothing. The ship owes them nothing. The Crown owes them nothing. They just stop eating."

"Under Seraphine's system, a portion of every voyage's earnings goes to a fund. If a man is lost, his family draws from the fund. His share, plus whatever the crew votes to add."

"The crew votes?"

"The crew votes. Every man sees the ledger. Every man knows his share. Nobody skims."

Dench was quiet for a long time. Then he said: "Tell Cutler I won't be at the next meeting."

Elias nodded. He didn't smile. But the nod carried weight. The ship's balance had shifted.

***

Kipp came to the galley at dusk.

Ortiz was at the stove, back turned, working something that smelled of pepper and onion. Cajun sat on the flour sack with the patience of a creature who knew dinner would arrive eventually.

"Can we make a second plate?" Kipp asked. "For the dock. At night."

Ortiz didn't turn around. "How much?"

"Enough for a big man."

"How many nights?"

"Until he stops comin'."

Ortiz tasted what was in the pot. Added salt. "He have a name?"

"Not yet."

The cook nodded once, still without turning. Kipp left. That night a plate sat on a coil of rope in the shadow of the crates, covered with a cloth against the dew, bread and cheese and dried fish, the same portion as any plate at any of Ortiz's tables.

On the dock, at night, the plate appeared and disappeared. Ortiz set it out. Kipp said nothing. The large man with the swollen eye came and took it, and each night he stayed a little longer — not approaching the ship, not announcing himself, just standing in the shadows between the crates, eating bread, watching the lantern on the quarterdeck with his one good eye.

On the third night, Kipp was sitting on the gangplank when the shadow arrived. The boy didn't look up from his string.

"Yer eye's healin'," Kipp said to the dark.

Silence. Then, from the shadows, a voice like gravel in a barrel: "Aye."

"Sorry about that."

More silence. Then: "No you're not."

Kipp grinned. "No. I'm not. But I'm sorry ye had to be standing where I had to hit ye."

The shadow shifted. Something that might have been a laugh — or might have been the sound a man makes when he encounters a concept his vocabulary can't hold.

"The cook makes good bread," the voice said.

"Aye. Best on the island. Come back tomorrow. He's making stew."

Silence. The shadow withdrew. The dock was empty.

Kipp sat on the gangplank and looked at the stars. His mother's voice came, unbidden as always — The Lord is close to the brokenhearted — and for once he let it stay instead of pushing it away. He let it sit in the air with the smell of salt and tar and Ortiz's bread, and he thought about the man with the ruined eye who came to eat in the dark.

The string went still. The boy sat. The harbor breathed.

***

Rafe watched all of it.

He watched from the quarterdeck where he had no business being, and from the bow where he pretended to check a line, and from the galley hatch where he stood in shadow and saw Gideon and Seraphine bent over the ledger with their heads close enough to touch. He watched Dench walk away from his faction. He watched the dock plate appear and disappear. He watched the crew talking in whispers that didn't include him.

He was losing. Not the argument — the argument was still sound, still the only honest assessment of their position. But it was losing to something it couldn't answer: the smell of bread, the weight of numbers, the sight of a boy feeding a monster, the idea that a ship could be a family and a family could be a future.

He stood at the rail in the dark and looked at the harbor. The whetstone was in his pocket. His hand found it. But he didn't take out the knife. Not tonight.

CHAPTER FOURTEEN

The Captain's Brand

The reports arrived at half past seven, as they always did.

A clerk carried the stack from the ground floor to the third and set it on the corner of the mahogany desk, aligned with the edge, as instructed. The stack was sorted by port of origin: Amsterdam first, then Rotterdam, then the coastal offices, then the colonial correspondences that arrived smelling of salt and months at sea. Each report bore a date, a port, a list of vessels arrived and departed, and the names of their captains.

Cornelius Vark moved through the Amsterdam report without expression. Ship names. Cargo manifests. Tonnage. Captains. His brown eyes tracked the columns with the patience of a mechanism that has never needed repair. He did not linger. Lingering suggested interest. Interest suggested weakness. The pocket watch on the desk ticked beside the inkwell, its rhythm the only sound on the third floor.

***

He found it on the fourth page. Halfway down the arrivals for the morning tide, entered in a clerk's careful hand:

Ship: Providence

Captain: Wry Slamyrbach.

Cargo: textiles, spices (eastern trade)

Moorage: Pier 7

His pen stopped above the page. For two seconds the third floor held nothing but the tick of the watch and the weight of a name that should have been dead.

Slamyrbach.

He knew the name. It occupied a closed file in the second drawer, the drawer reserved for 'resolved' accounts. He opened it. The file was thin. A single page: a promissory note bearing the name Wry Slamyrbach in a hand that now struck him as too careful — too deliberate, the penmanship of a man writing a name that was not his own. The debt amount was smudged. The original clerk had been careless with the entry, and the clerk was no longer employed. Beneath the note, in Thresh's hand: Account closed. Collected.

'Collected.' Thresh's word for the act that closed accounts permanently.

Vark reconstructed. The debt had been incurred through an intermediary — a man who was not a captain, who did not own a ship. A clerk. The brother of a woman in one of the island establishments. The signature on the note had been accepted because signatures *were* accepted. The ledger did not verify the hand. The hand held the quill, the quill touched the page, the page entered the system, and the system did not ask questions that would slow its operation.

The man Thresh had 'collected' was that clerk. Not a captain. Not a man who arrived in Amsterdam harbor with a ship called the Providence and a cargo hold full of eastern goods.

If the man who signed was not the man who owed, then the man who owed was still alive. And a living captain with a working vessel was an asset the dead clerk had never been.

Vark closed the file. He returned it to the drawer and consulted the pocket watch. Seven fifty-one. He wrote a message to Thresh — two lines, no signature — and rang for the clerk.

***

The Providence was still unloading at dusk.

Pier 7 was loud with it — stevedores hauling crates up from the hold, merchants' agents checking manifests against inventory, a foreman shouting in two languages at men who understood neither. Lanterns had been lit along the pier, their light catching the fog that rolled off the Zuiderzee in the late hours and turned the harbor into something half-real. Ropes creaked. Pulleys groaned. The smell of wet hemp and spice and bilge water hung in the November air, thick enough to taste.

The Captain stood at the stern rail with a manifest in his hand, checking each crate as it came up. He was broad-shouldered and weathered, his fur mantle dark against the fog.

Thresh and three men sat in a small boat on the harbor side of the Providence — the dark side, the side that faced away from the pier and the lanterns and the foreman's attention. They had been there for an hour, waiting for the commotion of unloading to provide what commotion always provides: cover. A busy dock sees nothing that isn't cargo.

The Captain came to the stern rail. He was alone. The crew was forward, managing the last of the hold. He leaned on the rail with the manifest, comparing a figure against the lamplight, his back to the water.

Thresh gave the signal.

Two men came over the rail in silence — practiced, quick, the coordinated movement of men who had done this before and would do it again. One clamped a cloth over the Captain's mouth. The other took his arms. The manifest slipped from his grip and fluttered down between the hull and the pier, catching the lamplight for an instant before the harbor water took it.

The Captain fought. He was stronger than they expected — the broad shoulders were not decoration — and for three seconds the rail shook and the boat knocked against the hull and someone swore in a voice that carried further than it should have. But the cloth was soaked with laudanum, and laudanum does not negotiate. The Captain's knees softened. His hands, which had been pulling a man's arm loose from his throat, slowed and then stopped. His weight settled against the men who held him.

They lowered him over the rail and into the boat. The boat pulled away from the Providence. On the pier, the stevedores continued hauling crates. The foreman continued shouting. No one noticed a thing.

***

The shack sat at the far end of the pier district, where the working docks gave way to the abandoned ones and the abandoned ones gave way to mud. It had been a chandler's store once, or a net-mender's workshop, or one of the dozen interchangeable structures the harbor produced and forgot. Its walls were damp planking because the roof leaked in three places. Its single window had no glass, only a shutter that hung from one hinge and let in the harbor wind.

Vark stood inside and regretted every decision that had brought him here.

He had not wanted to come. He did not visit docks or buildings that smelled of rot and bilge. But the matter required his presence — not because Thresh could not handle it alone, but because the terms needed to come from the man who set them, delivered in person. When the Captain's memory reassembled itself in the days that followed, the face behind the terms would be real and not a dream.

A brazier sat on the dirt floor, its coals breathing orange in the draft from the broken window. The fire crackled softly. An iron rod rested across the coals, its tip buried in the heat. The end that protruded bore the shape of three digits, reversed for pressing: 589.

A single lantern hung from a nail near the open window. The harbor wind found it and set it swinging — slow, rhythmic, the shadows on the walls lurching with each pass. The light made the shack larger and smaller by turns, the corners appearing and disappearing, the Captain's slumped body on the chair shifting from substance to silhouette and back. The fire in the brazier threw its own light — lower, redder, steadier — and between the two sources the shack became a place of moving shapes that would, in the Captain's broken memory, feel less like a room and more like the inside of a fever.

Vark pulled his coat tighter. The cold was not the kind he was accustomed to — not the clean cold of the Keizersgracht in November, but a wet cold that came up through the dirt floor and settled in the joints. He wanted the familiar surroundings of his office.

Instead he had this: a shack, a fire, an unconscious captain, and Thresh, who was checking the iron's temperature with the professional calm of a man testing a blade's edge before use.

"He's under," Thresh said. "Deep. The dosage was generous."

"Generosity is not what I asked for. I asked for compliance."

"You have both."

Thresh gathered the Captain's hair in one fist and pulled the head forward, exposing the nape of the neck. The skin there was pale where the collar and the hair had shielded it from years of weather. It looked, in the firelight, like a page that had never been written on.

Thresh lifted the iron from the coals. It glowed — not the bright orange of fresh heat, but the dull, deep red of metal that has absorbed enough to do its work and is ready. The number at its tip shimmered in the moving air.

The next number on the list. Sequential. The list did not skip. It did not repeat. Each number was a man, and each man was a line in a ledger, and there was no column in the ledger for the sound a man's skin makes when it meets iron at that temperature.

Thresh pressed. The hiss was small and sharp — a sound that belonged in a smithy, not in the dark of a harbor shack with a lantern swaying and a man who could not cry out because his tongue was a dead thing in his mouth. The smell rose: hair first, then flesh, acrid and sweet, climbing through the room and out the open window.

The Captain's body convulsed. His fists clenched and a sound came from his throat that was not a word. Vark's eyes caught the rings — silver on the thumbs, unusual — and moved on.

Thresh held the iron for a count of four, then lifted it. The number sat in the Captain's neck: 589. Raised, red, weeping at the edges. It would scar white and remain for life.

"Marks are for men who think they belong to no one," Thresh murmured, close to the Captain's ear. His breath was warm and stale. Honeyed and rotten.

Vark stepped forward. He did not raise his voice. "Captain Slamyrbach. You will not remember this clearly. That is by design. But you will remember the mark, because the mark will remind you. You carry a debt. It is recorded in my ledger. It is now recorded on your skin. The two records will agree for as long as the debt remains unpaid."

The Captain's eyes opened. Not fully — the laudanum held him in the shallows, where the world arrived through water and faces swam in lantern-light. His mouth worked. The word came out broken, barely a sound:

"How... much?"

Vark considered. The original sum — the smudged figure on the dead clerk's note — was unrecoverable. The clerk who had entered it was no longer employed, and the entry itself had been made carelessly, the ink feathered past legibility. He could have named a round number. Five hundred. Six hundred. Something that sounded calculated.

He looked at the mark on the Captain's neck. The number was still bright. Still weeping. Still legible.

"Five hundred and eighty-nine pieces of eight."

He said it once, clearly, without repetition. The amount was not calculated — not consciously. It was the number that was already there, the next entry on the list, the brand on the neck. But Vark was a man whose mind trafficked in numbers and some part of him — the part that never stopped counting — knew what 589 contained: five times eight times nine, three hundred and sixty, a full circle. A compass sailed to completion and arriving at the same point. He did not think this. The number thought it for him. The man, the debt, and the proof of both, bound in three digits that would follow Captain Wry Slamyrbach across every ocean he sailed for as long as Cornelius Vark chose to let them.

The Captain's eyes closed. The laudanum pulled him back under. The lantern swung. The shadows traded places on the walls.

"Return him to his ship," Vark said. He pulled his coat straight, buttoned the collar against the harbor damp, and walked to the door. He paused at the threshold. The shack offended him — its smell, its disorder, its indifference to the systems that governed the rest of his world. Next time, Thresh would handle the details alone, and the details would arrive at the third floor in writing, where they belonged.

He stepped into the night and walked back toward the Keizersgracht.

***

They returned the Captain after midnight.

The boat came alongside the Providence in the dark. Amsterdam was sleeping — the canals still, the windows shuttered, the harbor watch at the far end of the quay where the taverns stayed open late and the watchmen found reasons to linger. Two of Thresh's men lifted the Captain and set him on the dock planking at the base of the gangplank, propped against a mooring post. His head lolled. His coat was damp with harbor spray. The brand at his neck was covered by his hair and his collar, invisible to anyone who didn't know to look.

The boat pulled away and the harbor water closed over its wake.

***

Gideon had noticed the absence two hours after the unloading finished.

The Captain had been at the stern rail checking the manifest. Then he was not. The manifest was gone too. Gideon checked the cabin. Empty. He checked the quarterdeck, the hold, the heads. He asked the crew. No one had seen the Captain leave the ship. No one had seen him on the pier.

Gideon sent four men into the streets. The taverns along the Zeedijk. The harbor offices. The chandlers and warehouses that stayed open late for captains settling accounts. He stood at the gangplank and watched them go, his hand on the silver earring, turning it the way his father turned the gold band.

The hours passed but the men did not return. The harbor quieted. Gideon paced the deck and did not sleep.

***

In the last hour before dawn, a shape appeared at the base of the gangplank.

It moved the way a man moves when his legs are not entirely his own. One hand found the gangplank rail. One boot found the first plank. Then the next. The climb was slow and ugly and stubborn, and it was made in silence, because the man making it did not yet trust his voice to carry words.

Wry made it to the deck. He stood there swaying, one hand on the rail, the harbor tilting beneath him in ways that had nothing to do with the tide. The back of his neck burned. His mouth tasted of laudanum and rum and something metallic that he could not name. The night was a hole. He remembered the manifest, the stern rail, and nothing after.

Ortiz found him.

The cook was awake because the cook was always awake at this hour — the bread would not start itself, and the coffee required attention before dawn if it was to be fit for men and not for punishment. He came up the galley hatch with a sack of flour on his shoulder and saw the Captain standing at the rail in the dark, listing like a ship with a fouled keel.

Ortiz set down the flour and crossed the deck, took the Captain's arm, and steered him below with the practiced efficiency of a man who has handled drunks and wounded men and who understood that the difference between them was a question best answered after coffee.

He eased the Captain into the chair. Wry flopped forward onto the desk, revealing the fresh brand on the back of his neck.

Ortiz was not a man who startled. He had been at sea long enough to know that the world produced horrors the way the galley produced biscuits — regularly, and in quantities that exceeded demand. But the brand on the Captain's neck stopped him. Three digits, raised and raw, the skin around them angry and weeping. Not a tattoo. Not a scar from a fight. A brand. The kind you put on cattle. The kind you put on men you do not consider men.

He cleaned the wound with vinegar and salt water. He dressed it with a strip of clean linen from the galley stores — the same linen he used for burns from the stove. He eased the Captain into his bunk, pulled the blanket over him, and stood for a moment looking at the man he had cooked for, and cursed at, and followed across two oceans.

There would be time for asking. There would not be time for asking if the Captain died of infection because a cook stood around wanting explanations instead of boiling water.

He closed the cabin door and went back to his flour.

***

The commotion came at first light.

The four crewmen returned to the ship in a ragged group, cold and frustrated, having searched every tavern and alley within a mile of the pier and found nothing. They came up the gangplank talking over each other, and Gideon met them at the rail with a face that had not slept and was not interested in excuses.

"Nothing," the first man said. "No one's seen him. Not at the Zeedijk, not at the harbor office, not at —"

Ortiz appeared at the galley hatch. He held a mug of coffee in one hand and a wooden spoon in the other, and his face wore the particular expression of a cook who has been disturbed during bread.

"The Captain is in his cabin," Ortiz said. "He is not feeling well. Nothing that rest and proper cooking cannot fix." He took a sip of his own coffee and grimaced at the commotion on deck. "It will have been the food at this port. I have said before — the Dutch cannot cook. They boil everything. A man cannot live on boiled everything."

Gideon stared at him. "He's been — he's in his cabin? Since when?"

"Since I put him there." Ortiz raised the spoon in the manner of a man closing a conversation. "He needs sleep. Not questions. Not four men stamping about the deck like cattle." He turned back to the galley. At the hatch he paused. "And tell those four to eat something. They look worse than the Captain, and they have no excuse."

Gideon went below. He opened the cabin door quietly. His father was asleep — or something close to it, the heavy unnatural sleep of a man whose body had been told to shut down and had obeyed. He stood in the doorway and looked at the blanket, the closed eyes, the stillness.

He turned to leave. At the door, a crumpled parchment caught his eye — stuffed into the breast pocket of his father's coat where it hung on the hook, its corner protruding at an angle that did not belong to the Captain's habits. His father folded things. He did not crumple them.

Gideon pulled it free. He unfolded it. He read it. His face did not change, but his hand tightened on the parchment until the edges pressed white lines into his fingers.

He folded it along its original creases, returned it to the breast pocket, and left the cabin without a word. His hand went to the earring and stayed there.

***

The next morning, at nine minutes past eight, a boy burst through the front door of the counting house on the Keizersgracht.

He was twelve, maybe thirteen. A dock runner — fast, underfed, loyal to the last coin. He was breathing as though he had sprinted from the Stadhuis, which he had. His cap was gone, his shirt untucked, his eyes too wide for his face.

Twelve clerks looked up from twelve desks. The silence that had filled the room since seven o'clock broke like a pane of glass.

The nearest clerk rose, took the boy by the elbow, and walked him to the third floor. The boy's breathing did not slow. The clerk knocked once and entered.

Vark sat behind the mahogany desk. The pocket watch read eight twelve. He was always ahead of schedule, and today was no different.

"The authorities, sir." The boy's voice split between the words. "From the Stadhuis. Men in coats. They're asking about the counting houses on the Keizersgracht. Allegations. Corruption."

Vark did not stand. He consulted the watch. He had perhaps fifteen minutes — the houses east of the church were more conspicuous and would be visited first. Fifteen minutes was sufficient.

The number was in his mind. It had been there since last night — since the iron in the shack, since the Captain's broken voice asking the only question that mattered, and receiving a simple answer; 589.

He spoke to the clerk. "The sign above the door. Remove it. Replace it with a number."

"Sir?"

"Five. Eight. Nine. Plain lettering. No ornamentation. Now."

The clerk went.

Vark descended to the ground floor. He stood at the front of the room — compact, plain, dark coat buttoned to the collar — and addressed twelve faces that had not been addressed directly since the last clerk was dismissed.

"The counting house is henceforth called 589. You will use this number in all correspondence. You will not explain it. Clients who ask will be told it is an administrative designation. It is not. But that is what they will be told."

He paused. Twelve quills held above twelve inkwells.

"Resume."

Outside, on the Keizersgracht, a clerk climbed a short ladder and pried the brass plate from above the door — a modest thing that read C. Vark, Merchant — and replaced it with three painted numerals that meant nothing to the men who walked the canal and everything to the man who watched from the window of the third floor.

The authorities arrived twenty minutes later. They found a building with a number for a name, a proprietor who answered their questions with patient courtesy, and twelve clerks whose penwork had not paused once during the visit.

They left satisfied. Vark watched them go from the third-floor window. The pocket watch read nine twenty-three. He was behind schedule. He did not enjoy being behind schedule.

But the morning had produced a captain, a brand, a debt, and a name for an enterprise that would, in time, reach across three oceans and bind two hundred men in chains made not of iron but of ink... 589.

He wound the watch. He returned to the reports.

CHAPTER FIFTEEN

A Girl Who Counted

The first sound she remembered was the scratching.

Nibs on parchment. Twelve of them, their scratching noise rising from the ground floor through the boards of the house on the Keizersgracht, arriving at her ear as a single sustained whisper — the sound of her father's machine, breathing.

She learned to count before she learned to read. Her father placed numbers in front of her the way other fathers placed dolls — without explanation, without sentiment, as a tool whose purpose would reveal itself in use. She was three when she could add, four when she could subtract, five when she sat at the kitchen table with a column of figures in her father's small precise hand and found the error on the seventh line that the clerks downstairs had missed.

He did not praise her. He corrected the column and took the paper back. But a fresh sheet waited the next morning, and the morning after that, and the sheets became her education — not the one her mother wanted, which involved scripture and needlework, but the one her father decided she would have, which involved the quiet art of making money speak.

Her mother fought this.

Annelise Vark was a healer. Not a physician — physicians were men with degrees from Leiden who charged fees that could feed a family for a month. Annelise was what the neighborhood had instead. She kept herbs on the second-floor windowsill — rosemary, thyme, chamomile, comfrey — and the smell of them braided through the counting house's ink-and-paper atmosphere like something alive threading through something dead.

She said it once, clearly, in the kitchen, while Seraphine sat at the table with a column of figures and her younger brother, Matthias, played at their mother's feet with a wooden horse.

"You are teaching her to count the world, Cornelius. You are not teaching her to live in it."

Vark looked at his wife across the kitchen table — across the column of figures, across the distance between a man who measured everything and a woman who healed everything — and said: "The world is counted, Annelise. The ones who know how to count survive."

"And the ones who only know the count? What do they become?"

He went upstairs without answering. The door closed. The nibs scratched below.

***

Matthias was three years younger. He had their mother's face — round, warm, built for expressions that changed like weather. He was loud where Seraphine was quiet, clumsy where she was precise.

Seraphine loved him completely, and the love expressed itself the only way she knew: she protected him. She walked him to the market when their mother was called to a bedside. She wiped his face when he ate. She taught him to count on his fingers — not because their father asked her to, but because counting was the language she had and she wanted to share it with the one person in the house who didn't yet know what counting cost.

Their mother taught Matthias the herbs. He absorbed it messily, joyfully. Seraphine watched and understood, without bitterness, that her mother was giving Matthias what she had not given Seraphine — not because she loved him more, but because she had lost the fight for Seraphine's education before Seraphine was old enough to know there was a fight.

***

Annelise died when Seraphine was twelve.

A fever that came on a winter's morning and built through the week with the patience of a thing that would not be argued with.

The healer who had healed half the Jordaan district could not heal herself.

She called Seraphine to the bedside on the seventh day. Matthias was downstairs with a neighbor. Vark was on the third floor. The nibs scratched below.

"You have your father's mind," Annelise said. Her voice was thin but her eyes were clear, "I could not change that. I tried. The numbers were always louder than the herbs."

Seraphine held her mother's hand. The hand was hot. The bones beneath the skin were bird-thin.

"But you have something he does not. You can see the people inside the numbers. He cannot. He never could. That is your weapon, Seraphine. Not the counting. The seeing. Promise me you will use it."

Seraphine promised. She was twelve. She didn't fully understand what she was promising. But the promise lodged in her the way a seed lodges in a crack in stone — finding no soil, needing none, waiting for the rain that would eventually come.

Annelise died that night. Quietly. Vark came down from the third floor and stood in the doorway and looked at his wife's body with the expression of a man who had loved something he could not count and was now unable to record the loss.

He went back upstairs. The scratching sound of the nibs below reseeded with every footstep.

Matthias cried for a week. Seraphine held him at night and told him the names of herbs — rosemary, thyme, chamomile, comfrey — because they were the only words of their mother's she had.

***

After Annelise, the house changed.

Not visibly — the building was the same, the canal was the same, the clerks scratched at the same desks. But the second-floor windowsill where the herbs had grown went bare. No one replaced the rosemary.

Vark moved Seraphine's education from the kitchen table to the records room on the fourth floor — not his office below, but the floor above it, where twenty years of ledgers sat shelved by year and region, leather-bound, the spines uniform. He gave her access to all of them.

"Learn the system," he told her. "Not the figures — the system. How a transaction moves from a dock in Nassau to a desk in Amsterdam. How a debt is created, recorded, collected, and renewed. How the money flows."

She learned. She was fourteen. She learned by absorption, by immersion, by sitting in a room full of numbers until the numbers stopped being figures and started being architecture.

And somewhere in the third month — she would remember it as a Thursday, because Thursdays were when the Nassau packet arrived and the ledgers were updated — she found the gap.

It was not hidden. The discrepancy between the figure a captain reported receiving for his cargo and the figure the counting house recorded receiving sat in the main column, in plain ink, separated from the truth by nothing more than the assumption that no one would ever compare the two.

She compared the two.

The gap was consistent. It appeared in every transaction, every captain, every port. The difference vanished into a column marked "administrative levies" that was, upon examination, a door that opened onto nothing.

She didn't tell her father. She understood — at fourteen, with her mother's promise lodged in her — that confrontation was the one tool her father was built to withstand. He would explain. He would justify. He would reframe the gap as a necessary cost of commerce. And his explanation would be accurate, and his justification would be sound, and the reframing would be true in every way except the one that mattered.

Instead she took a pencil. She hid it in the binding of a Bible that sat on her bedside table — a Bible Annelise had given her, a Bible she kept because the smell of rosemary still clung to the pages.

In the margins of that Bible, in handwriting so small it could be mistaken for an imperfection in the paper, she began to write the real numbers. The captain's number beside the ledger's number. The gap between them. The date, the port, the cargo, the name.

The counter-record grew, over months, into something her father would have recognized if he had ever opened the book. Of course he would not. Cornelius Vark assumed his daughter's Bible was devotional rather than operational, and it was the one miscalculation in a career otherwise free of them.

***

She left Amsterdam at twenty. She asked no permission, made no announcement. She packed one bag, took the Bible with its three years of margins, and booked passage on a merchant brig to the Caribbean.

She left a letter for Matthias — not for her father, for her brother. Matthias was seventeen, apprenticed to a surgeon near the harbor, his mother's son with his mother's hands. The letter told him she was safe, but didn't tell him where she was going or why.

She left nothing for Vark. He would know soon enough. A man who tracked every debt across three oceans would track his daughter across one. She counted on this — on him sending someone to find her, and on the time between her departure and their arrival being long enough to build what she needed to build. The counting, as always, was precise.

***

Nassau was not what the ledgers described.

The ledgers described a port. Revenue streams, docking fees, cargo manifests, the clean geometry of commerce reduced to columns. Nassau was not columns. Nassau was heat and noise and the smell of rum and rot and the particular desperation of a place where every man was one bad month from drowning and knew it.

She understood, in the first week, that the counter-ledger she had built in the Bible's margins would not be enough. A record of fraud is evidence. Evidence requires a court, a magistrate, a system of justice that cares about the gap between what is written and what is true. Nassau had no such system. Her father's system was the court and the magistrate and the judge, and the judge did not rule against himself.

She needed something else. Not evidence — architecture. A replacement. A system that did what her father's did — recorded transactions, verified accounts, maintained the flow of commerce — but did it in the open. Visible and distributed. Held by many hands instead of one.

She rented a room at the Red Mercy because the Red Mercy was the one place in Nassau where a woman with a ledger would not be questioned. The women there understood disguise because they understood survival. Seraphine wore the dresses, but she didn't sell what the dresses advertised. The women who worked beside her knew this and said nothing, because solidarity in a house like the Red Mercy was practiced, not spoken.

Three years. Three years of building the open ledger one merchant at a time. Three years of holding her mother's promise in one hand and her father's method in the other, and discovering that the method was the weapon and the promise was the reason to aim it.

Churches burned. Ledgers survived. She believed this. And yet the Bible had outlasted both — still smelling of rosemary and a second-floor windowsill, still holding a mother who had seen the people inside the numbers before Seraphine knew there were people to see.

And then, on a morning like any other, a ship arrived in the harbor.

She watched it from the Red Mercy's upper window — the Providence, sails furled, kissing a dock that groaned beneath her. She watched the captain come down the gangplank last, broad-shouldered, fur mantle dark against the morning heat. A younger man stood beside him who carried the same jaw and the same blue eyes — a son, she guessed, or a mirror the years hadn't found yet.

Then a boy appeared on the wharf. No herald. Just motion — vaulting a coil of rope, skimming past a fishmonger's cart, hands blurring at a fruit stall. She saw him steal two apples and toss one to a child crouched in an alley mouth without breaking stride. Red hair. Barefoot. Fast and small and belonging to no one.

She turned from the window and went back to the numbers. The Bible sat on the bedside table, its margins full, its work done. The Bible had been the seed. The ledger was the tree.

She picked up her pencil and returned to the column she'd been working. Another ship in the harbor. Another crew. She would learn their numbers soon enough.

CHAPTER SIXTEEN

The Lesser Evil

The pain woke him before dawn.

It came the way it always came — not as a sharp thing but as a tightening, a band of heat across the lower back that cinched like a belt pulled one notch past bearable. He lay in his bunk and breathed through it and waited for it to pass.

It didn't pass. It had been getting worse since Nassau — the climbs up the hill, the tension in his shoulders that never left, and that the ship's bunk did nothing to undo.

He sat up. The cabin was dark. The painting on the wall was a shadow. The rings on his thumbs were warm — they were always warm now, holding back enough of the pain to keep him functional. He'd tested the theory once, taking them off for a night. He did not test it again.

He dressed. He buckled the cutlass and scabbard to his belt and climbed the companionway to the deck, where the harbor air hit him and the first gray light was turning Nassau from shadow into shape.

Elias was at the rail, as he usually was always at this hour.

"Back?" the Bosun said. Not a question.

"Back," Wry confirmed.

Elias said nothing more. He'd been watching Wry's back for twenty years — the way the Captain moved, the way he compensated, the way he held himself too carefully on bad days and not carefully enough on worse ones. Elias was the only man on the ship who knew the full history of what lived in that spine, because Elias had been there for the worst of it.

***

Gideon had been twelve. Wry had been forty-six. The damage from the mountain had spent two decades spreading quietly, the way a crack in a hull spreads — not from new storms but from the first one that made it. By forty-six the crack had become a fault line.

The laudanum came from a ship's surgeon in Bridgetown. A small brown bottle with no label. "Three drops in water. No more than four. It will take the edge off."

It took more than the edge off. The pain dissolved, the tension melted, the world went soft and manageable. He could train Gideon without grimacing. He could haul a line without his vision narrowing. He could sit at the table with Lianor at night and be present instead of absent.

Three drops became four. Four became six. The bottle was a tool. A crutch. It let him be the father Gideon needed during the years Gideon needed him most.

By the third year, the laudanum had stopped being a tool and started being a need. The need had its own schedule — morning, midday, evening, night — and the schedule was no longer optional. The drops no longer dissolved the pain. They dissolved the man. The piercing blue eyes went hazy. The steady hands trembled before the first dose. The voice that could carry across a deck in a storm went soft and uncertain in the cabin at night.

Lianor watched her husband disappear by degrees into a brown bottle. She prayed. She prayed in the mountains and at the table and in the bed beside him while he tossed in his sleep. She trusted that the man she'd married was still in there, behind the haze, behind the need, and that he would find his own way out. The decision would be his alone or it would not hold.

She was right.

It came one morning — not a special morning, not an anniversary or a crisis. Just a morning when he reached for the drawer and his hand stopped. The bottle was full and right there. His fingers were on the handle.

But Gideon was on deck. He could hear the boy's voice through the cabin wall — sixteen now, almost a man, calling out a bearing to

Elias, practicing for the day when the bearing would matter. Four years of watching his father slowly dissolve, and still the voice was clear, still full of trust.

Wry understood that the bottle was stealing the thing the boy counted on most – his presence.

He closed the drawer and never opened it again.

The withdrawal was Hell. He wished he was dead. He wished it with a sincerity that frightened him. The things that came when the bottle stopped were real in the dark, real in the shaking, real in the voice that whispered from inside his own skull that the drawer was right there and the pain would stop and no one would know and no one would blame him.

He cried. He raged at the bottle, at the surgeon who'd given it to him, at the spine that had started it, at the young fool on the mountain who had trained in secret and broken what could not be unbroken.

He snapped at men who didn't deserve it and apologized to men who didn't expect it. He held the wheel with hands that wouldn't stop trembling and the crew bore it without comment.

Lianor held him at night when the shaking was at its worst.

It was Elias who offered the bridge. Weeks into the withdrawal, when the worst had passed but the want had not, he came to the cabin one evening with a flask of rum. Good rum. He poured two measures and pushed one across the desk. The Captain had never been a drinking man.

"You need a floor," Elias said. "Something under the pain that keeps you from falling through. The drops were a trapdoor. This is a floor. Rough, but it holds."

Wry drank. It was not the warm dissolution of the laudanum. It was heat and burn and the knowledge that the pain was still there and would always be there. The rum didn't take it away. It put a floor under it.

"The lesser evil," Wry said.

“The lesser evil,” Elias agreed.

The rum stayed. The evening measure, and sometimes the afternoon when the evening didn’t arrive before the pain. Not sobriety. Not victory. Management.

Gideon watched with those blue eyes that saw everything and understood little. But one morning — a morning when the trembling had stopped and the Captain stood at the wheel with something in his face that hadn’t been there for months — the boy came to the quarterdeck and stood beside his father and said nothing at all.

Wry put his arm around the boy’s shoulders and turned his face into the wind so no one would see that the wind wasn’t the reason his eyes were wet.

***

The apothecary stall was on the corner of Harbor Street, three doors from the chandler’s. It sold herbs, tinctures, poultices, and small brown bottles with no labels. Wry saw it every time he walked through the market.

He didn’t stop. But today the pain was worse. Today the climb to the Red Mercy had left something in his spine that the rings couldn’t quiet and the rum couldn’t floor.

He stopped.

The apothecary was a thin man with careful hands. He saw Wry looking at the bottles and waited.

“Laudanum?” the apothecary said.

The word hung in the air.

Wry’s hand moved. Not to his pocket — to his thumb. Grace. The silver was warm.

He stood at the stall for a long time. Long enough that the harbor noise faded and the old need rose from wherever he’d buried it and said: I’m still here. I’ve always been here. One bottle. Just one.

"No," Wry said.

He walked away. His back screamed. His hands were steady.

At the Providence, Elias was at the rail. He saw the Captain's face and read it, then produced the flask, poured a measure, and set it on the rail.

Wry slammed it back in a single swallow. The rum burned. The pain stayed. The floor held.

"Bad day," Elias said.

"They're all bad days. Some are just louder."

Elias took the flask back. He didn't say anything else, because everything that needed saying had been said years ago in a cabin with a drawer that stayed closed.

Today the floor held.

CHAPTER SEVENTEEN

The Distant Shore

Wry bought fifty acres of volcanic soil on an island so remote that the maps disagreed about its position. He did it on the advice of a merchant in a harbor tavern who may or may not have been sober, using money that he and Lianor had earned delivering cargo and setting bones. It was a gamble. He would be the first to admit this. The merchant said the land was cheap. This was true. The merchant said the soil was fertile. This also was true. The merchant said the island was beautiful, and safe, and that a man who bought land there today would be wealthy tomorrow. This was the part that was not true — or not true yet. Or maybe it was true only if you waited long.

Wry bought it anyway. He bought it because the numbers suggested that fifty acres of fertile land in a place where no one was buying could not stay cheap forever. He bought it because the alternative was another season at sea chasing diminishing returns in an age when the letters of marque were expiring and the privateers were becoming pirates. And he bought it because Lianor, when he brought the idea to her, looked at him with her dark level eyes and said: "If you believe it, do it."

Gideon was only five at the time.

***

They arrived in the rainy season, which no one had mentioned. The land was green to the point of aggression with the jungle pressing in from every side. The volcanic soil when solid was like black gravel and sharp as glass to the bare feet. In other places when it rained it became a substance that was neither solid nor liquid but something in between that sucked at boots and swallowed tools and expressed a general hostility toward the concept of construction.

Gideon loved it — with total commitment and no reservation, the way only a five-year-old can. He chased crabs on the black sand beach and geckos in the forest. He climbed trees and fell in streams.

The cottage took shape over months. Wry cut timber from the forest with patience and a generous helping of brute force. The boy carried things that were too heavy for him and hammered nails that bent, and asked questions; why does the wall go there, why does the beam go here, why does it matter if the line is straight. Wry answered every one, because a boy who asks *why* is a boy who will one day know *how*, and with each passing day he was learning how.

The cottage grew under their hands — four walls, a floor, windows that faced the sea. A porch where Wry sat in the evenings with the boy beside him and the green book in his hands, his present child dozing against his shoulder, and his absent child living between the lines.

***

Lianor came every other week. She was working at a hospital in their hometown on a smaller island — almost a day by canoe, a journey she made with the uncomplaining regularity of a woman who had weathered far worse crossings and considered a day in a canoe a minor inconvenience.

On one visit she brought a puppy.

He arrived in a basket — white as sea foam, a ball of fluff and devotion that launched himself at Gideon and never looked back. The boy named him Timmy. There was no discussion. The dog became his shadow — on the beach, in the half-built cottage, underfoot during every project.

***

They fished. Not with sport in mind but with food — casting from the rocks where the reef dropped away into blue-black water.

One afternoon the line snagged on something heavy. Not a fish — the pull was wrong, dead weight without fight. They hauled it up together, father and son, the line cutting into Wry's palms.

What came over the edge was a chest — small, barnacled, the wood half-eaten by salt and time, trailing weed like a beard. It was from a vessel that had gone down years before, maybe decades, settling on the reef to wait for a boy's fishing line to find it.

Inside, wrapped in oilcloth that had mostly held, was a ship's log. The captain's own hand — careful script, fading ink, entries dated and numbered. Every voyage. Every cargo. Every transaction recorded.

Gideon wanted to read it like a story. Wry read it like a ledger.

The numbers didn't match. The captain had recorded one figure for the cargo sold at port and a different figure — always lower, always by the same margin — for the shares paid to the crew. The gap between the two was consistent, deliberate, repeated voyage after voyage. It was theft, plain and simple — not piracy, not violence, but bookkeeping. The quietest crime. The crew had been cheated by the man they trusted to keep the record, because the record was his and no one else could see it.

Wry showed Gideon. The boy was eight — too young for the mathematics but not too young for the injustice. Children understand unfairness the way they understand gravity: completely, without nuance.

"Why didn't someone check?" Gideon asked.

"Because no one else had the book," Wry said.

The boy looked at the log — the careful script, the lie repeated so many times it had become a fact — and said: "Then everyone should have the book."

Wry set the log on the shelf in the cottage beside the green book. He didn't forget it. Years later, when a woman named Seraphine would spread her ledger on the galley table and show him a system where every transaction was recorded in multiple copies held by multiple parties, Wry would remember the boy on the rocks and the eight-year-old's verdict that had been, it turned out, the answer to everything.

That evening, with the boy asleep and the lantern low, he brought it to Lianor.

He had been thinking about the shares. A captain took double — that was the way of it, the custom that no one questioned and no one justified, because custom doesn't require justification. But the captain in the log had taken double and then some, and the men who'd trusted him had died never knowing.

"I was thinking," he said. "About my share."

She waited.

"If I took one share instead of two — kept the second in a common fund for the crew, held in the open — it would be theirs. A floor under them. Something for the years when the sea stops giving."

She didn't hesitate. "We can make do without it. Our needs are simple. Do the thing you know is right."

The crew would assume it was generosity, or principle. It was simpler than either. They had enough, and enough was a kind of wealth most captains never found.

Years later, when Seraphine's ledger would grow into a pension system that reached across the trade, the crew would call it a revolution. To Wry it would look like a woman across a kitchen table telling him what he already knew.

***

The roof went on in a storm.

Lianor's last visit before they left for the north. The roof had to go on — metal sheeting, hurricane-proof — and the weather did not wait for them. The storm announced itself the way tropical storms do — not with warning but with a change in pressure that Wry felt in his spine before he saw it in the sky. The barometer dropped. The wind shifted. The birds went silent. And the roof was only half-finished.

They worked against the wind. Wry on the ridge beam, Lianor beside him — the healer with the nails, the captain with the hammer. Gideon, ten years old and strong enough to matter, passed the sheeting up the ladder. The wind caught the metal and turned it into a sail. He held on with a strength and determination that was beyond his age because his father was on the roof, and his mother was on the roof, and the only way they would be dry that night is if they worked together as one.

The rain came. Wry hammered the last sheet in horizontal rain, the water sheeting off the metal they were fastening, the wind screaming through the gap. Wry's back seized twice. He worked through it because the roof didn't care about his back and neither did the storm.

The storm hit full force that night. The three of them sat inside the cottage and listened to the metal roof take the storm's full weight. The wind howled. The rain hammered. The jungle outside bent and cracked and surrendered.

The roof held and the cottage held.

Gideon sat between his parents with Timmy shaking in his lap, but the boy was not afraid.

***

They moved north when Gideon was ten.

The harbor town needed a full-time healer. Lianor's visits to the island had been visits away from work she couldn't leave indefinitely. They packed and set sail. They left the cottage standing on its volcanic soil with its hurricane-proof roof and its view of the sea where a boy and a dog had spent five years learning that the world was built by hands.

Timmy came. He adapted the way dogs adapt — completely, without nostalgia, content to be wherever his boy was because his boy was his whole world.

The north was harder and richer. Wry invested again — more properties in the harbor town, buildings that needed work. He and Gideon renovated, repaired, and expanded. In the remote north you use what you have. You improvise. You don't complain about the tool you don't have — you make do with the one you've got.

The boy became a teenager and had to learn to navigate uncharted emotions. In private, he turned to drawing as an expression of his voice, a voice he was only beginning to learn the sound of. Charcoal, paper, in the margins of his school books, anything he could mark. He drew the mountains and the cabin and the harbor town and his father — though he would not show those to anyone. The drawing became his language for the things he couldn't say yet.

Timmy grew old. The white fluff thinned. The muzzle went gray. The energy that had chased crabs and barked at waterfalls became a slower thing — a warmth that preferred laps to trails and that dozed in patches of sun.

Lianor brought him to the hospital. Timmy became a full-time resident, padding the halls on stiff legs, sitting beside beds, laying his head on the laps of seniors who had outlived their own companions and needed the warmth of something alive that asked nothing and gave everything. He was, in his way, a healer — Lianor's colleague, working without credentials, prescribing nothing but presence.

He died at the hospital, surrounded by the people he had comforted. Gideon was fourteen. He drew the dog from memory that night — the white fur, the dark eyes, the tail that had never stopped wagging until it did. The drawing was good. It was the best thing he'd made. And the goodness of it was the first time Gideon understood that his art could hold what his heart couldn't carry alone.

***

They sold the acreage on the island at a tidy profit and the money was enough to buy a ship. Most men would have pocketed half and played it safe. Wry spent nearly every penny on cargo.

He found the Providence in a southern port. She was neither warship nor merchant barge but a working vessel — sound hull, good lines, room for a crew of thirty and cargo enough to make a voyage pay. She was not beautiful in the way that ships in stories are beautiful. She was beautiful in the way the cottage had been beautiful: solid, honest, built to hold.

He bought her outright, named her, and filled her hold with everything a remote settlement needed and couldn't make for itself. It was a calculated risk, the kind Wry had learned to take: never foolish, but always leaning into the wind.

With a green crew, a wide-eyed son, and a fair wind, he headed north — to the mountains and to Lianor.

It was during this maiden voyage that Gideon rose to First Mate because no one else could have held the post. Not by favoritism — by competence. The crew saw what Wry saw: a young man who listened before he spoke, who checked the rigging before he checked his pride.

Wry had no trouble finding crewmen because Wry's reputation preceded him — not as the fastest captain or the richest haul, but as the man whose word held. In a world where captains cheated on shares, watered the rum, and abandoned men in ports they couldn't afford to leave, word on the docks was that Wry paid what he promised. He shared what he earned. He treated every man aboard as a man. The Providence became known not for speed or cargo but for something rarer: honesty.

The ship was the third thing Wry had built. After the cottage on the island, after the properties in the north. Each had taught the same lesson: measure true, build honest, and the thing you make will hold.

CHAPTER EIGHTEEN

The Woman on the Mountain

Lianor's story did not begin on a mountain. It began in China, where her mother had been born to a concubine in a home where love was political and survival was negotiated. That woman had found something the household could not contain: a faith that burned quietly, the way embers burn beneath ash. The faith passed through the generations the way a lantern passes through a dark hallway — not by explaining the light, but by carrying it.

Lianor was born in Malaysia, in a town where the sea was warm and the markets were loud and the temple bells rang at hours that had nothing to do with the God her mother prayed to. She was quiet. She watched. She had her mother's eyes and her mother's hands, and a gift no one in the family could account for: a mind that understood the body the way some minds understand music. At twelve she sat beside a dying woman and learned — not from a book but from the sitting — that death is not an enemy but a threshold, and that the healer's work is not to block the door but to hold the hand of the one who crosses it.

***

The family pooled their money — aunts, uncles, cousins — and sent her to a port city in the northern colonies. She was seventeen. She arrived with a trunk, a letter of introduction to a hospital that trained healers, and a Bible her mother had pressed into her hands at the dock. "He will go before you," her mother said.

He did. But He did not make it easy.

In a sense, the hospital saved her. In the wards, language mattered less. The body speaks the same tongue everywhere — pain is pain, fever is fever, the sound a mother makes when her child is sick needs no translation. Lianor's hands found their purpose. By the second year the loneliness had not disappeared but had been joined by something stronger: the certainty that she was where she was meant to be, doing what she was made to do.

She finished her training, and the hospital offered her a place on the ward. In her second year, the colonial governor's office announced a new honor: a distinction, granted in the Queen's name, to recognize exceptional skill and compassion in the healing arts. Lianor's name was put forward. She didn't know what to do with the attention. She put the letter in a drawer and went back to the ward.

But the letter traveled further than she did. A teaching hospital in England read the citation and wrote to her. They were studying the diseases that ate from within and they were recruiting healers who had shown not only aptitude, but the willingness to sit with what could not be fixed.

She sailed in autumn.

***

The ward was on the third floor. Sixteen beds. Windows faced a courtyard where someone had planted roses that no one watered and that grew anyway, which Lianor took as a sign of something, though she was not yet sure what.

The work was different from anything she had done. In the northern colony, healing had been immediate — fevers broke, bones set, babies arrived. Here the answer was slower. Here the disease moved on its own schedule, and the work was not to cure — not always, not often — but to understand. To map the thing as it moved.

And she met Mrs. Fenn.

Eleanor Fenn was fifty-three. A seamstress whose body had begun to unstitch itself from the inside — breast first, then bones. By the time she arrived on the ward, the moving was done. She did not want pity. She said this on the first day with the economy of a woman who had measured cloth her whole life and knew exactly how much fabric a sentence needed. "I can see it in your face. You think you ought to save me. You can't. So we'll skip that part and get to the part where you're useful." The useful part was listening. Mrs. Fenn had no one left to tell her story to, and her story wanted telling. "The body is a garment," she said once, when the pain had retreated enough for metaphor. "Well-made, if you're lucky. But every garment wears. The seams go first. Then the fabric. Then you're left holding the thread and wondering where the dress went."

Lianor adjusted her morphine. She changed her dressings. She did the things a healer does when healing is no longer the verb — the smaller things, the holding things.

One evening Mrs. Fenn died quietly while Lianor was holding her hand. The hand relaxed and the breath stopped. Lianor sat with her for twenty minutes after, because her mother had sat with the dying and believed the sitting mattered, and this was the part she could not set down.

She stayed in England for two years. She learned that the gap between what medicine could do and what the dying needed was not a failure but a room — one that only certain people could enter, carrying nothing but presence and the belief that presence was enough. She sailed west.

***

The years between England and the harbor town left marks she did not show and Wry did not ask about. She had been hurt — not physically, or not only physically, but in the way that trust is hurt, which is the deepest way. The hurt had driven her not from faith but deeper into it. She was attending a small church in the harbor town when Wry walked in.

***

He was thirty. She was thirty-two.

He had come ashore carrying a back that hurt and a list of losses he was still learning to live with. He worked in a chandlery near the harbor — selling rope and pitch and sailcloth to the ships he wished he were sailing on.

They were two people leaning on the same God at the same time and did not yet know it. He had come to the church for the sermons. He had settled into the conviction that God had called him to be single for the rest of his life, and he was making peace with that. He was not looking for a woman. She was not looking for a man. She had closed those books.

They were an unlikely match; he was a kite, she was an anchor. What neither of them expected was joy. Not the loud kind — the quiet kind, the kind that arrives without announcement and sits in the room so naturally you don't notice it until it's been there for weeks.

He noticed her the way a man notices a fixed point in a room. She sat in the third pew. She didn't sing louder than she meant. She listened to the sermon the way she listened to a patient's breathing — with attention that was searching.

The pastor introduced them after the fourth week. Wry shook her hand and felt his own calluses against her palm — the hand of a sailor, weathered by rope and salt, meeting the hand of a woman who healed for a living. She didn't flinch from the roughness. She looked at him directly.

"You're a sailor," she said.

"Was," he said.

"That's not what your hands say."

They spoke after services. Then before services. Then on Wednesdays, then when neither of them could think of a reason to be in the same street, but both of them were.

He brought her fish. This was not romantic. It was practical — he had caught more than he could eat and she lived alone and fish does not keep. But she cooked it. And she invited him to eat it with her. She burned it. The rice stuck to the pot and the fish blackened on one side and the kitchen filled with smoke so she opened the window and they ate it anyway — the burnt fish and the crunchy rice — at her kitchen table in the evening light.

He did not complain and he did not leave. She told him later that this had been the test, though she had not planned it as one. If he had stayed for the cooking, she would have worried. He stayed despite it, and she knew.

"I have a daughter I do not see," he told her. "In France."

"I know. The pastor told me."

"What else did he tell you?"

"That you are stubborn. That your back is worse than you admit. That you're a dreamer. That you pray like a man who has recently learned how and is not sure he's doing it right." She paused. "I did not need him to tell me the last one. You hold the hymnal like it might bite you."

He laughed. It surprised him. She watched him laugh the way she watched everything.

Two months later he asked if he could court her. He used the word "court" because it was the word with weight.

"You may," she said. "But I will be slow."

"I have nowhere to be."

"That's not true. You have the sea."

"The sea will wait."

She looked at him for a long moment. The wonder of a woman who had decided, after years of evidence to the contrary, that it might be possible for a man to mean what he said.

"Then court me," she said. "And we will see what God does with it."

What God did with it took four months. Four months of walks along the harbor. Four months of meals at her table, and his. Four months of the gradual, careful, almost geological process of two people learning to trust each other with the parts of themselves they had learned to hide.

He proposed on the porch of her small house, in the evening, with no ring because he had not planned it — the words came out the way weather comes, not because he decided but because the pressure had built and the sky could no longer hold it.

"I want to build something with you," he said. "Not a ship. Not a voyage. A life. I want to wake up in the same place twice. I want to know where I'll be in a year. I have never wanted that before, and I am not young enough to ignore it."

"You are asking me to marry a man who belongs to the sea."

"I am asking you to marry a man who is learning to belong to the land."

"Those are not the same thing."

"No. They are not. But I am both of them, and I am asking."

She took his hand. She held it with the knowledge of what she was holding and the willingness to hold it anyway.

"Yes," she said. "But we will do it properly."

They went to the pastor. The pastor refused — six months was not enough. He counseled them to wait. He was not wrong. But he was not right either.

It was the captain of the ship Wry had sailed in on who married them. He was still in port, and he had the authority. The ceremony was simple. A spring morning in the harbor, the air carrying the sweetness of cherry blossoms from the trees that lined the waterfront, pink petals drifting on a light breeze that seemed to have arranged itself for the occasion.

When the moment came to place the band on Lianor's finger, Wry's hands — the hands that had never trembled on a line, not in gale, not in heavy seas — shook. Just once. Just enough for Lianor to feel and say nothing.

After, they walked along the harbor. Lianor took Wry's arm. Not because she needed steadying — but because the taking was its own language, and the language said: I am here. I choose this. The road ahead is not walked alone.

***

Gideon was born the following spring, in the small house near the water, delivered by a midwife Lianor had trained.

The early years were quiet ones. Wry sailed short runs. Lianor kept her practice in the harbor town. The boy grew between them — passing from his mother's hands to his father's ship and back again, learning the weight of both.

When Gideon was five, they bought the fifty acres on the volcanic island and Wry began building the cottage. When he was ten, they moved north to the harbor town, where Lianor became the community's only healer and Wry's runs grew longer.

The mountains changed her. Not her faith — the faith had been steady since China — but the shape of her days. She walked the ridgeline in the quiet hours with her Bible and her prayers and came home with the particular steadiness of a woman whose strength came from somewhere she didn't need to explain.

She prayed for Wry every day he was at sea — not the anxious prayer of a woman who fears, but the quiet prayer of a woman who trusts the God who goes before. She prayed for Gideon. For the daughter in France. And in later years, for the boy with the red hair who had appeared in Wry's letters like a character in a story she hadn't expected.

In the evenings, when the prayers were said and the fireweed was turning the hillside the color of a sunset that had decided to stay, she sat on the porch and looked at the mountains and waited. Not with anxiety. Not with longing. With the patience of a woman who had learned that the people you love come back when you've built a place worth returning to.

CHAPTER NINETEEN

Sword Play

It started with the children.

Kipp's harbor children — the network he'd built from bread and charcoal drawings — arrived at the Providence before dawn. Three of them running barefoot and out of breath. The girl with the scar reached the gangplank first.

"Men," she said. "Coming from the ridge. Lots of them. They've got the battery."

Kipp was on deck before she'd finished. He grabbed her shoulder — not rough, steadying.

"How many?"

"Twenty. Maybe more. The big one's with them — the one with the eye."

The battery — Fort Nassau's old gun emplacement on the ridge above the harbor. Three cannon that hadn't been fired in years but still commanded the anchorage. Whoever held the battery held the harbor. Every ship at anchor sat beneath those guns.

Kipp turned and ran for the companionway. "Captain!"

***

Having heard the commotion, Wry came on deck with the cutlass on his hip, the three flintlock pistols crossed in their leather rig against his chest, and the pain in his spine. He wore the look on his face that said the storm was here and the time for preparation was past.

Elias was already at his shoulder. The Bosun had slept in his boots, something he'd learned to do when the air tasted wrong, and the air had tasted wrong for a week.

"Thresh has the battery," Wry said. It was not a question.

"Aye. And we've got a problem below." Elias kept his voice for Wry alone. "Cutler's missing. Harkin and the Plymouth brothers too. They went over the side sometime after midnight. Quiet about it."

Rafe hadn't just left — he'd gone to Thresh. The hungry man and the enforcer, united by the only currency they shared: the understanding that the ledger had to be destroyed and the Captain had to fall.

"How many do we have?"

"Twenty-two who'll fight. Ortiz has a cleaver and opinions." A pause. "The woman won't leave the ledger."

"She shouldn't have to."

Wry's hand went to Grace. The silver was warm. The copper etching caught the first light.

"Gideon." His son was already there, standing at the rail, waiting.

"Take ten men. Circle through the market alleys and come up behind the battery from the east. Don't engage until you hear me."

"Hear what?"

"Something loud."

Wry turned to Elias. "Hold the ship. Send a runner to Brandy at the Blue Anchor. If this goes wrong, she gets Seraphine and the ledger to open water. That's the priority."

He held the Bosun's gaze. "Not me. Not the ship. The ledger."

Elias's jaw worked. He reached into his coat and held out the flask.

Wry shook his head. "After."

The Bosun pocketed it without comment.

"Kipp."

The boy was at the gangplank, bouncing on his toes, grinning like the morning was a gift he'd been expecting.

"Stay with Elias. Stay on the ship."

"Captain —"

"Stay. On. The ship."

Kipp's face fought a war between obedience and every instinct he possessed. Obedience won, but barely, and everyone who saw it knew it.

Wry took twelve men and went up the ridge.

***

Elias heard them before he saw them.

He was on the quarterdeck checking the stern lines when the sound came — not from the ridge where the Captain had gone, but from the water. Oars. Muffled, but not muffled enough. Six men in a longboat, pulling hard for the Providence's starboard side, the side that faced away from the harbor and away from the eyes of anyone watching the ridge.

Thresh hadn't sent all his men to the battery. He'd kept six in reserve. Take the ship while the Captain takes the bait.

Below, in the bow, Kipp sat cross-legged in a hammock with a strip of leather, a length of cord. His fingers worked the way they always worked — quickly, precisely, the cord feeding through the leather with the rhythm of a thing being born rather than made. He heard nothing — when Kipp's hands were busy, the world had to knock twice.

"Ortiz!" Elias's voice carried below without rising. The Bosun did not shout when shouting would give away the count. "Company. Starboard."

Ortiz appeared at the galley hatch with a cleaver in each hand and a look on his face that said the menu had just changed.

Two of Thresh's men never made the rail. Elias met the first at the gunwale with a belaying pin that put him back in the water before his second boot touched the deck. The second caught a coil of heavy line across the face, thrown with the arm that had hauled rigging for twenty years, and went over backward into the longboat with a sound like a sack of grain hitting a barn floor.

Four made it aboard.

They were dock muscle — the same breed as the men on the ridge, hired for size and willingness, not skill. But four men with blades on the deck of a ship held by a bosun and a cook is not a problem you solve with contempt.

Elias drew his cutlass. The first man came at him with more enthusiasm than sense, and Elias gave him the short lesson — parry, step, pommel to the jaw. The man sat down hard on the deck and stayed there. The second was better. He pressed Elias back along the rail with quick cuts that kept the Bosun's feet moving, and on the third exchange he found the angle and knocked the cutlass from Elias's grip. It skittered across the planking and came to rest against the capstan.

Elias stood disarmed, his back to the mast, the man advancing.

The cleaver came from the galley side of the ship. It crossed the full width of the deck in a spinning arc that caught the morning light in flashes — a wheel of steel turning end over end through the salt air. Cajun, who had been perched on the rail between the two fights with the detached interest of a theater critic, launched herself skyward with a yowl as the blade passed through the space her head had occupied a quarter-second before.

The cleaver hit Thresh's man between the shoulder blades with a sound that no one on the Providence would describe afterward and no one would forget. The force of it sent him forward and over the rail. He hit the water and did not come up.

"Mi cuchilla!" Ortiz roared from the galley hatch, shaking his fist at the harbor. "That was my best cleaver, you thieving son of a —" The rest was Spanish and unrepeatable and went on for some time. Two men remained on deck. They looked at each other. They looked at Elias, who was disarmed but did not look disarmed. He reached above his head, gripped the rim of the oak water barrel lashed to the mast — full, two hundred pounds if it was an ounce — and tore it free from its lashing with a sound of snapping rope and groaning wood.

He lifted it over his head. The muscles in his arms and shoulders stood out like cables drawn taut on a winch. He held it there for one breath — long enough for both men to understand what was about to happen — and brought it down.

It caught the first man square on the head. The barrel shattered. The man and his companion went down in a cascade of oak staves and two hundred pounds of water that turned the deck into a shallow river. One lay motionless, blood threading through the water from his scalp. The other scrambled to his feet, howling like a whipped dog, and threw himself over the rail.

Kipp came up the companionway into the light. He stood in the hatch with the leather sling dangling from one hand, blinking at a deck he did not recognize — two inches of water, oak staves everywhere, a man face-down in the flood, and Elias standing over the wreckage breathing like a bull, his arms still raised as though the barrel were a ghost he hadn't finished putting down.

Two men remained in the longboat. They had watched the cleaver. They had heard the barrel.

Now they watched Ortiz emerge fully from the galley hatch with a second cleaver, a boning knife, and what appeared to be a large iron ladle, all held in two hands with the organizational fury of a man whose kitchen has been interrupted. Cajun landed on his shoulder, fur bristling, tail lashing, looking like the smallest and angriest figurehead ever mounted on a Spanish cook.

The two men in the longboat put their backs into the oars and pulled for open water as if the devil himself had offered to race them.

Elias stood on the deck in an inch of water, breathing hard, surrounded by the wreckage of one barrel, two men, and one longboat's worth of ambition. He looked at Ortiz. Ortiz looked at him. Cajun looked at both of them with the expression of a creature who had very nearly been decapitated by her own cook's cleaver and intended to add this to a list that was already long.

***

The path from the harbor climbed through scrub and coral rubble, steep enough to make Wry's back announce each step. He climbed anyway. The dawn was breaking over Nassau in colors that had no business being beautiful on a morning that was going to be ugly.

Thresh met them at the battery wall.

He stood on the parapet with the composure of a man who has already arranged the board. Behind him, twenty men — hired blades, the kind who appear when coin appears and disappear when it stops. Rafe stood at Thresh's right hand, knife drawn, his face carrying the expression of a man who has chosen and is not looking back. The scar on his cheek — Cajun's gift — caught the morning light.

And Cael. Towering behind them, still as the battery wall itself.

"Captain Slamyrbach." Thresh's voice carried down the slope — measured, rehearsed, every syllable placed. "You have something that belongs to my employer."

"Your employer's daughter isn't property."

"Everything is property, Captain. Some things simply haven't been appraised yet." Thresh's long fingers rested on the hilt of a sword that was too fine for a man who did someone else's killing. "The ledger. Bring it to me, and you may walk away with your crew, your ship, your life. My employer is a reasonable man."

"Your employer killed a man for a debt he forged. That's not reason. That's arithmetic with a body count."

Thresh's expression didn't change. "The offer expires with the tide, Captain. After that, the cannons speak."

The three guns sat in their emplacements — rusted, ancient, but loaded, the slow match coiled and ready beside each one. The Providence sat in the harbor below, directly in the line of fire.

"Rafe." Wry said the name past Thresh, as though Thresh were furniture. "You can still walk back."

Rafe met his eyes. Something crossed his face — fast, involuntary, then gone. "There's nothing to walk back to, Captain. There never was. You just couldn't see it because you were too busy building a family out of men who needed coin."

"Dench didn't think so."

Something moved behind Rafe's eyes — but he buried it before it could be named.

"Dench made his choice. I've made mine."

***

The fight began the way most fights begin — not with a signal but with a silence that broke.

Thresh's men came down the slope. Wry's men went up to meet them. Steel hit steel and the sound filled the morning. The birds fled the ridge. The dogs in the alleys below began to howl. Nassau had seen a thousand fights and would probably see a thousand more, so it barely looked up from its coffee.

The first pistol spoke before the cutlass. A man had circled wide to come in behind Dench — belaying pin raised, quiet about it — and Wry's shot took him in the shoulder and spun him into the dirt. Dench didn't turn. He didn't need to. The sound of the Captain's pistol behind him was a language he'd learned to trust.

The second pistol misfired. The flint sparked, the pan flashed, but the barrel did nothing — the damp morning air had kissed the powder and the kiss was fatal. The man coming at Wry didn't know it had misfired, and Wry didn't have time to explain. He threw himself sideways — the third pistol falling from its rig as he hit the ground The throw saved his life, but cost his back. Something shifted low in his spine — not the old wire but a new one, sharper — and his legs went uncertain beneath him.

The cutlass was already in his hand. He moved through the forms the teacher had built into him — the geometry of attack and retreat, the angles that open when an opponent overcommits, the spaces that close when patience holds. Grace and Harmony hummed on his thumbs. The blade sang. The rings answered his motive with warmth that spread from his hands through his arms to the center of his chest, and for a few minutes — three, maybe four — he was the man the teacher had made: still, centered, clean.

The first man came high and open and Wry took his wrist apart with a cut so short it barely traveled — a flick from the elbow, the blade rotating through the man's guard like a key turning a lock. The second came smarter, low and angled, and Wry gave him the parry the teacher called "the door" — accepting the force, redirecting it past his hip, then stepping through the space it left and putting the pommel into the man's jaw. The third came with a friend. Wry let them crowd each other. He dropped his weight, pivoted on the back foot, and the cutlass drew a single line across both men's reach — a stroke that started as defense and finished as a work of art. They fell in different directions, but one didn't rise. The coral rang under the dropped steel.

Then his back broke the contract.

It came — a seizure, a full lock, the wire across his spine pulling tight and then tighter and then past tight into something that turned his vision white and his legs into suggestions. The cutlass wavered. A hired blade saw the opening and drove forward. Elias wasn't there. Gideon wasn't there. The crew was fighting, scattered across the slope —

A rock hit the hired blade in the temple. Small, sharp, thrown with the accuracy of a boy who had been hitting things from a distance since he could hold a stone.

Kipp. He was halfway up the slope, barefoot on the coral, a sling in one hand — not the string, a proper sling fashioned from leather and cord in the hours he was supposed to be staying on the ship. He loaded and threw with a fluid economy of motion that suggested considerable practice. A second stone found a second man's knee. A third whistled past Thresh's ear and cracked the coral wall behind him.

"I told you to stay on the ship!"

"Aye, and the ship told me to come here! Yer back's gone, Captain. Let me be yer legs."

Wry found his footing, retrieved the cutlass from the dirt, and put himself back in line — damaged, leaning slightly, but upright. He was still standing and that's what mattered.

Suddenly, the sound changed. From the east side of the battery — the slope Thresh hadn't fortified because the approach was too steep — came the sound of men moving fast. Gideon's ten, arriving exactly where Wry had sent them, coming over the wall with a force that had been building in silence and was done with it.

Gideon came first. He fought his father's fight — the same geometry, the same patience, the same forms — but without the damage, without the wire in the spine. He fought the way Wry had fought at twenty-five: clean and fast and full of the particular fury of a young man protecting the people he loves.

Thresh's hired men broke. They had been paid for muscle, not loyalty, and the pay had not included the possibility that the target would hit back from two directions. They scattered — three dropped their weapons, two ran for the harbor, the rest followed in a rout that was as complete as it was sudden.

Rafe didn't run. He stood at the battery wall with his knife and his decision and watched his hired army dissolve around him.

Thresh didn't run either. He drew the fine sword. It cleared the scabbard with a sound that was almost musical. He advanced on Wry with the deliberate patience of someone who has closed accounts before and knows exactly how it is done.

Wry raised the cutlass. His back screamed. He held the blade steady.

The exchange was brief and brutal and very nearly equal. Thresh was skilled — more than skilled, technically excellent — and his reach was long and his sword faster than the cutlass. But Wry had thirty years of sea-fighting behind the blade, and thirty years of sea-fighting teaches things that expensive instruction does not: that a man fighting in pain fights smarter than a man fighting fresh because he cannot afford to be wrong. The rings on Wry's thumbs were warm with a heat that had never yet lied to him.

Steel met steel. Thresh probed. Wry refused the angles he was offered and made his own. The fine sword sought openings and found them closed. The cutlass sought the same and was turned. They circled on the coral in the growing light, two men who understood the same language and were arguing in it, and the argument was close.

Then Thresh found the back. He feinted left, drew Wry's parry, and stepped right into the space it opened — not a killing stroke but a shove, a shoulder into Wry's left side, calculated to catch the spine. It worked. Wry's vision went white. His legs betrayed him. He went to one knee on the coral and the cutlass dropped.

Thresh stepped back. He looked at Wry on the ground with an expression that held no pleasure — only the professional assessment of a man taking inventory.

"The girl or the gun, Captain," he said quietly. "Choose."

Cael chose for him.

The enormous man had been standing behind Thresh throughout the fight. He had not drawn a weapon, had not moved. He had stood like stone, waiting for the order that would send him forward.

The order came. "Cael. Finish him."

Cael looked at Thresh. He looked at Wry, on one knee with his spine broken and his blade in the dirt. He looked at Kipp, who stood ten paces away with the sling and a fresh stone seated and a face that held no fear — the same boy who had blinded his eye and fed him bread in the dark, whose courage made no sense and whose kindness made less.

The bread. The dock. The plate that Ortiz had set out without comment or ceremony, the same size as all the others. The first secret he had ever kept from Thresh.

Cael turned. Not toward Wry. Toward Thresh.

He stepped between them and filled the space the way he filled doorways: completely. He drew no weapon, spoke no word. His turned back said everything that needed saying.

Thresh stared. For the first time since the fight began, something moved behind his eyes that he hadn't planned for. A weapon he'd owned for years had just decided to be something else.

"Cael." The name was a command stripped down to its bones.

Cael said nothing.

Thresh calculated: the sword, the giant, the captain on one knee, Gideon's men on the wall, the hired muscle gone. The cannon loaded but useless — you cannot fire a cannon at a man standing three feet in front of you. The calculus was thorough, and the calculus was over.

He sheathed the sword. He turned and walked down the ridge toward the harbor. But his walk was not retreat, it was repositioning.

Wry watched him go. Rafe watched him go too. Then he drove his knife into the battery wall to the hilt and left it there. He looked at Wry. Not at Thresh's retreating back. Not at Gideon. At Wry. The look lasted two seconds and offered nothing. Then he walked down the ridge in the opposite direction from Thresh. No word. No backward look.

***

Wry stayed on one knee for a long time.

The rings cooled. The cutlass rested in the dirt. His back had made its decision, but he had not been consulted.

Gideon crouched beside him. "Can you stand?"

"Give me a minute."

"Take two." His son's hand was on his shoulder.

Kipp appeared. The sling was over his shoulder and his grin was where it usually was — from ear to ear.

“Told ye the ship sent me,” he said.

“The ship is wood,” Wry said. “It doesn’t send anyone.”

“Tell that to the parrot. He’s been screaming since ye left.”

And despite the pain, despite the morning, despite the blood and the cannon and the men who had gone, Wry laughed. It was short and it hurt and it was real, and the sound of it carried down the ridge to the harbor where the Providence sat waiting. When Elias heard it, his shoulders dropped a fraction, and he reached for the flask.

Cael stood at the battery wall. He had not moved since Thresh left. He looked at the Captain, at the boy, at the son. He looked at his own hands — the hands that had done Thresh’s work for fifteen years and had just, for the first time, done his own.

Then he looked at Kipp’s feet.

He walked to the boy. Kipp looked up at him — all the way up, the way you look at a cliff face or a mast or a thing that used to be terrifying and is now just very, very tall.

Cael bent down and lifted him effortlessly and set him on his shoulders the way a father sets his child.

Kipp grabbed a fistful of the giant’s hair for balance and laughed — surprised, the laugh of a boy who has just discovered that the monster under the bed is actually a very large chair.

“Yer tall,” Kipp said.

“Aye,” said Cael.

It was the most he’d said all morning.

They came down the ridge together — the giant and the boy, Gideon and his father behind them, the crew falling in around them all — and the morning opened over Nassau with the particular clarity that follows violence: every color sharper, every sound cleaner, every breath earned.

***

The Providence was waiting.

Cael came up the gangplank first, Kipp still riding his shoulders, the boy's bleeding feet leaving bright red polka dots on the giant's chest. The crew parted for them — not in fear but in the particular silence of men watching something they don't yet have a word for.

Wry came aboard last. He leaned on a length of broken railing he'd picked up on his walk from the battery, and on Gideon, and on the rail, and on whatever else would hold him..., and when his boots hit the deck he stopped.

The planking was wet. Not sea-spray wet — soaked, and pink in places where it had no business being pink. Splinters of oak lay scattered across the deck like the bones of something that had been broken with enthusiasm. A belaying pin rested against the scuppers, and it had not been there that morning.

Wry looked at the deck. He looked at Elias.

"Some sailors mistook the Providence for a good place to get a free lunch," Elias said. His voice loud enough to be heard on the docks.

Ortiz leaned in the galley hatch, arms folded, a cleaver conspicuously absent from his belt. "To my great dismay," he said, "they didn't want to stay for dessert."

Wry looked at Kipp.

Kipp shrugged from the height of Cael's shoulders. "Didn't see a thing, Cap'n."

And for once, the boy was telling the absolute truth.

Cael set him down on a tall crate. Kipp's feet were cut to ribbons. The coral was as sharp as broken glass, and the boy hadn't owned shoes in years. Cael unwound the sash from his waist — the wide cloth belt that had once held a scimitar — and tore it into strips without hesitation. He knelt and wrapped the boy's feet with hands that were enormous and surprisingly careful, the way a man handles something small that matters.

Kipp watched him work and said nothing, which was the rarest thing the boy had ever done. Ortiz watched from the companionway and also said nothing.

Wry made it to the quarterdeck. He lowered himself into the canvas chair.

Cajun was in the chair before he sat. She turned twice, settled into his lap, and began to purr with the self-satisfied authority of a creature that has never doubted its welcome. Cipher dropped from the yardarm to Wry's left shoulder and immediately began working at the silver earring as though confirming by feel that it was still there and still his.

The cat looked at Cipher. Cipher looked at the cat. For a moment, the old war flickered. Then Cajun put her head down on Wry's thigh. Cipher settled his feathers. No contest. Just two creatures who had spent a morning waiting for the one thing they agreed on to come home, and who were, for now, willing to share him.

"Idiots," Wry said. The word meant something else entirely.

When Cael finished wrapping his feet Kipp's eyes met his. Neither spoke, but the seed that had been planted took water. "Your eye hasn't healed yet," Kipp said. Then he pulled the sling off his shoulder and wrapped it around Cael's injured eye. "It just needs more rest."

"Aye," said Cael.

Kipp leapt up on the crate, planted his fists on his hips, and shouted so loud it sent Cipher retreating to the yardarm.

"Eyes steady!"

Only the wind replied. He motioned for Cael to stand, and when the giant rose they were face to face. Kipp looked into his one good eye, put his arm around the huge neck, and looked out at the crew.

Elias looked at Gideon. Gideon looked at the Captain. Wry squinted in the sunlight, a hint of a grin forming.

"Eyes steady," Elias said.

"Blades sharp," Kipp answered.

The crew found it. "Blades sharp."

Kipp looked at the Captain and winked. Wry stood from the chair — slowly, with the cane, with the cost — and looked at the boy.

"Hearts true," he said. Not a bellow. Just the words, spoken the way they were meant to be spoken. The harbor heard them anyway.

***

From below, the smell of Ortiz's cooking reached the quarterdeck — peppers, bread, coffee.

They gathered without being called. The table had enough food set out for all of them because Ortiz had heard the sound of hunger before anyone had walked through the door.

There was a plate at the end of the bench that hadn't been there before. Same size as the others. No comment. No ceremony. Just a plate.

Cael dragged a crate across the floor that should have taken two men, and sat down at the end of the bench and looked at it for a long time. Then he picked up the spoon.

Seraphine came from where she'd been with the ledger and helped Ortiz without a word — feeding people after a battle was its own kind of accounting. Every plate a line item, every equal portion a proof that the system held.

She set a plate in front of Gideon. Their eyes met across the table — not the careful, restrained look of before, but open. She smiled. He held the glance a beat longer than necessary. Then they both looked away, and the table pretended not to notice.

Elias held out the flask. Wry took it. One measure, as agreed. The rum was rough and warm and tasted like the end of something.

Kipp watched all of it from his crate — the Captain, Cajun, Cipher, the family at the table, the giant eating slowly at the far end, the glance between Seraphine and Gideon, Elias and the flask. His hands were still in his lap for once. The string was nowhere. He was composing, filing each detail with the patient precision of someone building a picture where there was no charcoal yet. He would find charcoal later. He always did.

Outside, the harbor went about its morning. The debt was still there — patient as Thresh had been patient, waiting for its own reckoning. But the ledger was safe, and the crew was fed, and the boy's feet would heal, and Cael was at the table.

For now, that was enough.

CHAPTER TWENTY

The Cannon's Answer

The harbor had gone copper in the late afternoon light, the water flat and still, the kind of stillness that doesn't last. Seraphine found Wry at the rail.

She carried the ledger under her arm the way she always carried it — close, guarded, the binding against her ribs. But her posture had changed since the morning. The composure was still there, the straight back, the gray-blue eyes that measured everything. But the measurement had arrived at a conclusion, and the conclusion was in her voice when she spoke.

"I am not sailing with you, Captain."

Wry looked at her. He had known this was coming. A woman who had spent three years building a system to replace her father's empire was not going to abandon it for a berth on a ship.

"The ledger needs to be here," she said. "In Nassau. In the hands of the merchants who will use it. If it sails away with you, it becomes a story. If it stays, it becomes a system." She paused. "Cael will stay with me."

"And Gideon knows?"

"Gideon knows."

Wry studied her — this woman had hit a man with a bottle in an alley, built a weapon out of arithmetic, and worn a dress she hated for three years because survival required it. His daughter's age, near enough. His daughter's stubbornness, exactly.

"You'll need more than Cael and a ledger."

"I'll need the merchants Ortiz has been talking to at the market. I'll need the harbor children Kipp organized. I'll need Brandy, who knows every ear in every wall." She met his eyes. "And I'll need your son to come back."

"He will."

"I know."

***

Cipher went rigid on his shoulder.

The macaw's claws bit through the mantle into skin. His feathers pressed flat against his body and his head turned hard toward the battery, one gold eye fixed on the treeline above the shore guns.

"Thresh," Cipher said.

Wry did not wait for a second opinion.

"Gideon." He kept his voice level. Gideon was already moving toward him from the foredeck after reading his father's posture. "Get her moving. Now. Every hand to sail."

Gideon's mouth opened and closed. He looked toward the battery, saw nothing yet, and trusted it anyway. He turned and his voice carried the length of the ship without shouting. "All hands! Make sail! Cast off all lines!"

Elias was at the bow. He threw the forward spring line off the bollard and shouted aft for someone to do the same at the stern. Two men scrambled to free the remaining lines while others ran up the ratlines. The Providence drifted from the dock, sluggish without canvas, her hull nudging the pilings as the land breeze pushed at her broadside.

Canvas dropped. The main topsail caught first, luffing and then filling as the evening breeze found it. The ship steadied and began to pull away from the wharf.

Too slow.

Wry turned the wheel and felt the rudder bite. The Providence swung her bow toward open water. Behind them, at the top of the rise where the battery sat above the harbor, figures moved between the cannons. He counted six, maybe eight. One of them was taller than the rest and moved with the quick, clipped stride of a man who believed himself in command.

Thresh.

The first cannon fired while the foresail was still being sheeted home. The sound rolled across the harbor flat and heavy, more percussion than explosion, and a column of water erupted thirty yards off the port quarter. Too far aft. They had not had time to aim.

"Hold steady!" Wry called to no one in particular. Everyone was already doing exactly what they should.

The second shot came faster. Thresh was driving his men. This one passed high overhead and Wry heard canvas tear — a ragged sound, brief and sharp, somewhere in the foretopsail. He glanced up. A hole the size of a man's head, nothing more. She would hold.

The Providence was finding her stride now. The land breeze was freshening as the day cooled, pushing them toward the harbor mouth as if the island itself wanted them gone. Gideon had every scrap of canvas drawing and the ship heeled gently to port, her wake beginning to hiss.

A third report from the battery. This one struck something. Wry felt it through the wheel — a shudder that traveled up from the starboard rail. He heard wood crack and a man cry out, not in agony but in alarm. Elias was already running toward the sound.

"Splinters!" someone called out. "Rail's gone amidship. Nobody down."

Wry let out a breath he had not been conscious of holding.

They were making the harbor mouth now, the headlands closing in on either side like the jaws of something that might still decide to bite. The fourth shot fell well short, skipping once across the surface and then sinking. They were pulling out of range.

Then the fifth deafening cannon fire, but it did not sound right.

The report was too loud and too brief, a flat crack instead of a boom, and it came with a secondary sound — a grinding, tearing noise that carried across the water. Wry turned to look. At the battery, smoke billowed sideways from one of the gun emplacements in a way that had nothing to do with a proper discharge. Men scattered from the position. One of them did not scatter. One of them was on the ground and others were pulling at him, dragging him back, and even from this distance Wry could see it was wrong. The barrel had burst or the charge had cooked off before the bore was clear.

Gideon appeared at his side. He was breathing hard from running the deck but his face was set.

"One of their guns let go," Wry said.

Gideon looked back at the battery, at the knot of men bent over the fallen gunner, and said nothing for a moment. Then: "We're clear. Open water in two minutes."

"Set a course south-southeast. We'll find a cove down the coast and see to the damage in the morning."

"The rail can be patched. Foretopsail has a hole but it's drawing fine."

"I know. I want a proper look in daylight."

Gideon nodded and went forward again.

The Providence slipped through the harbor mouth and into open sea. The last of the sunlight lay in a band across the water ahead of them, amber going to red, and the ship sailed through it and out the other side into the gathering dark. Behind them the battery had gone quiet. No more guns. Either Thresh had spent his ammunition, or the burst cannon had taken the fight out of his men, or both.

Wry kept his hands on the wheel. Cipher resettled on his shoulder, feathers loosening now, the tension draining out of him as the adrenaline subsided.

There was nothing behind them now that required the Captain's attention and everything ahead that did. Ahead lay the ship, the crew, the dark water, and the morning.

He turned the wheel a quarter point and held it there, and the Providence bore away into the night.

CHAPTER TWENTY ONE

Reckoning

They found the cove six miles south of Nassau, a shallow cut in the coastline sheltered by a limestone bluff on its western side. Gideon brought the Providence in under reduced sail and they anchored in three fathoms with the bow pointed toward open water. Nobody slept much. At first light Elias took two men aloft to inspect the foretopsail and Wry walked the starboard rail with Gideon, running his hands along the splintered section where the cannonball had struck.

The damage was manageable. A six-foot section of rail was shattered and the stanchions beneath it cracked but not severed. The foretopsail had a hole that could be patched at sea. Nothing that would slow them.

Thresh was gone. He'd left Nassau on a sloop that sailed with the evening tide, heading east, back to Amsterdam and the man who paid him. The battery gambit had failed. His borrowed crew was scattered, one of his own guns had burst, and he had nothing to bring Vark but a report of what hadn't worked. Nassau held no more use for him.

Rafe was gone. No one saw him leave. No one knew which ship he'd taken or which port he'd aimed for. He left no message, no explanation, no forwarding address. He left a knife driven into the battery wall and didn't come back for it. Harkin and the Plymouth brothers were gone with him, or gone separately — it didn't matter. The faction was dissolved.

***

They stayed in the cove to make repairs. The days that followed were days for counting. Counting the men who were still there. Counting the ones who weren't. Counting the cost, which was measured not in coin but in the things that had shifted — loyalties, positions, the geography of who stood where and what they were willing to stand for.

Four men gone, and the ship wore their absence the way a body wears a pulled tooth: the structure holds, but the gap is there every time you open your mouth. Harkin had been quick aloft — whatever else he was — and the rigging work that had been his now fell to men who were slower and knew it. The watches stretched. Men who had stood four hours now stood six.

Elias oversaw the repairs with the meticulous attention of a man who believes that a ship's condition is a moral statement, and the statement he intended to make was: we are not finished.

The second morning, Gideon found Elias on the foredeck before dawn, splicing a line that should have been spliced the day before by a man who was no longer aboard. The Bosun's hands moved with their usual precision, but Gideon noticed what he would not have noticed six months ago: Elias was slower. Not in his hands — in his shoulders. In the half-second pause where a man gathers the energy for the next thing. Elias was pulling double weight and had been since the battery.

"I'll take the morning watch," Gideon said.

Elias didn't look up from the splice. "You stood the night watch."

"I'll take the morning watch," Gideon said again.

Elias looked up then. What he found in the younger man's face was not pity, which he would have refused, but the simple math of a ship that needed more hands than it had and a First Mate who understood that the math started with him.

"The longboat needs a look," Elias said. "She was taking water yesterday." Which was the closest he'd ever come to saying thank you, and both of them knew it.

Kipp noticed the gaps too. On the second evening he moved from his usual spot at the edge of the group to the middle of the bench, closing one of the gaps with his body so the gap would no longer be the first thing you saw.

***

On the evening of the third day, Wry called them together.

They gathered in the galley — the same table, the same plates, the same equal portions. Ortiz started them off with coffee and bread but didn't sit down, because there was never time to sit when there was food to manage.

Before the crew gathered, Wry had gone below alone to the sea chest that sat beneath the stern windows. He knelt. The kneeling cost him.

He lifted the lid, removed the charts, the rolled leather, the navigational tools. He found the seam in the grain — invisible unless you knew where to press — and lifted the false bottom.

Gold coins, mostly. Some silver. A few small stones from the Orient that caught the lamplight. A captain's share — years of it, voyage after voyage. The second share he was entitled to, set aside instead of spent, every time.

He counted out a share for Dench — enough to buy land, build a house, bring a wife and two boys from Plymouth. He wrapped it in oilcloth and placed it in a leather pouch.

He replaced the false bottom. He closed the lid. He pressed both palms flat against the chest — the old gesture, the covenant. The chest was lighter now. Not empty. Lighter.

He put the pouch in his coat and went to the galley.

***

Wry stood at the head of the table. Gideon was seated at his right, and Seraphine to his left. The ledger lay on the table in front of him.

"The debt is dead," he said. "It was never mine. The signature was forged by a man now buried in a harbor he never should have drowned in. The number — five hundred and eighty-nine pieces of eight — was a fiction, enforced by a banker who deals in other people's chains. The debt is not reduced. It is not forgiven. It is not deferred. It does not exist — it never existed. And any man, merchant, or magistrate who claims otherwise will answer to this crew, this ledger" —

He slammed his left hand down on the ledger. A puff of dust rose from the pages. The gold ring on his pinky glowed softly.

He looked around at the faces. "...and every name recorded in it."

Wry looked at Seraphine. "Nassau is yours now — not your father's. The ledger stays with the woman who built it. The system will take root because the men at this table will carry it into every port they sail to, and the merchants who see it work will want it for themselves."

Seraphine inclined her head — the small, exact gesture of a woman receiving an acknowledgment rather than an instruction.

He looked at Cael, who sat enormous and silent at the end of the bench, his plate clean. "You stay with her. Not because you're the biggest thing in Nassau — because you chose." Cael matched his gaze, but didn't speak.

"On that ridge, when Thresh gave the order, you chose. A man who chooses once can be trusted to choose again."

Cael nodded. Slow, but the weight of it showed.

Seraphine looked at Cael. Something passed between them — not warmth, not yet, but the recognition of an arrangement that would, over time, become something neither of them had a name for. She had the ledger. He had the shoulders. Together they would be difficult to move.

"The repairs are made. We're going home. All of us. The ship is taking me north, to Lianor, to the mountains." He turned to Gideon. "And then the Providence comes back. With a new captain at her helm."

Gideon didn't speak. His hand went to his earring — the old gesture — and stayed there.

"You've earned her," Wry said. "Not by blood — by work. She's a good ship. She needs a captain who'll keep her honest. That's you."

The table was still. Elias straightened at the hatch and said, in the voice he used for weather and for truth:

"Eyes steady."

"Eyes steady," the crew answered.

"Blades sharp."

"Blades sharp."

Wry let the breath go. He looked at his son. His voice was not loud.

"Hearts true."

"Hearts true," the crew said.

Gideon did not lower his hand from the earring. He did not need to. The ship was his.

"And the crew?" he asked.

"Elias is your First Mate."

Elias's arms unfolded. The jaw loosened a fraction. "Someone's got to check the joinery."

"Ortiz stays with the ship. The crew stays. Kipp stays — he sails with you." Wry looked at the boy. "If you want."

"I want."

"You'll work. You'll learn. You'll stop stealing apples."

"I'll work and I'll learn. The apples I make no promises about."

The table laughed. Even Elias. Even Cael, who produced a sound like a boulder shifting in a riverbed that was, upon examination, a laugh.

Wry looked at Dench. The gunner with the bad knees sat with his hands around his coffee.

"When we arrive, Dench stays in the north."

The table went quiet. Dench looked up.

"Your knees are done with the sea. Your wife deserves a husband who comes home and stays home. Lianor needs help — the town is growing, the work is more than one healer can manage. You're steady, you learn fast, and you've got hands that can do more than clean a gun." He paused. "Write to your wife. Tell her to bring the boys. There's land. There's work. There's a woman who'll teach you what she knows, and what she knows can keep a family fed for the rest of your life."

Dench's hands were still around the coffee. They weren't shaking now.

"Aye, Captain," he said.

Wry reached into his coat and set the leather pouch on the table. It landed with the sound of coin.

"Every captain takes a double share," Wry said. "That's the custom. But this ship doesn't follow that custom. Every voyage, my second share went into a fund — held in trust for the men who sailed with me. For the day a man's knees give out" — he looked toward Dench — "or his family needs him home."

He looked around the table. "In that fund is your money. Earned by me, set aside for you. Every man at this table has a share waiting."

He lightly tossed the pouch to Dench. It landed with weight. "This is yours. You've sailed long enough and given enough. Take it home to your boys."

Dench looked at the pouch. He didn't touch it. "You took the same share as us," he said. "This whole time."

"Lianor and I don't need more. We never did."

The table was quiet. Rafe had shouted about pensions. What he didn't know is that the Captain had been building one the whole time, quietly, without a word.

Ortiz wiped his eyes with the back of his wrist and blamed the peppers.

Dench picked up the pouch. He held it against his chest. His jaw worked once. "My boys," he said. "They don't know what their father looks like anymore."

"Then go fix that," Wry said.

Elias cleared his throat. The crew shifted. Something was happening that Wry had not been told about.

Ortiz reached beneath the bench and produced a length of dark wood, wrapped loosely in sailcloth. He set it on the table with the care of a man presenting a dish he has spent a long time preparing.

"From the crew," Elias said. "All of us."

Wry unwrapped the cloth. A cane. Dark hardwood, straight-grained, the shaft polished to a warmth that caught the lamplight. The handle was carved — simple, functional, shaped to fit a grip. He turned it in his hands. It was well-made and thoughtful.

"It came down to the ship the morning of the battery," Elias said. "We'd had the carpenter restoring it for a fortnight. The boy carrying it took one look at the cannon smoke and set it inside the companionway, then ran for cover. It sat there through the fight."

A cane, and a cane was what a man with a broken back needed — and the crew had seen the need before he had admitted it, and had acted before they'd been asked.

"It's a fine stick," Wry said. "Thank you."

"Twist the handle," Kipp said. The boy was grinning wide enough to split.

Wry looked at him. He looked at Elias, whose face betrayed nothing. He looked at Ortiz, who was studying the ceiling.

He twisted the handle. It turned a quarter rotation and released with a click, and the blade slid free of the shaft with a whisper that filled the galley like a held breath.

Damascus steel. The blade caught the lamplight and broke it into patterns — the layered ripple of metal folded and folded again, hundreds of times, centuries of tradition hammered into a single edge. It was slender, light, alive in his hand in a way that only steel of this quality could be. The edge was so fine it disappeared when he turned it sideways.

The galley went quiet. Wry held the blade and did not speak. His thumb found the flat and ran along the pattern the way a man reads something in a language he learned long ago.

"Where did you find this?" His voice had changed.

Elias did not answer at once. When he did, his voice was lower than it had been all evening.

"It was my father's," he said. "Came off a ship out of the east when I was a boy. He carried it most of his life. I carried it after him. No son to pass it to, no brother left to mind it. A blade like that doesn't want a shelf. It wants a hand."

He looked at Wry.

"I thought a long while about whose hand it would fit. It wasn't a hard thought in the end."

Wry slid the blade back into the shaft. The click of it seating home was small and final. He set the cane on the table and looked at it — not as a cane anymore, not as a gift, but as the last weapon he would carry, made by hands that understood what his hands had learned on a mountain a lifetime ago.

"It's not a stick," he said.

"No, Captain," Elias said. "It's not."

Wry looked at him across the table. Twenty years of shared watches and unspoken reckonings. There was nothing left to say that hadn't been said by the gift itself.

Seraphine sat with her hand resting on the closed ledger. For a moment — so brief she might have imagined it — the leather under her palm felt warm. The ledger's work was not finished. But its survival was assured.

***

In the days that followed, Wry spent most of his time in his chair on the quarterdeck. His back had locked after the battery fight and showed no interest in unlocking. The cutlass was conspicuously absent. The cane rested against the back of the chair. For the first time in years the scabbard did not hang at his hip, and the men who noticed said nothing, because the absence said enough.

In the privacy of his cabin, in the small hours when the ship was quiet, he taught himself to draw the Damascus blade from the shaft with the same fluid motions the teacher had trained into his hands with the cutlass — the same geometry, the same economy, the wrist rotating through the twist of the handle and the thin sword clearing the shaft in a single stroke. The blade was shorter than the cutlass. It was there just in case, and just in case was a country Wry Slamyrbach had lived in long enough to keep a residence.

Cajun stayed in his lap. Cipher stayed on his shoulder.

***

The repairs took two more days. On the third evening the Providence weighed anchor and left the cove, sailing north along the coast under reduced canvas. No lanterns on deck. Gideon worked the ship by the stars and the moon and the shape of the shore he'd been studying for weeks. They rounded the headland south of Nassau two hours before midnight and struck sail half a mile from the harbor mouth, drifting on the tide until her anchors held in six fathoms of dark water.

She was close enough to see the town's lamps scattered along the waterfront. She was far enough that no watch on the quay would see her.

***

Seraphine was at the starboard rail, the ledger under her arm. She was looking at Nassau the way a woman looks at a house she has chosen.

Gideon came up beside her. He did not speak for a long moment. The ship rocked gently under them. Somewhere in the rigging a block creaked, and somewhere below a man laughed in his sleep.

"You're coming back," she said. Not a question.

"I'm coming back."

She turned to face him. "Promise me with something other than words."

He reached for her hand. She let him take it. The touch was the first — the first time skin met skin between them, no ledger, no numbers, no pretense. His hand was rough. Hers was small and cool.

"I'll come back," he said.

"You'd better. I'll have the books ready for audit."

***

They brought the skiff alongside in the last of the dark. Cael went down first, the boat shifting under his weight and steadying again. Seraphine came to the rail last. She had wrapped the ledger in oilcloth and tied it with sailor's twine. A shawl was drawn close about her shoulders against the pre-dawn chill. She paused at the top of the ladder.

Gideon stood across from her. Neither of them spoke. He did not touch her. He did not need to. The hand on the rail and the hand on the rail were close enough that the ship's breathing moved them together.

She went down the ladder.

***

Gideon stood at the starboard rail and watched.

The eastern sky was not yet light, but the dark had softened — that particular grayness that precedes dawn by perhaps a quarter hour, when the moon is setting low over the water and casting a silver road across the harbor. The skiff pulled away from the Providence's hull. He could make out Cael at the oars, huge and steady, the slow rhythm of the stroke. He could make out the small shape seated behind the giant — wrapped in the shawl, the book held against her chest the way a child is held.

His hand found the earring. The silver was cool.

He did not look away.

***

Seraphine sat in the stern of the skiff. Cael pulled in long even strokes and the water whispered against the hull and the ledger was heavy against her ribs and the ledger was warm.

She watched the Providence.

The ship was already beginning to grow smaller. Her sails were going up one by one — foresail first, then the main, then the topsails, pale against the dark water, catching the first hint of the east. Men moved in the rigging. She could not see their faces. She could see Gideon at the rail.

The ship turned her bow north. The sails filled. She leaned into the wind and began to move — slowly at first, the way large things begin to move, and then with the steady gathering pace of a vessel finding her heading.

Seraphine held the ledger. Her eyes did not leave the Providence until the hull had shrunk to a silhouette against the brightening horizon and the silhouette had shrunk to a shape and the shape had shrunk to a point of sail.

Then the sun came up over Nassau. Gold spilled across the water between the skiff and the ship. The point of sail caught the light, held it for a breath, and slipped past it into the north.

Cael pulled the oars. The harbor drew close.

Seraphine wiped her face once with the edge of the shawl, and did not do it again.

CHAPTER TWENTY TWO

The Grand Banks

The voyage north began in silence.

Not the tense silence of men who had something to say — the spent silence of men who had said everything and done everything and were now, for the first time in weeks, allowed to do nothing but sail. Nassau shrank behind them. The harbor, the battery ridge, the rooftops and masts — all of it flattened into a line, then a shadow, then a memory. Gideon stood at the helm and watched it go and did not look back after the last rooftop vanished, because a captain who looks back is a captain who hasn't committed to the heading.

He gave the first order that was entirely his own somewhere north of the Bahama banks, where the Gulf Stream swung east and the shoulder of the continent tilted away.

"North," Gideon said. "We ride the Stream."

Elias nodded. He didn't add anything. The nod was the test — not of the heading, which was sound, but of the space between the order and the response. A first mate who hesitates teaches the crew to hesitate. Elias did not hesitate.

Wry heard the order from the quarterdeck chair. He said nothing. Cajun was in his lap. The cane rested against the chair within reach. His thumb found Grace and turned it once, the old habit, and the silver was warm.

***

The Caribbean fell away over three days. The water changed — turquoise to green to a deep Atlantic blue that held no bottom and gave no comfort. The Stream took them up the long shoulder of the continent, a warm river inside the cold sea, carrying the ship faster than the wind alone could explain. Cape Canaveral passed in the distance to port, a low green smudge seen only by the lookouts. The Carolinas after that. The Chesapeake. Names on charts, coastlines the crew heard of but did not see, because the Stream ran wide of the shore and Gideon held her to it.

A merchant brig crossed their wake on the second morning, northbound out of Charleston with a high deck-load under canvas. Sails full, bow clean, making for Boston or Halifax. She saw them, made her colors, and went on. Kipp watched her go with the interest of a boy who had never seen so many ships pass on open water.

Wry watched too. From the chair at first. Then he rose — slowly, the cane under his right hand — and went to the starboard rail. The merchant was already a shape against the northern haze. Wry's other hand found the rail. He stood there for a long minute, looking at water he had sailed before. Not speaking. Not explaining. Just reading the blue and the green of it, the way the Stream ran against the wind, the tilt of the light on the swell.

He had been a younger man when he'd last seen this water. He had been a father then too, but a different kind. The kind that believed the sea gave back more than it took.

He did not say any of this. He turned, found the cane under his hand again, and went back to the chair. Cajun waited.

From the foremast crosstrees, Kipp watched his Captain cross the deck. He did not draw the moment. He held it. Some things were not for charcoal.

***

Kipp spent the first week learning to be crew instead of passenger. The boy who had vaulted coils of rope on the Nassau docks discovered that a ship at sea demanded a different kind of agility — not the quick, instinctive movement of the streets but the repetitive labor of a vessel that needed every hand pulling in the same direction. He hauled lines. He scrubbed decks. He climbed the ratlines for the first time and froze halfway up, clinging to the shrouds with his eyes shut and his knuckles white, until Elias's voice reached him from below — calm, unhurried:

"Look at your hands, not the water."

Kipp looked at his hands. His hands were holding rope. Rope was something he understood. He climbed.

By the third day aloft he was faster than the older hands. By the fifth he was racing them, and Elias had to tell him twice to stop showing off because showing off in the rigging was how boys became memories.

The string came out at night. He sat on the foredeck after his watch, cross-legged, knotting and unknotting in the dark. But the knots were changing. The patterns his mother's hands had made were becoming something else. Sailor's knots. Bowlines, clove hitches, sheet bends. His fingers absorbed them the way they absorbed everything — by repetition, by feel, by the understanding that a knot is a knot whether it's made of wool or hemp or string, and the hand that knows one knows them all.

Ortiz fed him double portions and didn't mention it.

***

The water grew colder as they moved north. It happened by degrees, each day a fraction cooler than the last, until one morning Kipp came on deck and his breath made a cloud and he stood staring at it with the baffled delight of a boy who had lived his whole life in the tropics and had just discovered that air could be seen.

"That's nothing," Dench said. "Wait till the Banks."

The word moved through the crew the way weather moves through rigging — a vibration, a tightening. The Banks. The Grand Banks. Where the Labrador Current ran cold out of the north and met the Stream coming warm out of the south, and the two of them argued in fog that could stand on its own, over shoals that would take a ship down in clear water. Men who had crossed them once spoke of them the way veterans speak of battles that should have killed them.

Most of the crew had never seen the Banks. Gideon had not. Elias and Wry had, twice, and the second time had cost them a spar and a man and a year of Wry's back.

***

“How bad?” Gideon asked his father.

They stood at the chart table in the Captain’s cabin, the coast of the American continent unrolled beneath the dividers and the eastern edge of the chart disappearing into the blank where the cartographers had written Banks in a hand that did not invite questions.

“Bad enough. You’ll remember. Not bad enough to kill us if you sail it right.” Wry set the dividers down.

“I don’t remember,” Gideon said.

Wry looked at him. “You were four. You were under a tarp with your mother below. Elias was at the foremast and I was at the wheel and we went into a nor’easter that had no business being where it was, because a nor’easter in August is a thing the sky doesn’t usually permit, and the sky that year was in a mood to make exceptions.”

“You sailed us through.”

“I sailed us into it. That was the wrong call. Elias will tell you so if you ask him and you might have to ask him twice because he’s too polite to volunteer it.” Wry’s hand rested flat on the chart. “I turned us into the teeth of it because I thought I could outrun the southern edge and meet the Stream on the far side. I couldn’t. We lost the mizzen topgallant. We lost a man named Hollis who was a better sailor than I deserved. We lost your mother’s trust for a month and I earned it back by telling her the truth of what I’d done, which is the only way trust is ever earned back.”

Gideon did not speak.

“I’m telling you this now because the Banks are ahead and you will be tempted to make the same call I made. The fog will come down and the wind will shift and the shoals will be close and the Stream will be inviting and you will think you can thread it. You can’t. No man can. You sail wide. You sound. You trust the lead more than the chart because the chart is a hope and the lead is a fact. You keep the ship south of the shoals and you let the fog have the north.”

“And the fog?”

"You'll lose sight of your own bow. You sail by lead and log and the taste of the water. The Labrador runs cold enough to drop the fog even in summer. In October it's worse. Sometimes the fog breaks on a mountain. The mountain is white. You steer away faster than you think."

"Ice."

"Ice. Strays off the Labrador. Most of them won't be there. One of them will. That's the one you sound for."

Gideon studied the chart. The blank space where the Banks lay. The cartographer's hand. The dividers resting where his father had set them down.

"How long?"

"Could be three days. Could be three weeks. The Banks decide."

"I'll sail wide."

"Aye," Wry said. The word carried more than agreement.

***

The storm came on a morning when the sky was the color of lead and the barometer had been falling since midnight.

Gideon had been at the helm for six hours. The chart was in his head now. Wide of the shoals, south of the tail, the lead going every hour and the lead coming back with bottom that said Banks in the feel of the sand on the tallow.

The fog came first. It came out of the north like a wall, gray and soft and total, and it swallowed the foremast before the lookout had finished calling it out. The world closed to the length of the ship. Then to the length of the quarterdeck. Then to the wheel and the man holding it and the two faces nearest — Elias at his right hand, Wry in the chair at the aft rail with Cajun in his lap and Cipher wedged against his shoulder and the cane across his knees.

Then the wind hit. It came from the northeast, proper to the storm Wry had named, and it backed around quarter by quarter as the front rolled over them. The sea came up under it with the short steep chop of water arguing with itself, the Labrador Current running cold out of the north and the Stream pushing warm from the south and the waves stacking sharp between them. The Providence rose and fell and rolled and rose again, moving in three dimensions at once as the currents argued over which way she should go.

"All hands," Gideon called. His voice carried the way his father's carried — not by volume but by clarity.

The sails came down to storm canvas. The hatches were battened. Ortiz secured the galley and made cold biscuit for the crew because there would be no fire until the Banks were behind them. Dench checked the gun lashings with his bad knees and his steady hands.

Rain came first. Then sleet. Then a hybrid of the two that stung the skin and froze on the rigging and turned the ropes into bars of ice that cut the hands of any man who gripped them.

Kipp's hands bled. He didn't mention it. He hauled the lines with the rest of them, his small body low to the deck, the wind trying to peel him off the ship. He had no gloves. None of the Caribbean men did. They worked with bare hands on frozen rope and learned what cold meant, and cold meant that your fingers stop telling you things. When your fingers go silent you hold tighter, because holding is all you have left.

Gideon held the helm. The wheel fought him the way it had fought his father in the first storm. His arms burned, his shoulders burned. His back held.

He thought of his father — not for guidance, for comparison. His father had held this wheel through worse, with a spine that was failing and a body that was breaking, and he had held it because holding was the decision and the decision had to be made fresh every minute.

Wry sat in the chair. His hand found Grace. His thumb turned the ring once, slowly, and the silver held the warmth of a thing that had ridden a pulse for forty years. He closed his eyes. He was not sleeping. He was listening. The shape of the wind was a shape he knew. The sound of the sea under this hull in this kind of water was a sound he had heard before, in a month that should not have carried it, from a wheel he had held with a younger back.

He did not speak. He did not open his eyes. His hand stayed on Grace.

Cajun burrowed deeper into his coat.

Elias was everywhere. He checked lashings that Harkin would have checked. He tested lines the Plymouth brothers would have tested. He called Gideon "Captain" once during the worst of it — not a question, not a test, just the word, spoken into the wind near the helm, and the word landed the way it was meant to land: as a fact.

***

The Banks took two days.

Two days of gray water and gray sky and gray fog so thick that men at the foremast could not see the quarterdeck. The lead went every half hour in the worst of it — Dench and two hands hauling the line, calling the soundings to Gideon through the wall of fog. Thirty fathoms. Twenty-eight. Twenty-five. The numbers coming up small and the ship holding her heading wide of them and the dividers in Gideon's head keeping pace with the lead.

No one slept. No one ate anything but cold biscuit and water. The men discovered that the Banks were a different kind of enemy — one that could not be beaten, only outwaited, because the Banks did not care whether the ship survived and the ship could not argue with something that did not care.

They cleared the Tail of the Banks on the second evening.

The wind dropped. Not gradually — it fell away as though someone had closed a door, and the silence that followed was so sudden and so complete that men stopped what they were doing and looked at each other, because the absence of the thing that had been trying to kill them was harder to trust than the thing itself.

The fog thinned an hour later. Then broke. Then lifted off the water in long pale rags that drifted east on a wind they could no longer feel. The stars came out — the northern stars, bright and cold and higher in the sky than any of the Caribbean men had ever seen them.

The open sea opened ahead of them. Dark water, deep water. The air was cold but the wind was manageable and the swell ran long and clean from the east, and the Providence settled into it with the grateful silence of a ship that has been tested and has passed.

Gideon's hands were still on the wheel. His knuckles were white. His arms were shaking. He looked at Elias.

"You can let go now, Captain," the First Mate said.

Gideon let go. Elias took the wheel. And Gideon stood at the helm of the Providence and felt, for the first time, the exhaustion of a man who has held something important through something terrible and has not let go.

***

Wry was in his chair. He had not moved from it for two days. Cajun was in his lap, her claws dug into his coat, her dignity shattered by forty-eight hours of being a cat in a corkscrew. Cipher had wedged himself between Wry"s shoulder and the chair back and had not emerged since the first swell hit, which was the longest the bird had been silent since Nassau.

Gideon turned from the wheel.

His father was looking at him. The blue eyes held the blue eyes. Neither man spoke. Whatever Gideon had been going to say sat unspoken in his throat, and whatever Wry had been going to say sat unspoken in his, and between them ran a current that needed neither.

Wry rose from the chair. Slowly. With the cane under his right hand. Cajun slid to the deck and stood indignant.

He crossed the space between them. Three steps, maybe four, the cane marking the time.

His hand found Gideon's shoulder. It rested there — weathered, scarred, the rings dull in the starlight, the grip not firm and not loose but simply present, the way a father's hand is present when a father has nothing left to teach and nothing left to withhold.

He held it for a breath. Then a second breath. Then he turned and went back to the chair.

Cajun climbed after him.

CHAPTER TWENTY THREE

Fog and Bones

Dawn came up clean.

A long, spent swell ran east — water that settles under a ship after a bad night. The Providence moved through it with the ease of a vessel that had been pushed to her edge, had found it, and had come back. Cajun was on deck again, stalking nothing with great dignity. Cipher was muttering on the yardarm — a low, private syllable, then another, the beginning of a bird finding his voice after two days of silence.

Gideon stood at the quarterdeck rail. Elias was at the wheel. The watch had changed once without Gideon noticing, which was the first time in weeks he had let the ship's clock slip past him without correction.

Wry came up from below. The cane first, then the man, then Cajun sliding past both of them to return to her rightful chair. He stood a moment at the hatch, breathing air that was cold and clean and did not smell of fog.

He crossed to the rail. He set his free hand next to his son's on the wood.

"The wide line worked," Gideon said.

"Aye," Wry said. "It usually does."

Elias, at the wheel, did not turn his head. But the corner of his mouth moved half a degree.

The ship ran east of north through the long morning. The swell eased. The wind held. The crew moved through the work of recovery — coiling line that had frozen and thawed and been fought with, checking lashings, replacing rope that had bled during the night. Dench inspected the gun stops and made small marks on a slate in a hand that only he could read. Ortiz got his fire back. The galley stovepipe gave up its first thin thread of smoke since the first swell of the storm, and the smoke rose straight and gave Gideon something to look at that was not the horizon.

***

Kipp drew.

He drew in the middle of the day, which was new for him. The drawings usually came at night, after the watch, on the foredeck with the string beside him and the charcoal resting on a folded scrap of sailcloth. Now he drew in the open light, because the light was finally generous enough to draw in and because the boy who had climbed the ratlines at the Banks had come down a different animal.

He drew the crew one by one. Ortiz at the stove, a copper pan in one hand and a wooden spoon in the other, his face half-turned to Kipp with an expression that was not a pose and not a smile and was the face Ortiz made when he was about to tell someone they were skinnier than their mother would have liked. Dench asleep against a coil of line, his bad knees stretched out, his face turned toward the weak sun, a scrap of sailcloth pulled across his chest. Elias at the rail — the jaw set, the eyes on the water, the First Mate's stillness that was not rest but a gathered readiness. Wry in the chair, always in the chair, with Cajun and Cipher and the cane in his grip and the not-smile that Kipp was getting closer to capturing with every attempt.

On the third day the bird came.

It came out of the east, low over the water, white with black wingtips and a yellow head that caught the morning light. A northern gannet. Its wingspan was wider than a man was tall. It rode the wind without a beat, turned once around the Providence as if measuring her, then settled into a station fifty yards off the starboard quarter and matched her speed.

The Caribbean men had never seen one. They watched it in silence, because the bird was bigger than their words for birds and their words would have lied about the size.

Kipp drew it. He drew the wingspan and the hook of the head and the solemn yellow crown. He did not get it right. He drew it again. The second was closer. The third he kept.

"Lonely-looking thing," Dench said.

"She's not lonely," Ortiz said, from the galley door. "She's scouting. Somewhere ahead of us there's more of her. They come from a place where the cliffs are white with them."

"You've seen it?"

"I've heard men who've seen it. They said they couldn't hear themselves think for the noise."

Kipp listened without looking up. His charcoal moved. The gannet held her station.

***

Land came on a gray morning — a darker line in the east at first, barely darker than the sea, and then the line rose into cliffs. Granite streaked with quartz. Black spruce running down to the waterline. Fog caught in the high valleys, breaking apart in patches as the sun rose.

Gideon held her close enough to read the shore and far enough to clear what the shore could hide. The chart in front of him showed a coast drawn by men who had drawn what they could see and left the rest honest — blanks marked bay and inlet where no inland reach had been surveyed, crosses where ships had been lost and the loss had been reported, thin hand-written letters spelling the names of coves a hundred years old and still in use.

They ran the coast for three days.

The water was dark in the lee of the cliffs, still as glass in the deep bays, broken only by the wake of the ship. Thin falls dropped from high ledges, silver threads against the black spruce, roaring only when the ship passed close. The cliffs rose in places so sheer that a man at the foremast could look up and see nothing but rock to the clouds. The silence between them had weight — not empty but full, the fullness of a held breath.

Kipp drew the coast. He drew it one headland at a time, and he did not finish it before the coast itself moved on.

The crew went quiet. Not cowed. Attentive. Caribbean men who had spent their lives on water that threw the sun back at them were sailing now through water that held it down. The green of the spruce was almost black. The granite was almost white. The world had sorted itself into contrasts a painter would have refused as too simple.

Wry stood at the rail more than he sat in the chair. The cane took his weight. Cipher rode his shoulder, quiet. Cajun stayed below.

***

They rounded a headland on the afternoon of the third day and the coast opened into a sheltered cove and the ruins were there.

No warning from the chart. The cartographer's hand had marked only *cove* and left the rest blank. The crew saw them together, in the order a man sees things he does not expect: first the shapes on shore, then the shapes as structures, then the structures as a purpose.

Stone tryworks collapsed into themselves. The fire-pits were still visible — circular, blackened, choked with grass. A timber-frame structure leaned against a rise of rock, three walls still standing and the fourth gone, its roof-beam punched through by a harpoon head that had rusted into the wood and become part of it. Behind the timber, a pile of bones as large as the cove itself. Vertebrae like wheels. Ribs like barrel staves. A jaw propped at an angle that suggested a man had set it there once for some reason, and the man had gone, and the jaw had stayed.

Gideon ordered the anchor down.

They lowered the boat. Gideon took Wry and Elias and Ortiz and two hands. Kipp came because no one said he could not. Wry with cane, moving slowly, was rowed into the cove with his son at the oar opposite Elias.

They walked the site.

No one spoke at first. The quiet had settled into the stones and the bones, and it was not going to move for the likes of them.

Ortiz crossed himself. He did it without performance, the way he did it in the galley when the soup had gone right. Dench, on the shore, had taken off his cap and was holding it against his chest.

Wry stopped at the timber. He put his hand on the harpoon. The iron was cold and rough with rust and still, under the rust, recognizably a blade. Whoever had driven it had driven it hard. It had not been pulled out because pulling it out had not been worth the trouble.

He moved on.

A stone slab was set into the ground near the tryworks. Square, flat, worked at the edges. Someone had carved marks across it in a hand no man aboard the Providence could read. Wry crouched — slowly — and looked.

The marks were in a language he did not know. That was certain. He ran his thumb across the first row. He did not know the letters or the shapes.

But he knew the layout.

Left column: short entries, spaced evenly. Middle column: numbers. Right column: totals, running down the slab and summed at the bottom in a mark that even in a language he could not read was unmistakably a line drawn beneath a figure.

A ledger. In stone. A tally of whales or barrels or oil or days, kept by men who had come from far enough away that their alphabet did not reach this coast, and kept carefully enough that the stone had been cut flat and the marks had been made in the right columns in the right order.

He looked at the stone for a long time.

Then he stood. The cane creaked. His back spoke.

"From long before our grandfathers," he said.

Elias, behind him, nodded once.

They walked back down to the beach.

Kipp stayed.

Kipp drew the bone pile. The proportions slightly wrong, the jaw tilted more than it was, the harpoon larger in the timber than it was in life. He drew the slab last, squared and honest, though he could not read a mark on it and did not try.

When Elias came up the beach to fetch him, the boy folded the drawings into his shirt and followed without a word.

The anchor came up on the tide. The Providence slipped out of the cove and the ruins slid astern and the coast took them back.

***

Two days after the cove, in a wide reach where the channel opened between two islands, the whales came.

They came up together, four of them, off the starboard quarter. Enormous. Longer than the Providence. Their backs broke the water with the slow roll of creatures who had no interest in hurrying, blue-gray in the morning light, the dorsal fins small and set far back on bodies that went on and on and on before the tails lifted and the tails went down and the dark water closed where the whales had been.

Ortiz crossed himself.

Kipp hung from the shrouds with his mouth open.

They surfaced again a minute later, in the same formation, closer. A spout rose twenty feet above the nearest one and stood in the air for a breath before the wind took it. The spout hung in the light. The water where the breath had been settled and flattened and was water again.

"Finners," Dench said, quietly. "Fin whales. I've seen one once. Never four."

One of the older hands — a man from Bridgetown who had sailed north with whaling fleets as a boy — nodded. "The big ones. Second-largest thing God made. The first is a blue whale and nobody aboard this ship has ever seen one and probably nobody ever will."

"How old does a whale get?" Kipp called down from the shrouds.

"Older than me."

"Older than the Captain?"

"Older than the Captain's grandfather."

The whales surfaced a third time, further off. Then a fourth, further still. On the fifth surfacing they were almost out of sight, a line of quiet backs moving east.

Wry watched them from the rail. His hand found Grace. He did not speak. What the Basques hunted were still here outliving the hunters.

He turned, and Gideon, at the wheel, saw his father's face and did not ask what the face had said.

***

The harbor town appeared on the morning of the sixth day.

They had come west out of the strait and into a wider reach, and the channel had opened out, and the coast on the starboard side had softened — granite giving way to lower hills, spruce mixed with pine and birch, a coast that had been lived on and was still being lived on. Smoke rose in thin threads from points on the shore. Someone burning a fire. Someone cooking. Someone home.

The outport was built into a cove where the shore bent east and a fresh-water stream came down between hills. Half a dozen houses. A long low building that was either a storehouse or a fish-curing station or both. Stages for drying cod built out over the shingle on spruce poles. Boats drawn up on the stones — small, open, clinker-built, the paint worn off to gray. A wooden chapel stood a little apart from the houses, its cross simple and weathered.

Gideon put the Providence in close, dropped anchor in eight fathoms, and lowered the boat. He took Wry with him. Elias. Ortiz.

Two hands for the oars. Kipp, because refusing Kipp was a thing no one had the energy for.

The shingle crunched under the bow.

A man came down from the houses. Past fifty, heavy-shouldered, a wool cap pulled low, hands that had mended a thousand nets. He stopped at the tide-line and watched them land without expression.

Gideon stepped out first. He raised his hands empty.

The man did not move.

Wry stepped down from the boat with Elias's help and his cane. He straightened, breathed once through the pain, and walked past his son to the tide-line.

He spoke in French.

Not ship French. Not trade French. The French of a boy who had grown up on a coast where French was the language of the fishmonger and the priest and the grandmother and the morning bread. It came out of him without thought, because the man at the tide-line had the face of a man who spoke French and the shingle under his boots had the feel of a shingle he had crossed as a child.

He gave his name. He gave his ship. He gave his errand — provisions, trade, nothing more. He asked the man's name with the courtesy of a guest asking a host.

The man's shoulders moved once — a small drop, the weight of a wariness held too long and set down. He answered. His French was not Wry's French. It was older in the bones, different in the cadence, a French that had left the old country a long time ago and had made its own way. But it was the same French, and the two men heard each other, and both of them knew they did.

His name was Théo. The town had no name on any chart and he did not offer one. He offered, instead, a hand.

Wry took it.

The trade was brief. Barrels of rum out of the Providence's hold. Two sacks of sugar. In return: salt cod, fresh bread, root vegetables that had come up out of the ground that week, a small jar of dark berry preserve Théo said would keep a man warm through a watch. Ortiz took the jar the way a priest takes a relic.

Kipp drew the outport.

He drew the stages and the boats and the chapel. He drew Théo — not from the front, from the side, the wool cap pulled low and the cheekbone catching the light. He drew an old woman at the chapel door who did not see him looking, her hands folded at her waist, her face turned toward the water.

Théo's wife came down from the nearest house with a small loaf wrapped in a cloth. She crossed the shingle without hurry. She held the loaf out to Wry with both hands, the way a loaf is held when it is a gift and not a sale.

"Pour la route," she said.

Wry took it with both hands. The bread was still warm.

He said thank you in French. The thank you came out in the French of the grandmother who had taught him to say it sixty years ago. Théo's wife heard it, and her face moved — not a smile, not yet — a recognition that a man whose grandmother had taught him in that cadence was a man whose people and her people had spoken to each other across a great deal of water once.

She went back to the house.

The chapel bell rang for evening while they were still on the shingle. It was a small bell. It carried across the cove the way small bells carry when there is nothing between them and the water — clean, thin, patient. It rang six times. The men at the stages stopped what they were doing. Théo uncovered his head.

Wry uncovered his.

The bell finished. Work resumed. The Providence rode at anchor in the cove and the bread was warm in Wry's hands.

They slept ashore one night in a lean-to Théo offered. They sailed with the tide the next morning.

Wry stood at the stern as the outport shrank. He watched it go the way a man watches a thing he has decided not to speak about yet.

Then he turned to the bow, and the Providence ran north, and the cove closed behind them.

***

The Gulf opened.

The channel widened into water broader than any the Caribbean men had seen that was not open ocean — a great protected sea, ringed with coasts on three sides, the fourth lost in haze. The light changed. The air had the clean salt of open water but the taste of forest under it. Fall was further along here than it had been on the coast — leaves on the distant hills had started to turn, and the turn was a color Kipp had no charcoal for.

The gannets came. Not the one that had ridden their wake. Hundreds. A column of them rising off an island far to the north, white against the gray cliffs, wheeling on the wind and dropping in turn to strike the water. The column held the air. The sound, when the Providence came near enough, was a sound no man aboard had ever heard — the cries of a colony, layered and continuous.

Kipp climbed the shrouds for a better look. He did not draw. His hands stayed on the ratlines. The charcoal could wait.

Ortiz, from the galley door, watched the gannets the way he watched anything that flew. He was quiet a long moment. Then he went back to his stove.

Bald eagles worked the shore. They sat on dead spruce along the cliff-tops, white heads and white tails and the heavy hooked beaks cocked to the water, and when one dropped it dropped with a weight that looked like a stone falling until the wings opened at the last second and a fish came up with it. Half the crew had never seen one. The other half had seen them only in pictures. Kipp drew three of them before breakfast.

The coast narrowed again on the afternoon of the second day. The channel they had been running bent west. To the north, across the water, mountains rose — not the cliffs of the coast they had just left, but real mountains, higher, snow already on the summits even this early in the season. The crew lined the rail.

Wry stood at the rail with his hand on the wood and the cane under his other hand. His son was at the wheel. The wind was at their stern. The coast on the port side was a coast he had been carrying in his head, or in a painting, for longer than he was willing to count.

The bay opened.

It opened the way a door opens when it has been waited for. The channel gave way and the water widened and the wind came round to the stern and the Providence leaned into it, and the coast on the port side turned west with her, and the mountains on the starboard shore held their snow against a sky going gold.

Gideon turned the wheel.

The Providence's bow came round. Her sails filled. The wind held.

No one spoke.

Wry's hand left the rail. It moved a few inches and stopped. His son was two steps away. The two of them stood on the same deck in the same wind and the bay opened ahead of them and the Providence ran west, and west was where the mountain was, and the mountain was where Lianor was, and Lianor was home.

CHAPTER TWENTY FOUR

The Mountain

The bay narrowed into an inlet on the second morning.

The channel they had been running west turned north, and the mountains on the starboard side closed in until they were no longer mountains across the water but mountains over the water, granite shoulders rising from a shore so close a man could read the trees. Spruce. Birch coming gold at the edges. A thin fall of water dropping from a high ledge, silver against the rock.

Gideon held the wheel. Wry stood at the rail with the cane.

"There," Wry said.

The word carried what it had to carry.

Gideon looked. The inlet ran deep into the highland, a cleft cut by water older than the rock around it. Halfway up the eastern slope a clearing showed through the spruce — small, deliberate, the kind of clearing a man makes once and tends after. Smoke rose from it, thin and steady.

He brought the Providence in. The water was deep enough to take her almost to the head of the inlet. Eight fathoms under the keel where she dropped anchor. The chain ran out and held.

They lowered the longboat.

Wry stepped over the gunwale with Elias's hand at his elbow and his cane in his free hand. Gideon at the bow oar. Two hands at the others. Cajun in Wry's lap with her claws set in his coat, dignified again. Cipher on his shoulder, silent, watching the shore the way the bird watched anything that mattered.

The shingle crunched under the bow.

She was on the beach.

Lianor stood in her wool coat and her boots, her dark hair threaded with gray, her healer's hands folded at her waist the way they folded when she was praying or waiting or doing both at once. She had known they were coming. She had not run down to the water. She had stood where she stood and let the inlet bring him.

Gideon pulled the bow up onto the stones. Wry climbed out slow — the hip protested, the cane took its share — and walked to her across the shingle.

She put her arms around him and held.

"You're late," she said.

"I'm here."

"I know."

***

The crew stayed four days.

Lianor fed them, healed what needed healing, and learned everything she needed to know about the men who had kept her husband alive without once asking a direct question.

She took them to the river on the second morning. The salmon were running. Ortiz stood waist-deep in water that made his teeth chatter and pulled fish from the current with the delight of a man who had spent years cooking and had just discovered the source. Kipp slipped twice and came up grinning both times. Dench watched from the bank with his bad knees stretched out and learned the trick of reading the water without taking a step.

She showed them the blueberry slopes. Low bush, the berries fat and dark, the short-season intensity of northern fruit. They picked in silence, filling buckets, staining their fingers purple. Kipp ate more than he picked and was unapologetic.

She showed them the mushroom meadows on the upper benches — which to take and which to leave. Dench listened with the attention of a man who is learning that the world contains things his knees can still reach.

On the second evening, at the fire on the beach with the salmon on the grill and the light failing in the way it failed in the north — slowly, reluctantly — Dench sat alone at the water's edge. The oilcloth pouch from the galley table rested in his lap. He had not opened it since Wry set it in front of him. He opened it now. He counted. He closed it. He pressed it against his chest and sat for a long time watching the inlet, and when he stood his knees still hurt but his back had straightened by three inches.

***

On the third evening Lianor gleaned.

She sat with Kipp first. The boy was shy with her — the first time anyone aboard had seen Kipp shy — because the Captain's wife occupied a place in his hierarchy somewhere between God and the teacher on the mountain. He showed her his drawings. She looked at each one with total, unhurried attention. When she reached the one of Wry in his chair, with Cajun and Cipher, she held it for a long time.

"You see him," she said.

"Aye."

"You see the thing he hides."

Kipp's fingers worked his string. "He's not hiding it. He just doesn't know it's there. The smile. The one that's always underneath."

She looked at the boy and saw what Wry had seen in the alleys of Nassau: a child whose generosity had survived everything that should have killed it.

She sat with the others one by one, trying to hide the methods of her interrogation. Then she came to Gideon last.

They sat on the porch in the long northern evening, the light refusing to leave. The earring caught what was left of it.

“He’s proud of you,” she said. “He won’t say it well. He’ll say it sideways, the way he says everything that matters. But he’s proud.”

“I know, Mom.”

“Do you know what you’re sailing back to?”

Gideon was quiet a moment.

“A woman with a ledger and a plan and stubbornness just like yours,” he said. “And an island that needs what she’s building.”

Lianor smiled.

“Your father fell in love with a woman who crossed an ocean. You’re falling in love with a woman who’s rebuilding one. The Slamyrbach men have a type.”

Gideon laughed — short, real, surprised by its own arrival. His father’s laugh.

***

On the fourth morning the wind came round to the south and the tide turned to favor a ship sailing out.

The crew began loading. Barrels of salmon. Buckets of blueberries. Sacks of dried mushrooms Ortiz planned to keep through the voyage. The Providence sat in the inlet, her masts bare against a sky going gold, waiting.

Wry stood at the cabin window with his hand on the frame and looked down at the beach where his crew was working and his son was at the water with the boats, and he did not move for a long time.

Then he set the cane and went down the trail.

CHAPTER TWENTY FIVE

Hearts True

Wry called Gideon to the beach.

The crew had paused in their loading. Word had moved among them the way word moved when a thing was about to happen — not announced, recognized. Elias stood at the bow of the longboat. Ortiz at the gunwale. Kipp on the stones, string forgotten in his hand. Dench with his cap held against his chest.

Wry held out his right hand. On the pinky, two rings stacked: a gold wedding band and above it a darker ring etched with red glyphs that seemed to shift in the light, as though the symbols were not carved but living.

He slid the ring with the red glyphs from his finger. It came off slowly, as though the finger did not want to release it. Beneath it, Lianor's gold band sat alone — the wedding ring, now the only ring on that hand. The ship had left him. The woman remained.

"This ring belongs to the Providence," Wry said. "And the Providence belongs to it."

He held it in the morning light. The red glyphs caught the gold of the sky and held it.

"It's been on my hand since the day I named her. It carries the ship the way the ship carries the crew — not by force but by bond. The man who wears it speaks for her."

He took Gideon's hand and slid the ring onto his son's finger.

It fit. Of course it fit — the hands were the same, and the ring knew the shape.

"You're the Captain now. The ship knows it. The ring knows it. And I —" His voice held. "I know it."

Lianor stood on the porch above the trail. She did not come down. This was between father and son. But her lips moved — the prayer, the constant prayer.

Gideon looked at the ring on his finger. The red glyphs were warm. Not from the air — from the years.

Then Wry reached into his coat and brought out a small leather pouch. Inside were three gold earrings — small hoops, identical.

"The ring is the ship," he said. "These are the family."

Elias produced the flask from his coat pocket without being asked. Wry took it, poured a measure over the awl, and pierced Gideon's ear a second time — quick, clean. Gideon winced but held. The gold hoop slid home beside the silver. Two in the left ear now. The silver from boyhood. The gold to mark a new chapter.

He turned to Kipp.

"Come here, boy."

Kipp came. Wry looked at him — twelve years old, red-haired, standing on cold stone with the patience of a boy who had walked on worse — and said:

"Gideon told me you don't have a family. He's wrong. You've had one since the night you hit a giant in the eye with a piece of string and fed him bread in the dark. This is how we mark it."

He pierced the boy's ear — quick, clean. Kipp winced but did not cry out. The gold hoop slid home.

Wry held out the third gold hoop and the awl to Gideon. His son took them without a word. He tilted his father's head gently, positioned the awl beside the silver hoop that had hung there since a boy's hand first earned its match, and drove the point through. Wry didn't flinch. The gold hoop slid home beside the silver.

"I'll hear when you call," Wry said.

"And I'll answer," Gideon said, tugging his earring.

Kipp's voice cracked. He steadied it by force.

"Then I'll be heard."

***

"One more thing," Wry said. "Walk with me."

They took the longboat out — just the two of them at the oars — and pulled across the inlet to where the Providence rode at anchor. They climbed aboard and went down to the cabin.

The sea chest sat beneath the stern windows where it had always sat. Wry knelt. Gideon saw him wince and reached to help, but Wry waved him off. He lifted the lid. He removed the charts, the leather, the tools. He found the seam in the grain and lifted the false bottom.

Gideon looked at what was underneath. His mouth opened. Closed. Opened again.

"Dench's share came out of this," Wry said. "The rest is here, waiting for the men it belongs to."

He looked at his son.

"The chest stays with the ship. It belongs to the Providence and to whoever captains her. You hold it. You answer for what's in it. You keep the count honest — every coin, every name, every share. No one skims. No one borrows. The men see the ledger if they ask."

"And when Seraphine's system takes hold?"

"Then the chest becomes a tradition instead of a necessity. But until it does, this is how we take care of our own. Family first. System second."

Wry replaced the false bottom. He closed the lid. He pressed both palms flat against the oak — the old gesture, the covenant — and held them there.

"All of this responsibility falls on your shoulders now," he said. "Not just the chest. The ship. Everything."

Gideon put his hand on the lid beside his father's — same hands, same oak, the covenant passing between them without a word.

Wry opened the lid once more. Beneath the charts, the green book. He lifted it out and put it in his coat. At the door he took the silver clasp from its hook, folded it into a square of linen, and put it in the pocket with the book.

They went back up to the deck and climbed down into the longboat, and rowed back across the inlet to the beach where the others were waiting. The chest stayed where it belonged — beneath the stern windows, oak and iron, older than the ship, waiting for the next captain to keep its count.

***

They left on the tide.

Wry stood on the beach with Lianor beside him and the cane in his hand and Cajun at his feet and watched the Providence turn in the inlet and catch the wind.

Cipher had stayed with the ship. His post was the yardarm, and the yardarm was going to Nassau, and the bird's loyalty was to the vessel. Wry had let him go. Some creatures belong to the sea.

From the deck, as the ship cleared the headland, came the chant. Elias's voice first:

"Eyes steady."

And the crew: "Eyes steady."

"Blades sharp."

"Blades sharp."

"Hearts true."

"Hearts true."

And from the yardarm, as the last echo of the chant rolled across the water, Cipher rose and let out a single cry — sharp, clear, unmistakable:

"Hearts true!"

The words rang off the highlands and came back, and then the bird settled, and the ship sailed on.

The sound carried across the water. It reached the beach where Wry stood. It reached him the way all true things reach the people they're meant for — not loudly, not dramatically, but with the clarity of voices that mean what they say.

He stood feeling the warmth of Grace on his left hand, while leaning on the cane, and the warmth of Lianor's hand in his right, and both hands were warmed.

They turned from the water and walked up the trail toward the cabin — slowly, because the cane set the pace now — and the Providence grew small on the inlet and then smaller and then gone.

The mountain held. The fireweed was turning. And the cabin was warm.

CHAPTER TWENTY SIX

The Machine Adapts

The counting house had lost two clerks.

Vark noticed the way he noticed everything — not by looking but by listening. The nib-scratching that served as the building's pulse had thinned. Ten pens now, where twelve had been. The rhythm was the same — relentless — but the sound occupied less of the room, the way a choir occupies less of a cathedral when two voices stop singing.

The absence was small. Small absences were the ones Vark watched most carefully, because large absences announced themselves and could be managed, while small ones accumulated in silence until the structure they supported was no longer the structure you had built.

He did not ask where the clerks had gone. He knew. One had left for a counting house on the Herengracht that offered three guilders more per month. The other had simply not returned — chair empty, desk clean, collar and pen left folded on the seat like a skin shed in the night. The collar was the detail that interested Vark. A man who leaves his collar behind is not seeking better employment. He is making a statement about the employment he had.

Vark picked up the collar, examined it, and set it in the drawer with the others. There were four now. Four collars in six months.

The Keizersgracht was the same — dark canal, spent sky, wind off the Zuiderzee. The Exchange hummed three streets away. But the hum had shifted pitch in ways that only a man who had spent forty years listening to money could detect. Fewer contracts clearing. Longer settlement times. A merchant on the Prinsengracht had begun accepting payment in a currency Vark did not control — bills drawn not on a single counting house but on a consortium of three, each one holding a copy of the same ledger. The practice had spread from Nassau.

He noted it, the way his clerks noted a variance in a column — with a small mark in the margin, to be investigated when the rest of the figures were settled.

***

Thresh arrived on the afternoon packet from Bridgetown — not from Nassau directly, because Nassau was no longer a port where he could walk openly. He had taken the long route, island to island, three weeks of travel that a single vessel could have covered in twelve days.

He came to the counting house at mid-afternoon, when the clerks were deepest in their work. He looked the same. Tall, lean, the long fingers loose at his sides. Salt-marked traveling clothes. A face that gave nothing until the book was opened.

Thresh stood. He had not been invited to sit, and the omission was not an oversight.

"The battery failed," Thresh said.

"Continue," Vark said.

Thresh gave the report. Facts first, interpretation never. The hired men broke when the captain's son flanked from the east. The captain fought with the blade and the rings until his spine failed him. A boy with a sling provided cover. The crew held.

"Cutler?"

"Gone. Walked off the ridge after the line broke. Took the Bristolman and the Plymouth brothers. He left his knife in the battery wall."

"And my property?"

"Cael turned. He stepped between me and the captain. Would not respond to command." A pause — the first in the conversation. "The boy had been feeding him. Bread. On the dock. At night, when my orders were to watch. He kept it from me."

Vark's brown eyes rested on Thresh. A tool that could be turned by bread was a tool with a flaw he had failed to identify. The failure was not Cael's. It was the system's — his system — for not accounting for a variable as elementary as hunger met with kindness. Kindness was not a factor his ledgers measured. He was beginning to understand that this was an error.

"And the ledger."

"In Nassau. Your daughter holds it. Cael stands with her." He paused. "The captain sailed north with his crew. His son has the Providence now — headed back to Nassau, by my reckoning." Another pause. "The captain is finished. She is not."

***

He rose and walked to the map.

Nassau sat where it always sat — a thumbprint at the edge of the web. But the web was changing. Three flags had been removed from the Atlantic board since his last inspection. Three ships whose captains had settled their debts — not through payment, but through documentation. They had produced counter-ledgers. Copies of the original contracts alongside records of every payment made, every fee charged, every penalty added. The numbers, laid beside each other, told a story that could not be argued with. Three captains freed. The system that had held two hundred men in debt across three oceans had been cracked not by cannon or mutiny but by arithmetic.

He studied the map. The trade routes had not changed. The ports had not moved. What had changed was the paper itself. The VOC had understood this two centuries ago — that the man who controls the record controls the transaction. Vark had inherited that understanding and refined it. Where the VOC used a single ledger held by a single company, Vark used a network of ledgers, each one creating a web of obligation so intricate that no single thread could be pulled without the whole structure trembling.

His daughter had seen the architecture beneath the figures. She had understood that the system was not designed to collect debt. It was designed to perpetuate it. And she had built the one thing that could break a perpetual system: a transparent one. Copies held by multiple parties. Every transaction visible. Every entry verified by comparison. The gap where his profit lived closed, because the gap could only exist where the ledger was singular, and singular was the one thing the open ledger was not.

The machine would stop. The figures said so, and figures did not negotiate.

He stood at the map and permitted himself, for the first time in forty years, the impulse to reject what the figures were telling him. The impulse was brief and specific: find the girl, recover the ledger, burn it, and rebuild the gap. He had the reach. Thresh had the hands. The old system could be restored in a season if the counter-ledger disappeared. The impulse lasted four seconds.

The figures would not change. Burning one ledger would not unburn the copies already in merchants' hands in Nassau, Port Royal, and Bridgetown. The method had spread past the point where a single act of destruction could contain it. He had taught his daughter well enough that she had made herself unnecessary to the system she built — the ledger did not need her to survive, only to start. It was, he admitted without pleasure, elegant.

The question was not whether the machine would stop. The question was what replaced it.

***

Thresh stood by the door, waiting.

"The minting house on the Warmoesstraat," Vark said. "You know it."

"De Groot."

"De Groot mints coin for four colonial governors and stamps trade tokens for eleven merchant houses. Last month he refused a contract extension with my house. The month before that, he extended terms to a consortium in Nassau that uses a distributed verification system for their bills of exchange."

Thresh said nothing. Currency and systems were not his language.

"The men who mint the coin have begun to realize that the coin is not the value. The record of the coin is the value. De Groot is positioning himself to mint not metal but trust." Vark's voice carried no bitterness. Bitterness was an emotion, and emotions were a cost he did not carry on his books. "The system that replaces mine will require infrastructure. Clerks. Standards. A network of verification that spans the same ports my debt network spans. Someone will build it. The question is whether that someone inherits the architecture I have already laid, or whether they build from nothing and waste a decade arriving where I already stand."

He walked to the window. Below, the canal was dark and slow, the last of the winter ice breaking into plates that ground against each other with the patience of a season that would not be hurried.

On the far bank a boy was pulling a sled loaded with parcels along the frozen edge of the Keizersgracht — leaning into the rope with his whole small body, boots sliding on the ice, breath clouding the air in quick white bursts. A delivery boy. One of the dozens who moved the paper that moved the money that moved the world, and who was paid in stuivers that would not buy him the boots he was wearing out.

The boy slipped. The sled tipped. Three parcels slid onto the ice, and the boy scrambled after them on his hands and knees, gathering them against his chest with the desperate efficiency of a child who knew that a lost parcel was a lost meal.

Vark watched. The boy recovered the parcels, righted the sled, and leaned into the rope again.

Vark turned from the window.

"Your methods belong to the system I built," he said. "Coercion. Enforcement. The brand. These were instruments of a closed ledger — they worked because the men who bore them could not see what was written about them. In a transparent system, the brand is visible. The coercion is documented. The methods become liabilities."

Thresh's face did not change. But his stillness deepened — the stillness of a man recalculating.

"I am not releasing you," Vark said. "I am reassigning you."

"Every one of those offices runs the old system. Every one of them holds a single ledger, maintained by a single clerk, visible to no one but the man who writes in it. Every one of them is vulnerable to exactly what my daughter has built."

"You want me to close them."

"I want you to convert them."

The word sat in the room. Convert. It was not a word that belonged in Thresh's vocabulary. Thresh's vocabulary was composed of verbs that ended in silence — enforce, collect, remove. Convert required speech. Persuasion. The particular skill of making a man believe that the thing he feared was the thing he needed.

"You will travel to each office," Vark said. "You will carry a copy of my daughter's system — the open ledger, the distributed record, the verification protocols. You will explain to each clerk and each correspondent that the counting house is adopting the new method. You will train them. You will answer their objections. You will not threaten them." He paused. "You will sell them."

"Begin with Curaçao," Vark said. "It is the smallest office and the most resistant. If you can convert De Klerk in Curaçao, the others will follow, because De Klerk is the man every other clerk watches, and the man every other clerk watches is the man who sets the pace."

Thresh looked at his own hands — the long fingers, the swordsman's hands, the hands that had closed accounts and opened wounds and carried the brand from port to port for twenty years. They were being asked to carry paper now.

"And if they refuse?"

"Then they will be replaced by men who do not. But the replacement will be administrative, not physical. The new system does not require your old methods, Thresh. It requires your reach. You know every port. You know every clerk. You know which men can be reasoned with and which must be shown proof before they move. That knowledge is worth more than the sword. I have always known this. I simply had no use for it until now."

Thresh stood in the room and felt, for the first time in his professional life, the particular vertigo of a man whose purpose has not been taken from him but reshaped — the same hands, the same reach, the same network of knowledge, aimed at a different outcome.

"Curaçao," Thresh said.

"The next packet sails Thursday."

Thresh looked at Vark — long, hard, the look of a man confirming in the other's eyes that what he has just heard is what was meant. Then, without speaking, he reached to his hip and unbuckled the rapier. The leather belt came free with a sound like a breath released. He wrapped it slowly around the scabbard — one turn, two, the practiced motions of a man who had buckled and unbuckled this weapon thousands of times and was doing it now for the last time.

He set it on the shelf beside the door. The wood received it without comment.

He walked through the door and descended the stairs. His boots carried a different weight. Not lighter — repurposed.

The front door opened and closed. Ten clerks scratched on.

***

Vark sat down at the desk. He took a fresh sheet of parchment — the same heavy cotton stock, the same watermark — and wrote to his daughter.

The letter was not long. But it was, by his standards, remarkable — not for what it said but for what it conceded, which was territory he had never conceded to any debtor, any merchant, any clerk, any captain in forty years of commerce.

He wrote: Your system works. I have studied the reports from Nassau, from Port Royal, from Bridgetown. The open ledger reduces fraud. The distributed record eliminates the single point of failure that has been the vulnerability of every counting house since the VOC. The shared security provision reduces crew attrition and increases the quality of men willing to sign, which increases the reliability of the cargo, which increases the value of the contracts. The numbers are sound.

He paused. The pen hovered. The nib held its drop of ink, waiting for the hand to commit.

He wrote: The machine I built was designed for a world where the man who held the ledger held the power. That world is ending. The world that replaces it will be one where the man who builds the system of verification — the architecture of trust — holds the power instead. You have built the first version of that system. It will need to scale. It will need standards, protocols, a network of clerks trained in the new method.

He wrote: I am not offering partnership. I am offering infrastructure. My network spans three continents. My clerks are trained. My correspondents are in place. What I lack is the system your ledger provides — the transparency that my architecture was built to prevent and that the market is now demanding. You have the method. I have the machinery. The combination is not sentimental. It is arithmetic.

He signed the letter. Not with the counting house's seal — not the pressed wax circle bearing only a number. He signed it with his name. Cornelius Vark. The pen formed the letters with the same precision it formed his figures, but the act was different. A number is a function. A name is an identity. He had not offered his identity to anyone in longer than he could remember.

He folded the letter and sealed it with wax — plain, unmarked. He rang the bell. A clerk appeared.

"The next packet to Nassau. Standard post."

The clerk took the letter and left. The door closed. The nib-scratching resumed below — ten nibs now, not twelve, and the two empty desks sat in the rows like missing teeth in a jaw that was still strong enough to bite but was, for the first time, aware of the gap.

Vark returned to his ledger. A coffee shipment from Suriname — margins narrower than a year ago, penalties harder to enforce. The captain on that route now carried a counter-ledger that documented every fee.

He did not permit himself the irony. He picked up the pen. But the line it wrote was not the line he had written for forty years. It was a new line — tentative, exploratory, the first entry in a ledger that did not yet have a name.

The Exchange hummed three streets away. The wind off the Zuiderzee cut through the afternoon. The canal ran dark and still. And Cornelius Vark began to adapt.

The counting house kept its count. But the count, for the first time in forty years, was changing.

CHAPTER TWENTY SEVEN

Home

The cabin was warm. The fire was small and steady — the fire Lianor had left burning because a fire in the hearth was a prayer and a promise. The herbs hung from the ceiling in bundles that scented the air with rosemary and thyme. Lianor's Bible sat on the table by the window, open to a page she'd been reading that morning — he didn't look at which one, because the conversation was hers, and the privacy of it was sacred.

The quiet was large. It was the largest thing in the room. Everything that had filled recent days — crew, noise, fishing, laughter, the smell of Ortiz's salmon, Kipp's voice cracking on the chant — was gone, and what remained was the mountain and the cabin and the woman and Cajun and the quiet.

Through the window, the hillside was ablaze. The fireweed had turned. Most people who passed through the north saw the plant in summer, when it stood tall and dense and burning with a magenta so vivid it stopped travelers mid-step. It was Lianor's favorite color, the color she said reminded her of the bougainvillea that climbed the courtyard walls of her childhood. But the fireweed gave its beauty twice. Now, late in the season, the blooms had gone to seed, and the hillside was transformed. The seed heads caught the low sun and turned to silk — long, luminous threads drifting in the wind like angels' hair, backlit and glowing, while the leaves beneath them deepened to a burnt red that held the last of the year's warmth in its color.

It was not a weed at all, despite its name. It was called Fireweed because it was the first thing to return after a forest fire — the healer of scorched earth, spreading across the blackened ground in a blanket of green and magenta, stitching the land back together the way Lianor stitched wounds: patiently and completely, leaving the soil richer than it was before the burning.

"Soup's on," Lianor said.

"In a minute."

He stood at the window and looked at the inlet. The water was still. The wake was gone. The place where the ship had been was just water now, and the water didn't remember.

"All right," he said. "Soup."

Earlier, Elias had carried a chest up from the beach. Not the sea chest — that stayed with the Providence. A new one. Smaller. Lianor had made it during the months Wry was at sea — carved from local cedar, the lid worked with images from their life in the north: the cabin, the mountains, the fireweed, a bear at a stream, a boy and a dog on a shingle beach. Her hands had shaped it the way her hands shaped everything.

Elias had set it down beneath the window, stood there for a moment with his hand on the lid, his jaw working. Twenty years of shared watches. He had touched the lid once, turned, and walked back down the trail toward the ship. Halfway to the beach, not looking back, he'd said it to himself:

"The joinery's sound."

Wry opened the chest. The green book was on top. He lifted it carefully and placed it on the shelf beside the others. Grace he hadn't earned. Grace he received anyway.

Beneath the green book, wrapped in a square of linen, lay the silver clasp. He held it in his palm. It was lighter than he remembered — lighter than twenty years of confessions whispered to it in the dark should have made it. He turned it once in the firelight. Then he placed it on the shelf beside the green book, where the lamplight could find it, and where it. Beneath that, rolled in cloth, was Kipp's final drawing — the one he had been trying to perfect for weeks. He unrolled it and held it up.

Lianor looked at it. The Captain in his chair. Cajun in his lap. Cipher on his shoulder. The not-smile. The rings on the thumbs. The scabbard hanging at his hip. The whole of a man drawn by a boy who had seen him clearly and put the seeing on paper with charcoal and the hand that was born to make things visible.

"He's good," she said.

"He's twelve. He'll be better."

She looked at the drawing again. Her finger traced Cipher — the settled feathers, the beak near the earring. "I've been replaced," she said. "The bird has your ear now."

"The bird has my earring. You have my ear."

She smiled. The smile he had sailed toward. The one that said: I knew you'd come back, because I know who you are, and who you are is a man who comes back.

He hung the drawing on the wall beside the painting. The painting showed the cabin from the outside — the mountains, the fireweed, the clearing. The drawing showed the man from the inside — the chair, the creatures, the quiet. Together they were a complete portrait of a life: the place and the person, the home and the man it was built for.

Lianor served the soup. They sat at the table. The fire was warm. The mountain was steady. Outside, the fireweed guarded the hillside.

They ate in the silence of two people who have said the important things and know that the rest will come — over days and weeks and the long quiet years that lay ahead. The soup was good. The bread was better. The company required nothing and gave everything.

Wry took a measure of rum from the flask. The lesser evil. The floor that held. He drank. The pain was there — it was always there, it would always be there. The rings eased it. The rum floored it. The woman across the table held the rest.

He looked at his right hand. Lianor's gold band sat alone on the pinky. The ship's ring was gone — on Gideon's finger now, somewhere on the Atlantic, carrying the red glyphs toward Nassau. The pinky felt lighter. The lightness was not loss. It was release.

Lianor bowed her head. Her lips moved. She prayed without ceasing, because that was who she was, and who she was had been enough to hold a family together across an ocean and through a storm and into the quiet that comes after.

The fire settled. The mountain held. The floor beneath his boots did not move — did not roll or pitch or tilt with the swell — and after years at sea, where the world was never still and a man's balance was a thing negotiated with every step, the stillness of solid ground felt like a kindness he had forgotten the earth could offer.

The night came on. Cajun climbed into Wry's lap uninvited and settled there with the authority of a creature who has outlasted every rival and knows it. Wry's hand found her back. Grace and Harmony caught the firelight, warm on his thumbs, the copper etchings gleaming.

And Wry Slamyrbach — privateer, captain, father, husband, debtor to no man — was home.

***

He sits on their mountainside looking out — where stone meets tide and the wind carries the taste of distances he has crossed and will not cross again. His beard, silvered with time, catches the last of the light. His hands, scarred from rope and blade, lie still in his lap, twisting the rings.

He has held many things with these hands. Most of them are gone now. What remains is enough.

He remembers the sea most vividly in fragments: a mast splintering under cannon fire. The desperate clutch of bloodied hands on rope. The roar of storm and flame, and then — dawn breaking after chaos. Waves alive with bioluminescence, glowing as though the ocean itself carried a secret fire. The ship cutting a luminous path through them, parting the waters as it sailed into the rising sun. At the helm, he had stood unyielding, his silhouette etched against the gilded horizon.

He touches the earrings in his left lobe — gold beside silver, two metals that do not alloy but have learned, through years of proximity, to belong together. He listens. Somewhere behind him, voices. A woman's laugh. A young man's shout. A boy's — no, a man's now — answering call. The sounds of a family he built not from blood alone, but from the raw materials of storm and debt and the stubborn refusal to drown.

***

That was the beginning. This is the end. And the end is enough.

Epilogue

The Providence ran south on a following wind.

Gideon stood at the helm and felt the ship. She moved under his hands the way she always had — responsive, honest, a vessel that told you what she needed if you listened. Elias stood at his right hand. Kipp was in the rigging, barefoot, the gold earring catching the sun. Ortiz was below, singing, turning Lianor's salmon into a meal that made the world feel kind.

The crew was smaller than it had been — but new hands had signed on at the inlet, men drawn by the Providence's reputation and the promise of fair shares, and the ship had enough arms to sail and enough voices to fill the watches. Cipher was on the yardarm, where he had always been and always would be, watching the sea with one eye cocked and muttering commentary that no one could translate but everyone understood.

On the third night out, the sky gave them something most of the crew had never seen. It began as a pale green shimmer along the northern horizon, faint enough that the first man to notice it thought his eyes were tired. Then it moved. It rose and spread and deepened, curtains of green and violet and magenta light rippling across the stars as though the sky itself were breathing. The colors shifted and the curtains folded and unfolded with a silence that made the spectacle stranger, because something that vast and that beautiful made no sound at all.

The crew came on deck. They stood at the rails and in the rigging and stared upward with their mouths open. Ortiz stood at the galley hatch with a spoon in one hand and his other hand on his heart. Kipp sat on the foremast crosstrees with his legs dangling, the green light washing his face, his string forgotten. Even Elias stood still and let himself enjoy the splendor.

No one spoke. The lights held them for the better part of an hour, and when they finally faded the stars returned brighter than before, as though the sky had cleaned itself for company.

Gideon stood at the helm through all of it, the ship's ring warm on his finger, and thought: this is what he meant. Look up.

***

By morning the highlands were a blue line on the horizon. By afternoon they were a memory. By evening they were nothing. The inlet was behind them, and ahead lay the Atlantic — the long run south down the eastern coast and on through the Caribbean to Nassau. The wind was fair and the ship was sound and the captain was young, and young captains do not count the miles. They count the days until they arrive.

When the last light faded and the watch was set and the ship was running true, Gideon went below.

The Captain's cabin. His father's cabin. The desk, the chair, the lamp that swung with the swell. The painting was gone — his father had taken it home. The walls were bare and the shelves were empty. The cabin was waiting to be filled by the man who would fill it, and there were years ahead to fill them.

He sat at the desk, opened the drawer and brought out a new ledger. New, thick, and leather-bound, the pages clean. The Captain's Log.

He reached for the quill.

It was an eagle's feather. He and his father had found it together on a ridge above the inlet — a high place where the wind stripped the words from your mouth and the sky was so close you could feel it leaning on your shoulders. The feather had been lying on the rock as though placed there by a hand that understood what it would be used for. His father had picked it up, turned it in the light, and said nothing. Wry had cut it into a quill that night and had written with it for years — the log entries, the letters to Lianor, the notes in the margins of charts. His voice, in ink, committed to paper through the spine of a bird that had flown higher than either of them ever would.

Now it was Gideon's. Passed to him with the ship and the ring and the crew and the weight. His father's quill, and his father's voice, was now his own.

He dipped the eagle feather in the ink — Indian ink, black as the water beneath the hull, permanent in a way that charcoal never was. He held it over the first blank page of the new log. The lamp swung. The ship moved. The ocean breathed.

He did not write. He drew.

The crew would have been surprised. Gideon had never drawn in front of them — not once, not on any watch or in any port. Drawing was the private thing, the discipline he had built alone. Kipp's gift was natural — the boy picked up charcoal and the world poured out of his fingers as though it had been waiting for permission. Gideon's was the opposite. He had wanted it, studied it, failed at it, and forced himself to continue failing until the failing became learning and the learning became skill. He drew in his bunk after the watch. He drew in margins that no one read. He drew the way his father had sat on packed earth on a mountaintop — without comfort, without progress, with only the stubborn refusal to quit.

Not Kipp's drawing this time. Not Cajun, not Cipher, not the not-smile that the boy had captured in charcoal. Gideon drew something else — something that had been forming behind his eyes since the beach, since the ring, since the chant faded across the water and his father's figure shrank against the gravel until the mountain held him and the distance took the rest.

His father's profile — the long beard, the piercing eye. And from the crown of the head, rising like thought made visible, a bare tree — leafless, winter-stripped, its branches reaching into a sky of heavy cloud where the moon broke through, full and low, casting light on the water below. Beneath the tree, beneath the moon, a solitary figure walked a shoreline alone — small against the vastness. The moonlight caught the wet sand and the figure's reflection and turned them into a single shimmering path.

It was not a portrait. It was a landscape of the man — the weight he carried in his mind like branches, the storms he'd weathered in the clouds behind him, the moon that found him anyway, and the long walk he'd taken alone before he found the people who would walk beside him.

The drawing filled the first page. It left no room for words, and words were not what it needed.

He put down the quill and looked at the drawing. It was the best thing he had ever drawn.

He climbed the companionway to the deck. The stars were out — all of them, the full Atlantic sky, brighter now than they had been before the lights, as though the aurora had swept the heavens clean. The map his father had taught him to read on a ridge above the inlet and in the rigging of this ship and in every lesson that had started with the words 'look up'.

He looked up.

The Providence sailed on and as the stars turned the new Captain set his course south, toward the eastern coast, toward Nassau, toward a woman, and toward the future, which was blank and waiting and his.

In the log below, the ink was drying. The eagle feather lay across the open page.

The story continues.

In the Maritimes, a man with six rings watches the horizon and waits for ships that come less and less often.

The settlement has grown. The fire is warm. The wife he sailed for half a lifetime to reach is here, every morning, every night, where she promised to be.

But Wry Slamyrbach was built for movement.

South of him, the Providence runs the Atlantic with Gideon at the wheel.

West of her, in Nassau, Seraphine guards a ledger that has begun to outgrow the room she keeps it in — and a letter from the north she has read more times than she will admit.

Three lives. One ocean between them. And the corridor between them, waiting to be opened.

Coming next...

Five Hundred Eighty Nine

A Song for the Voyage

Drink to the storms we've survived
And the doldrums that nearly took our lives
Drink to the captains gone down with their ships
And the queens with their loose and treacherous lips

Five hundred and eighty-nine pieces of eight
Pay them up
Or seal your fate
Five hundred and eighty-nine pieces of eight
Pay them up
Before it's too late

Drink to the blonde haired maiden so fair
And the sailor who never got back there
Drink to the curse's song in the night
And the cold breath of dawn
Like the first morning light
To the stowaway cat who steals the fish
And the cook's meat cleaver that was too quick
It took of his tail, to the mast he fled
To lick his wounds, and erase the red

Five hundred and eighty-nine pieces of eight
Pay them up

Or seal your fate
Five hundred and eighty-nine pieces of eight
Pay them up
Before it's too late

Drink to the call of the sea
And the songs she still sings to me
Drink to the cutlass
The pistol
And blade
The boy that I was
And the man that they made

Five hundred and eighty-nine pieces of eight
Pay them up
Or seal your fate
Five hundred and eighty-nine pieces of eight
Pay them up
Before it's too late

Five hundred and eighty-nine pieces of eight
Pay them up
Or seal your fate
Five hundred and eighty-nine pieces of eight
Pay them up
Before it's too late

About the Author and the Story

Leo is a father, an artist, and a dreamer, but more than that — a student of the distance between who we are and who we're becoming. The 'seed' to this story began many years ago inspired by the 1972 song, *Brandy* (You're a Fine Girl) by 'Looking Glass'. He wrote *Rings That Bind* the way its characters build ships and ledgers — one plank, one line, one honest entry at a time.

The novel grew from a simple question: what do we owe the people who sail with us? Not in the transactional sense — not debts on paper — but in the way a crew depends on its captain, parents shape their children, and the systems we build outlive the hands that built them. During the genesis of the writing of this story, it slowly and unintentionally became semi-autobiographical in nature.

The story is set in the early 1700s, but the questions belong to any era where ordinary people find themselves caught between machines that count them, and the relationships that can't be counted.

At its core, this is a book about legacy — not the kind carved in stone, but the kind passed hand to hand, like a ring, a feather, or a way of looking at the stars. It's about the work of becoming someone worth following, and the grace of finding people worth walking beside.

If you take anything from these pages, let it be this: the ledger that matters most is the one that has a column for humanity.

May you find the *Grace*

to live in peace with your Creator,

and the *Harmony*

to live in peace with your fellow man.

M. Leo Doucet

a.k.a Wry Slamyrbach

Acknowledgments

This novel was written with the assistance of AI over the course of a year and 20 rewrites. The story, the characters, and the voice are mine. The tool helped me build what I could see but couldn't always reach alone.

www.ingramcontent.com/pod-product-compliance
Lightning Source LLC
LaVergne TN
LVHW090557110826
845146LV00001B/163

* 9 7 9 8 9 9 5 7 9 7 6 1 6 *